DOWNBURST

RACHEL HATCH BOOK TWO

LT RYAN

with

BRIAN SHEA

LIQUID MIND MEDIA, LLC

THE RACHEL HATCH SERIES

Drift

Downburst

Fever Burn

Smoke Signal

Firewalk

Whitewater

Aftershock

Whirlwind

Tsunami

Fastrope

Sidewinder (Coming Soon)

RACHEL HATCH SHORT STORIES

Fractured

Proving Ground

The Gauntlet

Join the LT Ryan reader family & receive a free copy of the Rachel Hatch story, Fractured. Click the link below to get started:

https://ltryan.com/rachel-hatch-newsletter-signup-1

Love Hatch? Noble? Maddie? Cassie? Get your very own Rachel Hatch merchandise today! Click the link below to find coffee mugs, t-shirts, and even signed copies of your favorite L.T. Ryan thrillers! https://ltryan. ink/EvG_

ONE

HE LOOKED DOWN at his watch for the second time in as many seconds, as if checking again was going to make him any less late than he already was. It was the bus driver's fault, but he couldn't use the excuse even if it were true. She never accepted anything but punctuality. And recently he'd failed in that area more times than he cared to admit.

Juan picked up the pace. His backpack was loaded to capacity and the weight tugged down on his shoulders. His stomach rumbled and he thought about stopping to retrieve the granola bar from the bottom of the pack. Precious seconds would be lost to the effort. He decided against appeasing his belly's audible protest and continued on without sustenance. Maybe Miss Garcia would give him a little time to snack before they began today's session. Doubtful, but the thought of it, regardless of its probability, gave him hope.

Rounding the corner onto Serrano Drive, a cold gust of wind blew his hat off. Juan spun to grab it as the brim bounced off his fingertips. It was a valiant effort, but like most of his athletic endeavors, he came up short. Trotting back, he picked up his hat and cinched it down to prevent a repeat episode.

As he turned to resume his jog toward his tutor's house, he heard the pulsing bass of a subwoofer. The thumping reverberated around the quiet of the street. The sound of it shook him to his very core, and Juan stopped dead in his tracks. He turned as the boxy front end of a rust-colored '80s Cadillac Fleetwood Brougham slowly eased around the corner of the street he'd just come from. The vehicle rolled to a stop alongside the curb.

The car's windows were heavily tinted and reflected the deep purple of the evening sky. It was impossible to see inside. The thumping continued, brake lights giving the plume of exhaust an eerie red hue, like the peel of a blood orange. He'd become all too familiar with the fruit when helping his father pack the crates at Gonzales' Grocery. His father's work had left their family with little in the way of financial security in the aftermath of his death, so Juan picked up where he left off, stocking the store's shelves.

At fifteen, he'd become the man of the family, and what little money he earned went to putting food on the table for his three younger sisters. He knew his only chance to help his family would be to graduate high school. But with the hours spent at the store, his grades had slipped, and now he spent his evenings with his teacher, Miss Garcia, who provided him with extra help.

The Cadillac idled. The V8 had a sputtery hum that seemed to jive with the music blaring from the aftermarket stereo system. Juan's heart began jackhammering uncontrollably. His fingers trembled, and the tips went numb. In his haste to get to his destination, he hadn't initially connected the dots. There were plenty of dangerous people in town. But he now knew who was in the Coupe and the knowledge paralyzed him with fear.

Juan sucked in a cool gulp of air mixed with exhaust, turned, and began running at a dead sprint toward his tutor's house. His thin legs carried the gangly lankiness of his frame in a wild, awkward gait. The load on his back slowed him down, swinging from side to side as he pushed the limits of his physical ability. The exertion left a metallic aftertaste in his mouth with each wheezy breath he took. Juan knew this was due to increased fluid pressure in his lungs. The pressure creates a leakage of red blood cells into the air sacs of the lungs and a subsequent release of hemoglobin from the cells. Juan aspired to be a doctor and spent much of his free time, what little there was, devouring any and all he could find on the human body and its mysterious functions. How he wished those hours of research provided him with the ability to access some untapped superhuman function that would enable him to outrun a car.

The engine behind him roared, the sound momentarily drowning out the boom of the music. A squeal of tires followed. His feet couldn't move across the cracked cement of the sidewalk fast enough. He looked ahead and could see the black metal guide rail leading up the steps to Miss Garcia's home. It would be close. But if he dug deep and gave everything he had, the possibility of reaching safety was within grasp.

Without looking back, he knew the car was gaining rapidly. He could hear it. Worse, he could sense it. Sense the evil intentions of its occupants. Juan needed to lighten his load to give himself the best chance. He shed his extra weight, releasing the burdensome straps without breaking stride. The bag fell behind him. Books spilled out on the ground as the metal teeth of the zipper separated upon impact.

Just ten steps to go and he'd be inside the house. He wheezed under the exertion and regretted not taking a blast from his inhaler before getting off the bus. It was buried with the granola bar at the bottom of his discarded pack.

Out of the corner of his left eye, he saw the car parallel to him. The rhythmic drumming reverberated in his rib cage, louder now because the back-passenger window was down. They were close now. His peripheral vision picked up the long black cylindrical barrel of a gun.

Somebody from the car yelled, "You don't never mess around with an Outlaw's girl!"

He'd walked Sophia home from school once. Juan knew she was Macho's sister. And he knew Macho was the head of the Luna Vista's notorious street gang. But she was nice. Different from the other kids at school. On their walk, they talked about life outside of Luna Vista. A vision of the future, however grandiose and unrealistic. It felt good to have a conversation with a girl. Especially one as beautiful as her.

Nothing happened on the walk. Although, in the days since, he'd dreamed about her. Juan created an alternate reality where he fantasized about running off with her to start a new life. He hadn't told her or anyone else about this. Now, running for his life, he wished he had kissed Sophia, or at least tried. Maybe, in some way, it would make his current circumstance more acceptable.

Two more steps and then the stairs. Two more. That's it. Safety awaited. Optimism gave way to reality with the deafening roar of gunfire.

Juan was slammed sideways with the impact as he toppled over less than a foot from the first step leading up to Miss Garcia's. He smelled an acrid smoke and tasted the metallic burn from his lung's exertion. The sour bitterness of blood overwhelmed his senses, filling his mouth and choking him.

Another blast of wind lashed at him, again knocking his hat free. This time he made no effort to retrieve it. He couldn't. His motionless body yielded to the trauma.

The tires from the car screeched as it raced off down the street and around the corner.

Juan heard the screen door open followed by a scream he could only assume was Miss Garcia's. He couldn't be certain because of the dark veil shrouding his view. A coldness wrapped around him. He thought of his mother and sisters. What would they do without him to help out? Who would stock the shelves and feed his family?

It was a question he would never learn the answer to.

"DID you see him go down? Like he got hit by a Mack truck. Punk bitch never had a chance." The boy rested the Remington 870 pump-action shotgun across his legs, admiring it. He stroked the long black barrel with his hand as if petting a lap dog. Although his face was hidden beneath the blue cloth of the bandana, it was obvious from the crinkled lines around his eyes that the boy who had just fired the gun was smiling.

Xavier Fuentes looked over at the gunman. Feeling his body shake, he worried the other boy would notice. He tucked his hands under his thighs, hiding them from view. Apparently, it didn't matter. The man next to him was oblivious. His only focus was on the shotgun.

"Yo, X. Hit this shit." The front passenger twisted in his seat with a fat joint pinched between his thumb and forefinger.

Embers glimmered at its burnt end, the smoke adding to the hazy layer already present in the car. Xavier took it. Putting it to his lips, he could feel that the previous user's moist saliva had dampened the paper. He pulled in hard, drawing a deep hit of the marijuana. The smoke burned his lungs as he held it. He was already high, higher than he could ever remember being, but it wasn't enough to block the image of the dying kid from his mind.

Releasing the aromatic smoke from his lungs, the heat of it tickled the back of his throat and caused him to cough. He handed the joint to his right, passing it off to Blaze, who pulled his face mask down before taking it. Blaze's real name was Mateo Rivera, but it had been years since anybody had called him that. He'd been a grade above Xavier before dropping out of school in the eighth grade. The Outlaws had claimed him and, as was the practice, gave him a new name.

The front passenger, Psycho, was a few years older. A big, wild-eyed kid with long hair he kept in tight cornrows. His skin was lighter than the rest of the group's and light brown freckles dotted his cheeks. He was the right-hand man to the gang's leader, Carlos "Macho" Ortiz. The two were inseparable, and Psycho would do violence to anyone who challenged Carlos. His explosive temper and the resulting injuries he put on others was the stuff of legend in the town. Thus, his name and reputation were forever intertwined.

Macho drove fast, quickly putting distance between them and the dead boy.

Sirens sounded in the distance. Xavier's hands continued to shake, and after passing the joint, he returned them to hiding under his thighs. He wasn't scared about the cops catching them. It wasn't even on his mental radar. Even if there had been a witness, nobody in Luna Vista would speak to the police. Especially about the Outlaws. Not unless they had a death wish. His fear stemmed from the trauma he had just witnessed. He had watched as his best friend since third grade was gunned down.

He knew the shotgun in Blaze's hand would be given to him soon and a similar task would be asked of him. It was the way of things here. A rite of passage in becoming an official member of the Outlaws. A title he never sought, but one he nonetheless bore.

Macho eyed him through the rearview mirror. "You ready for tomorrow, right? It's the first step in comin' up. Earn your place in the pack."

Xavier tried to look tough. Puffing up his chest and sitting up straight, he gave a smile. It was weak at best. He wondered if Macho bought the act.

Tomorrow night would be when he proved himself worthy. Everybody in the gang had to go through it. Some fared better than others, but nobody came out unscathed.

One thing was certain. Tomorrow night, regardless of the outcome, there would be blood.

TWO

SHE SAT LISTENING to the rising and falling buzz of the engine. The air freshener clipped to the vent was supposed to make the older-model Camry smell like a new car. Instead, it barely masked the stench left behind by the previous renter, who'd clearly violated the rental company's non-smoking agreement. The end result smelled as though potpourri had been heated in a used ashtray. Hatch lowered the windows a crack, letting the cool breeze purge the air around her in cyclonic fashion, and then turned off the car.

Sitting in silence, Hatch evaluated the exterior of the building. It stood out amid the bleak desert backdrop. One road, an arterial spurt from the main one, led to the dead-end where she now waited. She was parked just past the building, behind a utility shed. The rounded nose of the Camry poked out a couple of inches, but the vehicle was positioned opposite any arriving traffic, making it difficult to spot unless looking for it. The muted beige of the car helped it blend with the bland, sandy surroundings.

There was little need to worry about visitors. The place looked long-since abandoned. Hatch wouldn't have been shocked to see a tumbleweed roll by while the leitmotif of *The Good, the Bad and the*

Ugly rang out in the background. The lock had been cut on the fenced entrance leading in and it appeared local vagrants had long since ignored the Keep Out sign posted to it.

Spray paint adorned the boarded-up windows and walls, giving an unwelcoming vibe to any person who might have accidentally ventured out this way. To Hatch, these overt displays of dominance were a sign of weakness. Those boasting in colorful epitaphs proved to be more bark than bite. When or if she bumped into those responsible, she expected to validate her assumption.

Over an hour had passed since she first pulled up to the location, and she still hadn't seen a single person come or go from the building. Experience had taught her observation was an underutilized skill. And patience to do it for long durations, even less so. One hour wasn't long for Hatch. During a sniper course, she'd once remained in position for three days waiting for the target to arrive. Three days of minimal movement and sleep, all in the hope of hitting a passing target that would present itself for less than thirty seconds. Hard to describe the release of pulling a trigger after seventy-two hours of mind-numbing waiting. In the crudest of terms, and the way she relayed it to one of her closest teammates, it was orgasmic. So, in comparison, sitting on a cushioned seat idle for an hour in a climate-controlled vehicle was a drop in the bucket.

She picked up the letter with the faded return address in the corner. It led here, to this exact location. A place which most likely looked very different twenty-one years ago. That or it was the most impressive attempt at urban camouflage she'd seen to date.

Hatch pulled the door handle. She was met with a resistant blast of sand-filled wind as she pushed the door open and stepped onto the packed earth below. As the wind subsided, she heard a rhythmic drumming sound off in the distance. At first, the repetitious beat sounded like the spinning of a Blackhawk's rotor blades. But after giving it more attention, she realized it was music. The source of which was a rapidly approaching car.

Shifting over to the utility shed's nearest wall, Hatch stepped out of view and waited. The noise amplified, announcing the arrival. A dark red Cadillac, the cause of the commotion, pulled up within a foot of the boarded double-door entrance of the main building. Hatch knew that from their position, if they looked to the right, her car's front bumper would be spotted. She'd worked up a non-violent contingency plan in which she'd pretend to be meeting a boyfriend out here for a private rendezvous. She always had an alternative action plan, should the ruse fail. If you fail to plan, then you plan to fail. Something her dad said. He hadn't coined the phrase, but he'd definitely drummed it into her head. Then the Army had taken her understanding of it to the next level. Hatch kept her focus on the car and hoped it wouldn't come to that. Things worked out better for other people if they didn't choose option B.

She wasn't here to pick a fight. Today was about gathering intelligence. Nothing more. And by the looks of the four exiting the rectangular-framed sedan, these were not the people she'd get it from. Their outer garments were all similar in color, dark navy blue from head to toe. One of them carried a shotgun. Without much mental exertion, Hatch immediately deduced these young men weren't an up-and-coming boy band looking for a quiet place to practice their routine.

Of the four, one stood out from the rest. He looked younger, less dangerous than the others. His face hadn't yet been hardened by crime. He stayed a few steps behind the three larger guys. His hands were stuffed in the pockets of his baggy jeans as he followed them into the building.

None of them paid any attention to the beige Camry, or the woman standing along the wall of the utility shed. Hatch's battle itch kicked in and she gave serious thought to making an uninvited entrance into the gang's hangout, but quickly dismissed it, realizing the futility of such a move. And the high probability of a negative outcome. Her fight was not with them.

The mailing address listed this location as Las Cruces, but the official name for this small town on the eastern outskirts of the more populated city was Luna Vista. Hatch decided she'd need to do a little digging around the local area to see if she could find anyone who knew what this place used to be, if anybody from those days was still in the area.

Loud music disturbed the still night again, similar to the car's, but this time the noise came from inside the building. The sun dipped below the horizon, casting the sky into a dazzling wash of purple and pink. The mountains to the east darkened in contrast. On the other side of those high ridges lay the expansive White Sands of New Mexico, a vast, desolate area used by the US military. The proximity of it to the now abandoned address of her father's last connection to a private covert operations group made more sense in that context.

Hatch used the noise from the building to mask her departure. She got back into the Camry and started it, pausing for a ten count. No movement. Nobody exited. She shifted into reverse and backed out from her concealed position.

The Camry exited past the open fence and she accelerated toward the main road. Hatch turned right, heading toward the town of Luna Vista.

NEON BATTLED for attention against a bright skyline. VACANCY glowed at the sign's base. The Moonbeam Motel was as good a place as any, and Hatch liked the fact the lot was empty except for a few scattered cars. Rooms were lined in a strip with the manager's office on the far left as she pulled the Camry in.

The motel was set back from the main road and was partially shrouded by a cluster of desert willows. A man wearing a lightweight buttoned-down short sleeve shirt was sweeping the walkway near the entrance to the main office. Dust kicked up with each stroke of the broom, surrounding the man like Pig Pen's cartoonish cloud.

As Hatch pulled into an empty parking spot, the man stopped mid-stroke and looked up. His skin, the dark color of chestnuts, was coated in a film of sweat. He wiped his forehead with the back of his hand and set the broom against the wall. Smiling broadly, he walked over to the office door and held it open as Hatch exited the car.

"Looking for a room?"

"I am."

The man tipped his head and outstretched his arm in a welcoming fashion. "Right this way."

Hatch walked through the open door and into the small office. A rectangular space heater on the floor at the base of the counter on the customer side pushed out a barely noticeable amount of heat. She looked down at it and hoped the rooms had more efficient units. Hatch had several exposures to hypothermia during her time in the military and was now more sensitive to the cold. She endured when necessary but preferred not to go into survival mode while staying in guest quarters.

The man must've noticed her examination of the heater because, as he walked around her to the other side of the counter, he said, "Don't worry. The rooms are equipped with a wall unit that will keep you nice and toasty."

"Good to know."

The man grabbed a small hand towel from his back pocket and wiped the sweat from his face. Single threads caught and hung in his stubble. "How many nights will you be staying with us?"

"Not sure. Can I pay as I go?"

"Sure." He paused, giving Hatch a measured look. "First time in Luna Vista?"

"Yes."

"Where are you visiting from?"

"Everywhere and nowhere."

"I don't understand."

"Sorry, just something I say." Hatch absently brushed back a piece of hair from her face, tucking it behind her ear. "I travel a lot."

"Oh, I see. I just saw the Colorado plates on the car and wondered. I've got family out that way. Beautiful country."

Hatch's recent experience in the Rocky Mountains left her bittersweet. She thought of her sister's kids, Daphne and Jake. And then her mind drifted to Dalton Savage and the offer he'd made. Giving her a chance at normal. An offer she'd turned down. Did she really have a choice? She looked at the man in front of her who expectantly waited for a response, obviously hoping for some type of connection.

"It's just a rental."

"Well, if you ever get a chance, I highly recommend you take some time and check it out. The mountains are amazing, much different from the range here."

Hatch nodded. She hoped when closure was reached, she would return. "I'll try to get out that way some day. Hopefully, sooner rather than later."

The man's smile faded, and he sighed. "You seem like a nice person, and I don't like to push paying customers away. By the number of cars in the lot, you can plainly see I could use the business."

"But...?"

"But this isn't the safest place to be." He lifted a crucifix attached to the simple chain around his neck and kissed it. "God knows I've done my best. But this area of town is extremely dangerous. Especially for outsiders."

"Doesn't seem so bad. I've seen worse."

"I'm just saying there are plenty of better places not too far away in Las Cruces. I can get you a map and show you, if you'd like?"

"I'd prefer to stay here."

The man shook his head and shrugged in resignation. He opened a drawer and pulled out a form. "Will you be paying cash or charge? But I should warn you, our credit card machine has been a little finicky lately."

"I prefer cash anyway. How much per night?"

"Forty. But if you'd like to book a room for the week, I can drop it to thirty-five a night."

Hatch pulled the cash from her wallet, handing the two twenties over to the man. "Forty will be fine. I doubt I'll be staying that long."

He took the money. Pulling out a small metal lockbox from the same drawer he'd gotten the form, the man took a small key and worked the lock open. He placed the cash inside and closed the lid, then looked up. "I have an incidentals form I'm going to need you to fill out. Just name and address stuff. And even though you're paying in cash, I am going to need a driver's license."

Hatch smiled, retrieving another twenty and placing it on the counter. "How about we leave that form blank?"

The man looked at the money and then up at Hatch. She was taller than him by a few inches. His eyes moved up and down, evaluating her. She was wearing a navy-blue fleece-lined windbreaker and khaki cargo pants. He began nodding, the motion indicating he had come to some satisfactory conclusion for her need for anonymity. Taking stock of her apparel coupled with the fact that she hadn't been phased by the man's reference to danger, he most likely assumed she was a federal agent.

And then the man did something she didn't expect. He pushed the twenty back toward her. "No need for that."

"Thanks." Hatch put the money away, impressed by the man, who obviously needed the cash, yet took the moral high ground and refused the subtle bribe. The simple gesture spoke volumes to his integrity.

He pulled a room key from a pegboard on the wall behind him and handed it over. "Room number three. Couple doors down from here. Can't miss it."

Hatch took the key and turned to leave. "Thanks."

"My name is Manuel. If you need anything, my family and I live in the far room, number twelve. Actually, I converted eleven and twelve, joining them together to form one room, but the door to eleven is sealed. Please, don't hesitate to knock if I'm not at the front desk."

"I should be fine but thank you." Hatch pushed the door open.

The chime above rang out her departure as she walked to her accommodations.

The room was small, and the furniture was a bit dated, but it was clean. Immaculate would have been a better word to describe it. A heavy scent of lemon emanated from the wood surfaces. The carpet, although worn bare in some spots, looked as if it had been cleaned by a professional-grade rug cleaner. Hatch had stayed in more luxurious places that paled in comparison to the effort put into the small strip of rooms.

She decided to shower and get a good night's sleep. Hatch wanted to get an early start.

THREE

EACH FOOTSTEP WAS light and quick. The cadence of breath in sync with every fifth heel strike of the sneaker. *Run as if your life depends on it*. She heard the words of her father as she picked up the pace. His philosophy was centered around pushing boundaries, both mental and physical. Ingrained at an early age and sharpened in recent years, Hatch lived up to his mantra. Here in a place somehow connected to his past, she pushed herself even harder.

No better way to find yourself than to get lost on a run. She didn't plot her morning's course, nor did she know how long or far she planned to go. Hatch took only the room key and some cash, tucking them into her waistband before heading out on the morning's trek.

It seemed like a good way to see the small town of Luna Vista. She had left the motel forty-seven minutes ago and her pace had been relentless. Even with the coldness of the morning, she worked up a decent sweat as she opened her stride on a long stretch of road. The terrain was flat, but the elevation, three-quarters of a mile high, put a strain on her lungs. A slight touch of hypoxia gave her an endorphin rush, making each step feel lighter and more disconnected than when she ran at sea level. It was a euphoric experience.

The smell of bacon caught her attention as she passed a corner diner. The saltiness of the rendered pig fat caused her to slow to a stop. Hatch walked back to the diner and stood on the sidewalk looking in through the plate glass windows. Her legs tingled from the exertion, but her stomach rumbled at the marvelous odors seeping out from the restaurant. The diner wasn't crowded. After taking a minute to stretch her thighs, Hatch entered.

Local diners were the hub of a small town, and she could think of no better place to start her fact-finding mission than inside the diner. There was a sign inviting patrons to seat themselves, but Hatch didn't want to take up a table, so she meandered over to the bar-styled counter. She took up a stool a few seats down from a plump gentleman in a heavy plaid coat, the orange and black of a hunter. He was reading the paper and slurping noisily from a mug of coffee and didn't break from his routine with her arrival.

An older man with bits of white stubble coating his ruddy jowls approached. He wore a paper hat, covering a head spotted with buzzed hair the same color as his unshaven face. His thick caterpillar brows furrowed as he approached, taking wary stock of the sweat-coated newcomer.

"Get you somethin' to drink, Miss?"

"Coffee's fine." She swallowed and the dryness in her throat caused her voice to crackle.

"And maybe a glass of water, too."

The man in plaid folded his paper and Hatch could feel his stare fall on her. He then grabbed his coffee, announcing his return to the morning's routine with a loud slurp. A moment later, a mug filled to the brim was set in front of her. The aroma had a boldness to it that Hatch enjoyed. She took a sip of it before rehydrating with water.

She picked up a menu stuffed between a napkin holder and bottle of ketchup. The stubbled man behind the counter waited patiently for her decision. It didn't take long.

"I'll have the Luna Vista special."

The man cocked an eyebrow. "That's a pretty big plate and it comes with a side of pancakes, too."

"Pretty sure I can handle it."

At that, the man's rough exterior softened. He smiled, drawing up his hound-dog-like cheeks. "One special, coming up."

She watched as the man who'd taken her order walked back to the grill. Hatch could see him still smiling as he cracked eggs and flipped the pancakes. He took great pleasure in building the pile of food for her. Must not be a menu item commonly ordered by the women of the town.

Hatch quietly enjoyed her coffee while she waited, taking the time to survey the other patrons by using the angled mirror above the cooking station. Only a handful of people were in the diner. There were murmured conversations amid the occasional clink and clatter of a dish or utensil. But at some point during her brief observation, each and every one of them took a moment to check her out. Growing up in a small town and having just recently revisited it, Hatch knew the distrust and guardedness with which outsiders were received.

And she felt it now.

"Enjoy." Two plates were set in front of her, one containing eggs, bacon, home fries, and toast. The other held three of the biggest pancakes Hatch had ever seen. She smiled, understanding the man's shock at her decision to place the order.

"Thanks. Mind if I get a refill on the coffee? I'm going to need it to wash down these pancakes."

The man laughed as he turned to get the pot.

He held the pot over the mug, bringing the black liquid back to its brim. Before he walked away again, Hatch asked, "Have you been in business long?"

The man set the pot on the counter. A small droplet of water sizzled under the heat of the pot's base. "I've been working this counter since this hair was as black as that there coffee. Why you asking?"

His voice was terse. Defensive to her inquiry. She dismissed it.

"My father had travelled out this way a long time back. That's why I wanted to check it out."

"Most people don't travel to Luna Vista. You sure he didn't mean Las Cruces? Much more touristy."

"I'm sure. He worked here for a bit."

"You don't say." He maintained his guard but leaned in and rested his forearms on the counter. "How long ago are we talking about?"

"A while. 'Bout thirty-plus years ago."

"Well, that's going back a while. I was here then. Not sure I'm going to remember, but I'm pretty good with names."

"Paul Hatch ring a bell?"

The man behind the counter scratched at his stubble. Giving a healthy pause, the answer came in the slow shake of his head. "Can't say it does."

The man in plaid stood abruptly. He tucked his paper under his arm and headed out the door.

Hatch said, "What do you know about that old abandoned warehouse on the outskirts of town?"

The man shrugged. "Not much to say about it. Been that way for years. There's been a couple businesses take up shop, but nothing seems to last there. I heard it's been taken over by a bunch of local punks and used as some kind of hangout."

"Can't the cops do anything about it?"

The man laughed and turned. Placing the pot back on the burner, he said, "That man who just walked out is the chief of police. Why don't you ask him?"

Hatch turned. The man in plaid had already slipped from view. There was no need to chase after him. She'd know where to find him should the need arise.

She cut into the eggs and began the task of taking on her second challenge of the morning, the Luna Vista Special.

The cook smiled at her efforts. "There is somebody else who may be able to help you out. Wilbur Smith's been here since before me.

He runs the gun shop across the street. Doesn't open up for a couple hours, but it might be worth talking to him."

"Thanks."

"I'm Harry Packer, by the way."

She held up her mug in a salutary fashion. "Rachel. But people just call me Hatch."

"Well, we serve lunch and dinner, also. So, don't be a stranger."

Hatch looked down at the mountain of food, giving a conciliatory smile. "I don't think I'll be hungry again for a long while."

"Can't say I didn't warn you."

Hatch set about devouring the meal. The long walk back would give her time to digest. She needed to shower off from the run and then pay the gun shop owner a visit.

The town of Luna Vista owed her some answers, and Hatch wasn't leaving until she had them.

FOUR

THE SHOWER WAS HOT. Not so much that it burned the skin, but enough so that steam filled the small space of the motel bathroom, coating the window and mirror in a foggy layer. She cut off the water and stood still. The water dripped down her body. She let the cool air surround her, tightening the pores of her skin before stepping out. The scar snaking its way up her right arm always tingled after a shower. It felt like a trickle of goosebumps spreading along its rough web of scar tissue. Her eyes followed a droplet as it traveled downward from her shoulder following the zigzags to her wrist. The memory of the day that caused the damage was never far from her mind, but always more prominent when the old wound was visible. She didn't let her mind drift too far down memory lane and grabbed the towel from the metal rack above the toilet.

It was closer to noon now. She'd taken her time on the walk back from the restaurant. She figured she'd take in as much of the town as she could in slow stride. There wasn't much to really take in. She came to understand why the motel owner tried to move her on to the bigger town of Las Cruces. It was readily apparent during her walk that this particular section of Luna Vista was rundown and poorly kept. Hatch had been in many a town like this in her travels and was not unaccustomed to poverty and the things that followed it. From first glance, it looked like there was little to no police action or presence in the town. As if law enforcement had turned a blind eye.

As she toweled off, Hatch heard voices. They were coming from the backside of the motel. She stepped back into the tub and tried to peer out through the small window. It was frosted glass designed to let light in but obscure any visibility. She listened for a moment to the muffled sounds of several male voices. Although the words weren't clear, she was able to discern the tone. And what she made out did not sound amicable.

Something inside Hatch activated her innate need to investigate. She quickly finished toweling off and dressed in jeans and a light-weight sweatshirt. Tugging on a pair of hard-toed hiking boots, she stepped outside. The cool air against her damp skin and wet hair was exhilarating. She made her way down the long, connected row of motel rooms. By the look of the parking lot, it seemed likely most were vacant.

Hatch passed by the office. Nobody was inside. She didn't see Manuel tending the walkway or anything else, for that matter. The voices behind the motel grew louder and she became concerned it might be him in trouble. Her pace quickened into a brisk jog.

As she rounded the corner of the building, bringing her to the backside of the motel, she heard the jeers more clearly.

"Give him everything you got. Crack that fool!" A man's voice said followed by a cackling laugh. "Blaze put it down on him. Don't hold nothing back! This ain't no time to take it easy on his ass."

Hatch stepped into view and saw a young boy in his mid-teens being pummeled by a short stocky man who looked to be only a few years older than the boy. Two other men watched on. One casually leaned against a Cadillac smoking a joint. She'd guessed it was this one who'd been calling out the taunts, guiding the action while the other two men carried out his bidding. A third man, taller and more physically impressive than the others, circled the downed teen. He had a lighter complexion and his hair was pulled back into cornrows. His eyes had a wildness to them, a hunger.

The teen propped himself up on all fours. His head down, looking at the dirt ground beneath him. The wild-eyed one with the cornrows rushed forward and swung his foot upward, like a place kicker trying to send a football through the uprights. The top of his foot struck the boy in the face with the laced portion of the Vans impacting perpendicular to the bridge of the boy's nose.

He whimpered but didn't cry out as his head whipped back. His body followed, tossing him flat on his back. A spurt of blood bubbled out from both nostrils. The young teen sputtered a blood-filled cough.

The two men, the short stocky one and the cornrowed kicker, began hooting and hollering at the injured boy as they circled him like hungry wolves looking for their next opportunity to pounce. The boy, still on his back, was barely moving and, from what Hatch could discern, was nearly unconscious. The odds were definitely not in this boy's favor and he was clearly outnumbered.

Hatch decided to level the playing field a bit and began her approach.

The injured teen had managed to roll to his side and begin the slow process of trying to stand once again. He was bleeding from several places on his face, the worst coming from his recently damaged nose. Scratches and abrasions along his arms were evidence of the fighting that had taken place prior to Hatch's arrival. She was impressed at the boy's stubborn resolve to stand once more. He was tougher than he looked, at least mentally if not by physical measures. She'd learned physical strength could always be taught, but mental fortitude was a born trait few had.

Each time he rose halfway to a standing position, one of the guys standing above him pummeled him back down. The short stocky one delivered a knee to the side of the boy's head. The boy collapsed. The fight was knocked from him. He lay in a slumped heap. The blood continued to drain from his broken nose and darkened the dry, cold dirt he rested on. Hatch could see the boy's chest rise and fall under heavy, labored breaths.

Hatch closed the distance enough to be able to insert herself into the problem.

"Three on one seems like pretty unfair odds if you ask me," Hatch said.

Her comment drew the attention of all three men, who looked over at her in surprise.

"Nobody asked you, bitch." The comment came from the one leaning against the older model Cadillac. Evaluating it more closely, she realized it was the same one she had seen yesterday outside of the abandoned warehouse.

Hatch continued to close the distance, more slowly now, between her and the two assaulters. Both men, the wild-eyed one with corn-rows and the shorter stocky one, stopped the beating they were giving the younger teen and directed their full attention to Hatch.

Both gave her a smile, not a welcoming one, but something bordering on the devious and somewhat deranged. Hatch had seen this in many past opponents. Larger more imposing men all thought they had an advantage over her. Many dismissed her because she was a woman, some because of her thin frame. Little did they know her body was tight with wiry muscles hidden under the loose-fitting sweatshirt she wore. To them she must've looked like an average person, a good Samaritan stopping to intervene. Well, she was a good Samaritan, and she did stop by to intervene. But she had no intention of doing it peacefully.

Now, she decided it was her turn to smile. And in doing so she could see it had a disorienting effect on the men. These thugs must have grown quite accustomed to intimidating people if not by their looks then by their actions. Both of which were on full display here today. Neither of which seemed to have any effect on Hatch.

The boy on the ground choked on a cough and groaned noisily. In his damaged condition, he was obviously unaware of why the beating had stopped. The slight reprieve of blows gave him time to begin his recovery. From the external damage and multiple shots she'd witnessed him taking, it was likely the boy was concussed.

The two thugs stepped around the moaning boy as if he weren't there. They treated him with the same regard as a discarded bit of trash on the ground.

Hatch recognized these men. They were the ones she'd seen while tucked behind the storage shed outside the abandoned building. Yesterday, she saw them with weapons and now wondered if they were armed. She, unfortunately, was not except for a small pocketknife she kept clipped to her front pocket.

"You heard my boy, Macho? Or are you deaf? This doesn't concern you." The stocky man said, wiping frothy spit from the corner of his mouth. "You stay here any longer and you'll be lying next to him." He eyed the boy on the ground.

"Best you get back to wherever it is you came from," the man by the car said. Macho, as the stocky man referred to him.

Hatch carefully assessed the situation. "That's not going to happen."

"Excuse me? Have you lost your mind, lady?" The stocky man looked at Macho and his cornrowed partner as if trying to understand her insolence.

"Maybe I have. I don't know. Or maybe you've gotta start thinking how crazy a person like me must be to face off against a group of thugs." She stopped moving forward and stilled her body. Bringing everything around her into full clarity. "If I were in your shoes, I'd be trying to see this situation a whole different way. I think you all should leave."

"Blaze, Psycho, check this bitch!" Macho said as he exhaled a deep lungful of smoke. "Teach her who the Outlaws are. And make sure it's a lesson she never forgets."

Two henchmen's smiles evaporated as they stepped forward, closing the distance to Hatch.

The one with cornrows, whom Hatch deemed to be Psycho due to the insane look in his eyes, took the lead. His arms were open, and he pushed out his chest like a peacock. As he walked slowly toward her, he began slapping his chest like an angry gorilla addressing a territorial threat. The problem with this overt display, intended as a means of intimidating an opponent, was that it was rooted in a deeply ingrained fear the man had most likely never assessed or even acknowledged. Hatch could smell weakness masked within the man's movements. As he sauntered closer, she decided her course of action.

Fighting multiple components is not much different than fighting a single adversary. The trick was turning many into one. A sort of "E Pluribus Unum" of combat. Hatch had spent extensive time training the finer points of hand-to-hand combat, studying under some of the best the military had to offer. The strategy was to keep one component in front of the other at all times. In doing so, it neutralized any secondary or tertiary attack from others in a group. It was a hard lesson to learn, and one filled with some memorable pain. The best lessons always were. But those battle-tested ones served her well on many occasions thereafter. It would appear today was proving to be another one of those days.

Psycho stopped three feet in front of her. His arms still wide. Hatch stood her ground, not giving an inch.

His right hand, held slightly above his head, was clenched into a tight fist. His movement telegraphed his intention. He would come crashing down on her face with an overhand right. He was taller than her 5'10" by an inch or two. And with the confidence with which he stepped forward, it was likely he had delivered this blow to multiple others in the past with success, including the boy on the ground.

She waited patiently, keeping her arms loose by her side. She moved outward, extending them in front of her chest. Hands open in a feigned gesture of weakness. The pose drew him in closer. Her outward display of fear seemed to give the man a boost of aggression. She saw the glimmer in his eye. He'd hurt women in the past and enjoyed it.

Psycho's fist rocketed down. "You stupid bitch!"

Hatch maintained her position until the last possible second. As soon as his fist was within a few inches of her face, she stepped in fast. Her calculated movement was a blur. The years of training exploded in milliseconds of rehearsed muscle memory.

Hatch shifted her bodyweight and stepped in hard with her right leg, splitting the gap in the man's unnecessarily wide stance. Her left arm came up as she moved, and her forearm jammed Psycho's descending blow into the crux of his elbow. The short stocky man was directly behind the taller man, effectively blocking his ability to engage Hatch.

Her block eliminated the potential strength and power of Psycho's blow. His kinetic energy stalled, and he was in an open, off-balance stance. Hatch drove her right elbow upward with impressive speed. The bony point of her elbow impacted underneath the man's chin. The mistake of talking crap during a fight left the mouth open, as in this case. As a result, the strike had a devastating effect. His jaw snapped shut. The bottom row of teeth smacked hard into the upper row with a loud crunching sound. She was hopeful it meant some of the teeth were broken or at the very least cracked.

Psycho staggered backward. His eyes rolled back in his head. Hatch knew he was out on his feet. His body swayed for a brief second before collapsing back into his friend, who was preparing his charge into the fray. Psycho fell into the other man, forcing the stocky one to catch him before casting the unconscious man aside.

In the shorter man's effort to right himself after being knocked off kilter, he was unable to come to a standing position before Hatch closed the distance. She delivered her next strike while the stocky man was still in a hunched half-squat. Hatch drove her knee forward, increasing its momentum by thrusting hard with her hip. Elbows and knees were much more devastating impact weapons. When delivered correctly, they carry a disastrous effect on their recipients.

The stocky man, who she deemed to be Blaze, didn't go down with one shot like his taller compatriot. Instead, he stumbled forward and grabbed wildly at her legs in a desperate attempt to take her down to the ground. Not wanting to turn this match into a ground fight with the heavier man, Hatch sprawled her legs out wide, reducing the ability for his grip to gain purchase on her thighs. She dropped her weight down onto his back. With his hands occupied, he was unable to break his collapse and was forced face first into the dirt below.

With her chest pressed tight to his back, Hatch spun herself around him and locked legs in under his hip. Keeping him pressed down, she slipped her left arm deep underneath the man's chin. She brought her right forearm across the base of the man's neck. Intertwining her arms and locking them in place, Hatch sunk in a rear naked choke hold.

Hatch squeezed her arms tight, cinching them down along the man's carotid arteries, effectively restricting blood flow which in turn restricted the oxygen to the brain. The human brain deprived of oxygen for approximately eight seconds will temporarily shut down causing a person to pass out. Ensuring this state of unconsciousness came quicker, she inhaled deeply, drawing the man in tight and closing off the final few millimeters of space between her arms and his neck. She counted down in her head from eight. By the time she got to the number three, the man went limp.

BY NATURAL COURSE OF ACTION, most fights do not take place for long in a standing position and usually end up on the ground. In situations when facing multiple adversaries, like this one, it was advantageous to spend as little time possible engaged in one-on-one ground battle. The more time Hatch spent entangled with the man left herself vulnerable to attack. She released her grip, pushed off on the unconscious man's back, and stood facing the ringleader.

He hadn't moved from his spot at the Cadillac, which wasn't all that surprising to Hatch. Her assault on the two men had been brutally efficient, only taking a matter of seconds.

His arms remained folded, and he was still leaning against the side of the Caddy. And if she properly read the man's facial expression, which was one of her specialties, she would label him impressed.

The man gave a slight nod, eyeballing the two downed men he'd sicced on her. She saw both of them were slowly beginning to regain their consciousness and roll about.

Macho began a slow cadence golf clap. "Impressive," he said without a hint of sarcasm.

"I'm not here to impress you."

His face grew serious and the clapping stopped. "I think you should take my compliment for what it is and be happy I don't do anything about what you just did to my two guys." His voice was not that of a hot-headed banger. His message's delivery was cold and calculated.

Hatch was approximately fifteen feet from him and, not sure of his intentions, she began weighing her options.

Macho kept his eyes on Hatch as he slowly pulled a pistol from the front of his waistband. He began tapping his index finger on the outside of the crescent trigger.

"So, that's how you want this to go? Afraid of a girl and you pull a pistol?" She wanted to buy time. Enough at least to come up with a plan for this new variable.

"Truth is, there's not much I am afraid of, lady. And that goes for you. But I can't have you come over my way, throwing hands and feet. Ain't nothin' fair about fighting." His stoic face softened just a bit. His lips moved as though they were going to bend into a thin smile. "I'm giving you an out. Time for you to go. Don't need no cops poking around 'cause I smoked a white girl. You can take my kindness and walk away. Or I can end this, here and now."

Hatch knew better than to push this envelope. There was no way she could close the distance, withdraw her pocketknife, and avoid the gunshot. There were tested theories amongst law enforcement and military circles that a person could close a twenty-one-foot gap before a person could get a shot off. Most of the demonstrations proving this were under very controlled environments. Not the dynamic real-world situation presented to her now. Every theory has its variables. Right now, that included the two men on the ground that were coming to a slow state of angered alertness. Plus, the fact that she had no weapon at the ready and Macho's pistol was out. This last factor alone negated the distance between them.

Macho continued his metronomic tapping of the trigger. Its taunting gesture gnawed at Hatch. Part of her, the deeply rooted never-give-up part, wanted to throw caution to the wind and attack. But the reason Hatch had survived this long in some of the world's most dangerous places was because she could put her drive mechanism in check. She also knew when and where to unleash it. This was not one of those times.

The younger teen was now alert and sitting up. She looked over at him. "He's coming with me."

"I don't think so." Macho looked at the boy who was bleeding from a cut above his eye. From the swelling around the bridge of his nose, it most likely was broken. Blood continued to drip from of both nostrils. The layers of blood encircled his mouth and created a dark goatee. "But I'm reasonable. Why don't you ask him for yourself?"

"How about it, kid?" she asked.

The injured boy scooted back and stood. It was obvious to Hatch he probably hadn't witnessed any of her interventions. His brow furrowed as he looked over at the two men who'd been beating the living crap out of him. He watched them in their semi-conscious state, and then looked back at Hatch. His brow began to unfurrow as his eyes widened.

The boy stepped back on wobbly legs and, for a moment, it looked as though he were going to collapse back onto the ground he'd just expended so much energy trying to get off of. He did a double take of Hatch. Understandably so. He'd been unconscious when she'd come to his aid, or at the very least, had been close to it. Now, the two men near him were in similar physical distress and here stood this woman, with hair still damp from the shower she'd left, who had come to his rescue.

"What the hell just happened?" The boy said, looking around at the ground. The two men pushed themselves up and were standing a few feet away from him.

"Your guardian angel appeared to save you," the ringleader said with a smug look of contempt. "She came to your rescue. Thank goodness she was here to save you from such an awful fate." His tone was overly sarcastic.

"I don't understand." The boy said, rubbing his head with one hand while wiping the blood on his sleeve with the other. He spat some blood from his mouth.

The ringleader looked at the boy. His lips curled into a smirk. "How about it, X? You want to go home with this sweet lady who came to save you from us horrible gangsters? Or are you an Outlaw who's ready to ride and die for his homies?"

The boy exhaled. A raspy wheezy cough came with it, one born of exertion and adrenaline.

She watched the boy's face. In it she saw the slightest of twitches. Hatch immediately recognized the spasm for what it was, a micro gesture. The body externalized thought in these subtle, barely notice-able releases. In the boy's miniscule twitch of his left check, she read his nonverbal confliction. *He didn't want to go with the ringleader.*

"You know me, Macho. I'm an Outlaw for life," the boy called X said with as much false bravado as he could muster.

Hatch watched as the boy walked toward the ringleader. She stepped toward him and thought about pulling him away from them, physically removing him. But she saw in the look the boy gave her, it would have been met with resistance. His eyes were contemptuous.

"I don't know who you are, lady. You don't know me. Or what you got yourself involved in."

She listened, not only to the boy's words, but more to his tone. Hatch could hear his attempt, as weak as it was, to sound tough like the other men. She saw through his act.

"You don't have to go with them. I can get you some help. Looks like your nose is broken. At least let me fix that."

The boy spit blood on the ground near Hatch's feet and gave a raspy laugh. "I don't need you to fix nothing." He walked away toward the ringleader.

Macho tucked the gun back into his waistband. The teenager stood before him. Macho slapped the boy's shoulder and then cupped his hand around the nape of his neck and pulled him in. Macho pressed his forehead to the boy's. "You did good today, X. Welcome to the Outlaws."

Psycho and Blaze, dazed but functional once again, started to step in the direction of Hatch. She squared to them again.

"You going to give her an opportunity to kick your ass one more time? Get your asses over here before you embarrass me anymore." Macho looked down at his cellphone. "We've got things to do and people to see."

Hatch stood still as the four men loaded up into the Cadillac. Her right arm tingled from the exertion.

The car sped off, kicking up dust from the unpaved lot. Hatch raised her hand to shield her eyes from the onslaught of dirt and debris. As it drove around the corner and was almost gone from view, Hatch saw the teen's head turn. He made eye contact with her.

A moment later, the vehicle roared out of sight.

FIVE

HATCH RETURNED to her room to finish drying her hair and thought about the boy in the back seat of the Cadillac. There was something about him that made her want to jump in her car and go after them. To chase them down and drag him away from those thugs. But she knew the way of the world. The things you want don't always translate into the things that happen. She also knew, better than most, circumstances dictate your future. In this case, it seemed as though whatever hold the gang had on the young boy, it was tight.

Hatch put the thought of the boy from her mind and entered the Camry. She was surprised at how cold New Mexico was. After leaving Colorado, she had assumed the southern locale would be warmer. But she'd found it was just as cold, if not colder, without the high mountains of Hawk's Landing to shield the wind. The Organ Mountains, off in the distance to the east, separated the town of Luna Vista from White Sands, but did little to provide much shelter from the hard blasts of icy wind. Each desert gust carried with it bits and pieces of sand and rock.

She now drove the same path she had run earlier in the day. The stretch of roadway zipped by much quicker in a car than on foot. The town seemed much smaller. She headed back to the diner and pulled up in front, parked in an angled space on the street, and got out.

The diner's owner and cook hustled out of the restaurant. "You're making quite an impression here in town," he said.

"How do you mean?" Hatch asked.

"Words out you stood up to those damned Outlaws." Harry smiled and gave a thumbs up. "About time somebody did."

Hatch gave a half smile.

"But I need to warn you." His face grew serious, as did his tone. "They're about as dangerous as they come. They may not look like much, but they've basically crippled this side of the town. Been that way around here for a good bit of time."

"They didn't seem like much to me. Pretty much amateur hour."

"You ever get a chance to talk to Wilbur over at the gun shop?"

"About to do that now. It's actually why I came back to town. I was hoping to catch him."

"You be careful out there, Miss Hatch—correction, just Hatch."

Hatch crossed the street to Vista Guns. Heavy steel bars lined the glass of the shop's storefront windows. The security measure was understandable, especially in light of witnessing the gang influence firsthand. This town didn't need the weapons inside to fall into the hands of the criminals. Hatch thought about the gun that the ring-leader, Macho, had displayed. She wondered where he'd acquired it.

She pushed open the door. A sensor chimed a digital three beep tone as she crossed the threshold. A head of messy dirty blond hair popped up from behind the counter. Hatch was greeted by a ruggedly handsome man in his thirties.

"Can I help you?"

Hatch wasn't expecting to see a younger man. "I was looking to speak with Wilbur Smith."

"Well I'm a Smith—just not the one you're looking for. Wilbur's my dad. He's out at a town meeting at the moment. I'm Gabe. Is there something I can help you with?"

The clerk looked to be around Hatch's age. He had kind eyes.

They were a soft powder blue. Even though temperatures had dipped low, his skin was a robust tan. Not that of a beach boy, more of someone who spends his time outdoors recreationally. *Maybe he was a runner, too,* she thought. Looking around the shop, it was more likely he was a hunter of some sort.

The man leaned on the counter. Hatch noticed the ripple of muscle in his forearms.

"I'm not so sure you'd be able to help me with what I'm looking for."

"Come again?"

"I'm looking for some information on that old abandoned warehouse on the outskirts of town. The one that looks as though time has long forgotten it. I talked to Harry over at the diner and he mentioned that your father's been running this business for over forty years. I was hoping he could tell me a little bit about the place and maybe point me in the direction of somebody who used to work there. It's a longshot, I know."

"Well, Harry's right about my father. He's a second-generation Luna Vista resident. Which makes him the longest living resident of our small town." He beamed with pride. "Not that it comes with much reward with the state of things lately. This place has really changed in recent years." The man cocked his head to the side and gave her a little smile. "I heard you met some of the people at the root of our problems."

"Man, word sure does travel fast around here. Is there some type of town twitter blog thing that every resident gets an instant play-by-play update the moment something happens?"

"Just small-town life, I guess. Not much happens around here. When it does, word spreads like wildfire. People around here, at least the good ones, try to take care of each other. We take care of our own. Ya know, look out for one another. And to do that you have to stay in contact. Each business on this strip of roadway is family-owned and family-run. You won't find any chain stores anywhere within the town limits. Closest one would be in Las Cruces, which is about a half hour drive west from here."

"I come from a pretty small town too. I know how things go. Gossip is king. Although in rural Colorado word doesn't seem to get around as quickly. People out there tend to keep to themselves." Hatch then thought of the recluse turned ally, Jed Russell, and wondered how the old man was recovering from the wounds sustained during their standoff.

"What part of Colorado?"

"Ever heard of Hawk's Landing?"

Gabe shook his head. "Nope. Never heard of it. I venture up to Colorado every once in a while. The elk hunting in Gunnison is pretty good, especially around mid-October. My father and I used to take a trip together every year, but in recent years his health started to come into question. His diabetes acts up a bit and while the exercise of tracking the big animals would do him good, he's become less inclined. I guess he just doesn't much like leaving the store anymore."

"It's just you and your dad? Nobody else around here to help with the store?"

"Yep. It's just us running things. If we both go, it's a period of time without anybody manning the shop. That means it's a period of time without us making any money. Even out here in our little Luna Vista, a man's still gotta make money if he wants to survive. Goodwill only goes so far."

"You're right about that."

"Plus, the last time he and I went out that way hunting, we returned to find that somebody had robbed our store. They broke in through the back. We had a small shipment of handguns, Smith and Wesson M&P 40 caliber semi-automatic pistols, still in the box that hadn't yet been shelved in the back-storage area." He shook his head. "Never recovered them."

Hatch thought about the ringleader, Macho, and the pistol he'd displayed. It wasn't a stretch to think the gang had stolen the guns he was referring to. She knew criminals found ways to get their hands on weapons regardless of governmental laws and regulations. Those restrictions sometimes slowed but never really stopped a criminal from getting a gun when they needed it.

"Maybe I can't tell you about things from thirty years ago, as I was only a toddler at the time, but I could show you around town." Gabe smiled.

"I thought you said there wasn't much to see around here?"

"Depends on where you go. You're standing at the dividing line of our small town. There's a nicer section. From what I hear, you decided to stay at the Moonbeam. That rundown motel isn't the nicest accommodations around. I could reach out to Agnes Pierce. She runs a little B&B on the other side. She makes a helluva breakfast. Might be worth checking out."

"Sounds nice, but I've already made arrangements with Manuel to stay at the Moonbeam for a couple of nights. And I don't like to welch on an agreement. Especially with a good hard-working man. I figured what little money I spend there, hopefully helps him and his family out a bit." Hatch offered a smile. "And trust me, I've stayed in much worse places than the Moonbeam."

Gabe cocked an eyebrow. "Yeah? Where is that?"

"Everywhere and nowhere."

"Pretty vague," he said.

"Didn't mean to be," Hatch said, realizing her standard comeback line could be perceived as off-putting. "Just something we used to say. It means I've been around a lot and seen a lot of places. Some forgettable and others not so much."

"Let me guess—you're military?"

Hatch's eyes narrowed. She never liked when people surmised anything about her. Especially if they had gathered it from just looking at her. She preferred to move anonymously among the population. To be just another face in the crowd. Albeit, her height caused her to stand out more than she'd like. Regardless, the gun store owner's son had pinpointed her origins in this brief exchange. As she thought about it, his ability to do this made sense. He'd spent his lifetime around weapons and the types of people who came into his store. If the information she had about this town, or at least that warehouse, was true, then for a time, Luna Vista was home to some former military special operations people. *Who knows, maybe some of them were still around now.*

"You got quiet for a moment. Did I say something wrong?" His smile faded. "It's just—I heard the way you handled those thugs. And now you're asking about the old warehouse. I figured you might be a bounty hunter or fugitive recovery agent. Our town is close enough to Las Cruces and not too far from the border. Not often, but every once in a while, we get a drifter come through here."

"You were right on your first guess. Although, it's been a bit since I've worn the uniform." She paused and looked at the man. He had the rugged build of a triathlete, but his biceps pressed tightly against the fabric of his shirt and his exposed forearms showed he was strong. "How about you? Did you serve?"

"Wanted to. I had everything set to go after graduating college. I decided I wanted to be a fighter pilot in the Air Force, but apparently colorblindness is something they frowned upon. Who knew?" Gabe looked down at the counter. "I still remember the disappointment. It really derailed me. I ended up coming back home to help with the store. And here I am ten years later."

Hatch just nodded. She knew the rigorous standards set by the military. And they were in place for a reason. She thought about her own situation and how those standards, or at least the military's interpretation of those standards, had left her at a crossroads and subsequently taken the one thing she loved more than anything in the world away from her. The military's decision to medically disqualify Hatch from returning to her unit left a bitter taste in her mouth. "I got out a little over a year ago."

"How long did you serve?"

"Fifteen years."

The man's eyes widened. "I'm impressed. I figured maybe you did a few years to pay for college. Officer or enlisted?"

"The best of both. I was a warrant officer. Earned my way up through the enlisted ranks."

"What did you do for a job?"

"I served in the Army's Criminal Investigations Division."

Gabe gave a nod of approval and then changed the subject. "It'd really be no trouble for me to show you around, if you'd like."

"Maybe later." He seemed harmless and the offer appeared genuine, but Hatch wasn't here on vacation. "What time do you think your father will be back?"

"Hard to say. Those town council meetings can get pretty heated. They last anywhere from a half hour to as long as three hours. It really just depends on what the issues are."

"Okay. Could you have your father give me a call at the Moonbeam? I'm staying in room number three." Hatch gave a friendly smile and turned to leave.

"Wait a minute." Gabe disappeared underneath the counter. After a couple seconds of noisy shuffling and closing of cabinets, he reappeared. He placed a small black handgun on the counter with the muzzle pointed off to the side and away from both of them. He looked at Hatch expectantly. "I think you might want to take this."

Hatch cocked her head and took one step closer. She looked down at the weapon. It was a Sig Sauer P229 Compact semi-automatic. It was a 9MM handgun. She was familiar with the weapon and had used it on several occasions during her time in the military. "It's great. But I'm really not here to buy a gun. Like I said before, I'm just here for some information and then depending on what that information is, I'll be leaving this town and heading on to the next."

"Consider it a loaner. Just until you get yourself situated and find whatever it is you're looking for."

"You guys loan guns here on a regular basis?" Hatch asked.

"Not by practice." The man smiled broadly. "But we also don't have people stand up to those thugs the way you did. I'm worried the odds might not be in your favor next time around. You seem like a good person, and I'd hate to see something bad happen to you."

Hatch looked at the gun a second time and then back at the man. She couldn't fault his logic. She knew to some degree he was right. She'd been lucky the man they called Macho had only brandished the gun and hadn't decided to fire it. And if, by chance, they crossed paths again, she doubted he'd be so lenient. Although, Hatch hoped that their dealings were done and that she'd be long gone sooner rather than later. But she was a realist and never planned on hopes and dreams. Hatch weighed her decisions in the cold hard reality that sometimes life was out of her control.

"Well, I'm going to need a box of ammo," she said, returning the man's smile.

Gabe reached under the counter again and pulled out a box containing fifty rounds of 9MM ammunition. He placed it on the counter next to the gun and pushed them closer to Hatch's side.

Hatch picked up the Sig, keeping the muzzle down and away, pressed the button located on the upper portion of the left side of the grip and released the magazine. It wasn't an ambidextrous mag release, but she knew how to compensate. She then opened the box and loaded ten rounds one by one into the magazine. Hatch then seated the magazine, guiding it with her index finger and using her palm to press it until she heard the click.

If Hatch carried a weapon, it was always in battery. Keeping the gun pointed down and away from the store clerk, she gripped the slide and racked it back. She then let it slam forward with a loud metallic thud. The action chambered a round. Hatch then ejected the magazine and set the weapon down on the counter. She took one more round from the box and topped off the magazine, maximizing its capacity, and reseated it back into the gun. The weapon was now combat ready with a full mag and one in the chamber. The only way Hatch ever carried a weapon.

Gabe watched her manipulate the gun. "Well, I don't think I need to ask you if you have ever handled this type of firearm before," the man said with a laugh.

Hatch smiled. "I know my way around the gun. And thanks."

Hatch then slid the weapon into the small of her back. The cold metal pressed against her flesh but the feel of it was good. She reached out with her left hand and the man shook it. Hatch had become left hand dominant since receiving the injury to her right arm. But she knew the real reason she now offered her left was more out of a self-consciousness regarding the scars and visible damage.

As she began walking out of the store, the man called back to her. "And don't hesitate to take me up on that offer. It's a standing one. Anytime you want to see a little bit of this town, let me know. And if you change your mind about your accommodations, just say the word and I'll get you in touch with Agnes."

"Thanks for the offer. I'll keep it in mind." Hatch then tapped the weapon that was now concealed underneath her sweatshirt and said, "Hopefully, I can return this to you in the same condition it is now."

SIX

XAVIER SAT on the beat-up couch. Its internal springs poked at his leg through the worn leather. His head hurt worse than any migraine he'd ever experienced. The throbbing expanded out from the epicenter of the damaged bridge of his nose, a relentless pounding in sync with every beat of his heart. He had stuffed some toilet paper up his nostrils. It had worked to slowly clot the blood inside his nose.

A broken mirror on the nearby wall provided him an opportunity to visually examine the damage to his face. His nose was a dark purple and the discoloration was starting to spread along his cheekbone under each eye, giving his medium complexion deep, dark rings like that of a raccoon. It was definitely broken. There was no doubt about that. But with the swelling, he couldn't tell whether it would heal straight or if he'd be cursed with a crooked nose for the rest of his life. A visible reminder of the beating he took marking his official entry into the Outlaws.

Macho rolled a joint while Psycho tapped out a small amount of cocaine onto a flat piece of mirrored glass set atop a table.

Blaze was sitting with his arms folded in anger. "You should've let me have a second chance with that bitch. I could've taken her, man. She just caught me off guard is all."

"You think she just caught you off guard? Just got lucky with both of you?" Macho looked at both men and held it until each one of them returned his gaze. "She flat out whooped your asses. Each one of you. In less than a minute and you were out cold. So, no. I wasn't going to let you take another shot at her. You'd just up and embarrass yourself. More importantly—embarrass me."

Psycho put a cut plastic straw inside his nose and ran the line on the table. He sat back, pinched the other nostril, and snorted loudly, pulling the powdered cocaine deep. When he released his breath with a big exhale, his eyes were wilder than normal. The cocaine hitting his bloodstream through the capillaries in his nasal cavity had an immediate effect on him.

"Why didn't you just smoke her?" Psycho rubbed the end of his nose. "Ain't like the cops around here are going to solve anything. Hell, even if they did, they'd be too scared to do anything about it. They know better."

"Pop that young'n yesterday and people know better than to talk because it's a local thing. But you go and shoot some woman we ain't never seen in this town before and who knows what kinda shitstorm that's going to bring down on us." Macho lit the end of the joint and took two quick pulls at it. Exhaling, he said, "The way she handled you two—maybe she's some investigator down here looking into things or something. But one thing I can tell you, if I had put her down, we'd be up to our necks in trouble. Trouble we don't need right now."

Blaze rubbed the side of his neck near his throat. The same spot where the woman had choked him. "So, she just gets a pass then? She gets to roam free, around *our* town, without a care in the world? Word gets out, people might think we gone soft."

Xavier looked over at hearing the man's comment, knowing the effect it would have on their leader. Macho's jaw was clenched shut.

Little ripples pulsing along his jawline were an indicator of the anger he was holding back.

"Ain't nobody around here going to think the Outlaws have gone soft. Get that through your thick head. But like I said, a bullet to that woman's skull ain't good for our operation."

Blaze sank back a little bit in the chair he was sitting in. "I didn't mean no disrespect, Macho. You know how we do. I'm just pissed that girl put me down like that. I just want to know we have a plan to take our pound of flesh."

Macho picked up the lighter he'd set down on the table next to the small bag of white powder. Psycho was now tapping his second line onto the mirrored glass. Macho lit the joint in his hand again. This time he took a longer pull and held it deep in his lungs. As he exhaled the thick smoke, he passed it over to the man who'd questioned his decision. Blaze took it in hand.

"We're going to get even with her. No question about that. And Xavier is going to help us get that figured out." Macho looked over to Xavier.

Xavier sat forward on the couch, his head still pounding, as Blaze passed the blunt to him. Without hesitation, he sucked in a lungful of the fragrant pot, hoping the tetrahydrocannabinol, or THC, would have a medicinal effect on his debilitating headache. "What do you need me to do, Macho?"

"We don't want to come at her right off the rip. She's obviously able to handle herself pretty well, and I'm not sure if she's here with anybody else. We're going to take a little time and get a feel for her before we move. But when we do, we need to make it look like a tragic accident."

Xavier cocked an eyebrow upward. "Accident? What do you mean?"

"You let me figure that out. But this is Luna Vista and people disappear around here all the damn time. It's a hard life living in our little town. Accidents happen all the time."

"How do you want me to help?" Xavier asked.

"If she's staying at your dad's crappy little motel, then I want you to keep an eye on her and figure out as much as you can about her."

Xavier nodded. He didn't let his offense at Macho's comment about his father's business show.

Psycho rubbed his jaw line and fiddled with one of his teeth. Not one for complaining, it was apparent to Xavier the man was in pain. He took a little bit of the white powder and rubbed it along his gum line near the loose tooth. And then with a deranged smile, he said, "Whatever you say. You know I'm always game."

Xavier watched the men who had just taken pleasure in beating him behind the motel during his initiation. And then he thought of the tough woman whom he'd never met but had risked her life for his. She'd stepped in on his behalf. Albeit, not her place to do so. But she had done it without promise of reward. And she'd done it unarmed against three very dangerous people. *What kind of a person does that for somebody they don't know?* And then he thought about what Macho had just said and how they were going to get their revenge on this woman. He didn't like it, not one bit. He hoped to find some way he could get her out of this mess before it cost her life.

He caught another glimpse of himself in the broken mirror. He then thought of his mother and what she was going to do to him when she saw his broken nose. She'd know who was responsible and although there was little she could do about it, she would be furious. But more upsetting than her anger toward him was the disappointed look he knew he'd see in her eyes. As if he had a choice in the matter. As if anyone in Luna Vista had a choice. Maybe those on the other side, but not here and not in the world that Xavier had grown to know.

The marijuana began to work its magic and the pounding subsided. He pushed back on the couch, trying to find a comfortable position without the spring's poke so, for at least a brief moment, he could relax and enjoy the high. Because he knew in the coming days there would be much more asked of him. Things he wouldn't want to do but would have no choice but to carry out.

Blaze turned the music up on the stereo and the booming bass reverberated in him, giving a rhythmic beat to the pulsing throb of his broken nose.

SEVEN

HATCH DROVE in the opposite direction of the Moonbeam. She decided to give herself a self-guided tour of the nicer side of Luna Vista. Afterward, she planned to drive out toward the desert mountain range of White Sands. It wasn't every day that she was in this part of the country, and although she didn't intend to stick around town long, she figured she might as well take a moment to explore her surroundings. Plus, kicking the proverbial hornet's nest with the local gang, she figured it was best if she made herself scarce for a few hours before returning to the motel.

Gabe, the gun store owner's son, was definitely right about one thing...there was a much nicer section to the town. After passing Harry's Diner, she seemed to pass through an invisible barrier between the two areas. The houses on the west side were run down and had a ghetto feel. The neighborhood she now drove through was its polar opposite. Each side of the street was lined with small, well-kept homes. Although, the grass had browned due to seasonal change, they weren't dirt-patched like the other side of town.

The homes themselves looked to be single-family ranches of fairly high quality. The cars in the driveways weren't rust-coated, broken-down heaps. For lack of better words, it was akin to Andy Griffith's Mayberry.

She took a turn onto another residential street. A pink house near an intersection caught her eye. Hatch hadn't seen a house in that color before and it caused her to stare. It looked like a Mary Kay top seller was rewarded with a house instead of the pearlized-pink Cadillac. Distracted, Hatch missed the stop sign at the corner. She hit the brakes but not in time to come to a complete stop and ended up slow rolling through it.

Moments later, she saw in her rearview mirror a black-and-white cruiser pulling up behind her. In that moment, she realized she hadn't seen much in the way of law enforcement since she'd been in town, minus the sheriff sitting in the diner earlier that morning. She couldn't imagine it being a big department. The headquarters was attached to the town hall. If she had to guess, it probably wasn't much bigger than the one she'd left in Hawk's Landing.

With the police car behind her, she suddenly felt uneasy, remembering the Sig Sauer Gabe had just given her. A loaded firearm was tucked neatly into the back of her waistband. A firearm which she had no license to carry.

Even with all her experience as a law enforcement agent for the U.S. Army, a cop by all rights, just one of a different uniform, she never liked the feeling of a police car in her rearview. The present circumstance unnerved her at the potential of being stopped. She'd worked with a lot of good cops over the years, great ones in fact. Men like Dalton Savage. But there was a percentage out there who took the job too seriously. And a pompous ass behind a badge was an ugly thing. In her time since she'd left the military, she'd run into a few who fell into that category as she drifted across the country and not all those experiences were pleasurable encounters.

She hoped the officer behind her would drive off and leave her be, letting her exit town uninterrupted.

As Hatch drove, she looked in the rearview mirror and knew this would not be the case. The patrolman had picked up his microphone and was radioing something in. Most likely her license plate, which would return to a rental agency out of Colorado. She knew, being a former cop herself, an out-of-state plate, and in particular a rental, driving around a small town would be a big red flag. She'd already given him the violation by rolling through the stop sign. With his hand on the mic, it was only a matter of time before he activated his lights and pulled her over. Her mind drifted to the gun pressed against the small of her back.

The cop's decision to put the mic up in eyeshot of her gave away his intention. It was something she had long ago learned to avoid. If you're going to radio something in behind the car you intended to stop, you wanted to hold that microphone low, below the steering column so it's not visible to the person you're behind. Bad guys picked up on such things. And in turn, they prepared for their response. Hatch had learned not to telegraph her movements.

The cruiser's overhead strobes activated. In the gray light of day, they weren't as impactful as if it had been night, but the message was received. A quick flip of his siren bellowed. Hatch began to yield and pulled to the right side of the roadway. Before coming to a complete stop along the curb line, she cantered her wheels outward to the left and then put the vehicle in park. Hatch did this purposefully. Cops around the country were trained when initiating a traffic stop to canter their wheels out to the left toward the flow of traffic. This was done as a precaution, in the event of a rear end collision with the police car, the turnout would redirect the impact away from the officer and stopped motorist. But Hatch didn't do it out of fear of impact. She did it as a way of tipping her hand. She hoped this officer behind her was savvy enough to notice the gesture. A moment later she had her answer.

Over the PA system, she heard the officer say, "Driver, please straighten your wheels and turn your vehicle off."

Step one in her deflection was complete. Hatch did as she was told, turning the steering wheel to the right and then cut the ignition. She waited and watched for the officer to exit the vehicle, which he did a moment later. Hatch then crossed her wrists across over each other and laid them over top of the steering wheel. It was another extra layer to show total compliance and to hopefully engage the officer's intuition.

The patrolman approached on the passenger side of the vehicle. She was impressed. Although extremely beneficial during motor vehicle stops, it was a tactic that was not commonly deployed by officers on the street. Hatch had learned the benefit of it from a field training officer. The technique of approaching from the passenger side gave the officer a different vantage point and view into the car, further enabling them to control the occupants of the vehicle more easily. And in a worst-case scenario, if something broke bad, gave them more of an advantage in a tactical situation. The fact that this officer had chosen to approach her car from the passenger side and his quick observation of her wheel's positioning meant he was, in her short summation and at bare minimum, a well-trained police officer.

He stood by the B pillar of the car, the portion of the vehicle's frame separating the front passenger compartment from the backseat. He stood approximately a foot from the vehicle and positioned himself to where he was partially visible through the passenger-side window. He was in a slightly bladed stance as he tapped lightly on the glass.

Hatch uncrossed her hands and depressed the button, lowering the window. The officer cantered his head and peered in on her, not fully exposing himself to the interior of the car. Another point in this officer's favor, further supporting her theory he was well-trained.

"Ma'am, I'm Officer Cartwright. The reason I stopped you this afternoon is you failed to come to a complete stop at the stop sign a couple streets back. Any reason you didn't come to a stop?"

"I guess I just missed it. I wasn't really paying attention, Officer. I apologize. I was checking out your town and the pink house caught my eye."

"Ma'am, do you have your driver's license on you?"

"I do. It's in my back pocket. I'll reach for it, if you don't mind?"

Hatch said these words on purpose. Again, working to draw the question out of the officer without pushing too hard.

"Go right ahead."

After lowering the window, Hatch had placed her hands back into their crossed position on the steering wheel. She now moved her right and reached for the wallet in her back pocket. She retrieved it and brought it back up in front of her. She then pulled out her license from the clear plastic encasement in the wallet. She leaned across the passenger seat and handed it out the window to the officer, exposing the scar tissue along her wrist in the process. She noticed the officer's eyes trail just a moment longer than they should have after he took the license. Hatch knew he noticed her damaged arm.

"Mind if I ask—are you police?" The officer examined the license in his hand.

"I was. Well, if you count being a military police officer to be police, then my answer is yes." Hatch was satisfied her multilayered deployment of hints had worked. She had, without overtly telling the man, exposed her experience.

The man smiled. "I think being in military police counts twice. It's two services rolled into one." He held onto the license but wasn't examining it as intently after hearing her claim.

"Thank you."

"I can see from the license and the rental car that you're not from around here. Are you still in the service?"

"No. Got out about a year ago."

"What brings you to Luna Vista, or are you just passing through?"

"I'm staying in town for a few days. My dad had come through here before I was born, and I've been retracing some of his steps since he passed."

"Did he live here? Or work here?"

"Still trying to figure that out. Haven't had much luck yet. From what I know, he worked at whatever business used to occupy that old abandoned warehouse on the outskirts of town."

"Always wondered what was in that building. It's been abandoned since I moved up this way."

"Not from around here?"

"I actually grew up in Wisconsin. I was looking for a change of pace. One night I just threw a dart at a map and this is where I landed."

"Sounds like as good a plan as any." Hatch gave a soft chuckle and removed her hands from the steering wheel. "Maybe I should try that. I'd probably have better luck."

Hatch watched as the officer relaxed his stance and was no longer in a defensive posture behind the B pillar of the side door. He now squared himself to her. He looked down at the license in his hand. "I've just got to run this real quick. Ya know—procedures and all."

"Of course."

Officer Cartwright stepped back from the door and moved toward the rear quarter of the car. He spoke into the microphone clipped to his lapel while keeping his eyes on Hatch. He returned in less than a minute.

"Here's your license back, Ma'am."

Hatch felt awkward being addressed as ma'am even though she knew it was most likely an indicator of the officer's upbringing rather than a remark about her age. She guessed she was only six or seven years older than the man. The patrolman did have a disarming charm to him. She imagined he would make a pretty good interrogator.

Taking the license in hand and slipping it back inside her wallet, Hatch shifted in her seat and felt the gun press into the small of her back on the left side. The little pinch of metal against her flesh reminded Hatch of the fine line she was walking.

"Well, enjoy your stay here in Luna Vista. If you need anything, you know where to find me."

As the patrolman turned to walk away, Hatch said, "Far be it from me to be one to nitpick but—"

Officer Cartwright turned and placed his hand on the top of the car, bent and leaned into the open window. "But what?"

"Seems to me you've got a little bit of a gang problem here in this quiet town. Kinda strange to have you out on this side, where as far as I can tell, there's not much going on in the way of criminal activity."

"What are you getting at?" His face was not as welcoming as it had been only moments before.

"I'm just saying. I've been in town for a short period of time and you'd have to be blind not to see what's happening on the other side. But I haven't seen any cops except your chief. Then I cross over into some imaginary line into Mayberry and am pulled over within three minutes."

Hatch watched the man's face redden, but he didn't speak. She wasn't certain if it was anger at the insinuation or embarrassment at its truth.

"You seem like a bright cop. And if my intuition serves me correctly—a good person. So, you tell me, what I'm missing here?"

Cartwright exhaled a long, slow breath. He looked down toward his chest and with his thumb gestured towards the body camera clipped under his lapel mic. "Ma'am, all I can tell you is that every citizen of this great town deserves protection and today my current assignment is over here on the eastern side. And that's where I came in contact with you after you failed to come to a complete stop. I'll be issuing you a verbal warning for the violation." He then rolled his eyes at his own comment.

"Thank you. I think you've more than answered my question. Will that be all, Officer Cartwright?"

He nodded. "You take care of yourself, Miss Hatch."

"Just call me Hatch. Everybody else does."

Cartwright gave her a friendly wink before turning and walking back toward his patrol car.

Hatch continued on toward the mountain range in the near distance. Feeling frustrated, she figured the best thing for her would be an intense hill workout.

EIGHT

HATCH ROUNDED the bend of dirt-covered roadway and the Moonbeam Motel came into view. It didn't appear any new guests had graced the establishment in her absence.

She pulled the Camry to a stop in front of her room and exited the vehicle. As she walked toward her door, she saw a small business card sticking out from the slit between the door and its frame near the knob. Hatch looked around to see if whoever had delivered the card was still around but didn't see anything or anybody out of the ordinary. Manuel's truck was parked near the main office. It was the only vehicle in the lot, aside from hers. A sign that business was obviously not doing well this week.

Hatch plucked the card and saw that it was Manuel's. Flipping it over, she found a handwritten note. *Please see me when you get in.*

She pocketed the card and walked toward the manager's office. Hatch entered to see Manuel standing behind the counter. With seemingly no business, he managed to stay very busy. He was holding a spray bottle and wiping down the counter.

He looked over at her and gave a genuine smile. Putting the

cleaning supplies aside and wiping his hands on his trousers, he rounded the corner and came over to Hatch. He extended his hand and gave hers a hearty shake. "I can't thank you enough for what you did for my family."

"I'm not sure what you're talking about."

Manuel released his grip on Hatch's hand. His smile still permeated his face. "You did what few others would've done."

"Manuel, I don't mean to be rude, but I really have no idea what you're referring to."

"This morning. What you did for my son."

Hatch instantly realized what he was talking about. Xavier was his son. *Did he know his son was now an official member of the gang? And aside from interrupting his beating, she'd effectively done nothing to change that.* "I think I did what any reasonable person would do. I saw somebody in trouble and offered my assistance."

"You beat up two of those gang members. Those are dangerous people, and I don't know anybody, reasonable or otherwise, who would've done what you did. Or could have."

Hatch just shrugged and offered a simple response, "You're welcome."

"My wife and I would like to invite you to dinner tonight."

Hatch thought about dismissing the invite and offering some lame excuse. But for some reason, she couldn't. "What time?"

"My wife's already started cooking. How does seven sound?"

Hatch looked at her watch. She had over an hour to freshen up. "Sounds good. I'll see you then."

Manuel gave a pleased look, his smile pushing his cheeks up and wrinkling the sun-soaked skin around the corners of his eyes.

She left the office and went to her room. As soon as the door closed behind her, she peeled off the sweat-soaked clothes from her run and turned the shower on. She had enough time to get cleaned up before going over to their room that had been converted into a home.

After freshening up with a quick shower, she opened up her phone and called home. It rang twice before someone picked up. Hatch's heart skipped a beat when she heard the sweet, lyrical sound of Daphne on the other end.

"Auntie Rachel!" she cried.

"Daphne, it's so good to hear your voice. I miss you."

"I miss you, too. Jake does too, although he's probably too cool to say it. Grandma is here, too. Everyone wants to say hello. How have you been?"

Daphne spoke a mile a minute, rattling off questions. It'd only been a little over a week since she'd last set foot in Hawk's Landing. But for Hatch, and apparently Daphne, it felt like an eternity. Hatch never thought she would miss her hometown. Never thought it would become something she'd want to return to after spending so many years avoiding it, fifteen to be exact. Now the desire to return to the quaint town set in the foothills of the Rocky Mountains was a foreign one. In her short time there, she'd become close with her niece and nephew. Hatch felt guilty for leaving them so soon after having become reacquainted, but also knew she would never be able to settle until she closed this chapter of her life...until she found the answers she was looking for.

"Daphne, I hope to be home soon. I've just got a couple things to take care of here before I can do that." Hatch wondered how much of what she had just said was the truth. She did intend to return but didn't know when that would be.

"Auntie Rachel, where are you right now?"

"I'm in a small town called Luna Vista."

"Luna means moon and vista means to see. Is it easier to see the moon where you are?"

Hatch laughed. Only Daphne seemed capable of being able to make her laugh in a natural, heartfelt way. "To be honest, I haven't checked, but I am staying in a hotel called the Moonbeam. So, there's that."

Daphne giggled. It was a lilting laugh, and the sound of it was music to Hatch's ears.

"Where is Luna Vista?" asked Daphne.

"It's in New Mexico near a small mountain range. Nothing like the Rockies. A lot more dust here, too."

"Is it snowing there? It's snowing here. A lot. Jake and I have been home from school for two days."

"No snow. Just dirt and wind." Hatch wished she could see the girl's face. It might be reason enough to abandon her flip phone and upgrade to a smartphone where they could video chat. "I hope you're not driving your grandmother crazy."

"Oh, maybe just a little bit." She giggled.

"Is grandma around?"

"She's right here. You want me to give her the phone?"

"That would be great. Thanks." Before Daphne got off the phone, Hatch said, "I love you." Three words she used sparingly, but with her young niece, they came without any reservation.

"I love you, too. Finish up whatever it is you're doing there and get home soon. We miss you."

A muffled handoff of the phone took place.

"Rachel? Surprised you called so soon." No judgment in her mother's voice. Just a simple declaration, and an honest one.

"To be honest, so am I."

"Is everything okay? Are you okay?"

"Yes. I mean—I think so." Hatch sighed louder than intended. "This is new for me, Mom. The little time I spent with those kids has changed me. It's really strange for me to miss a place."

"It's not something to be ashamed of. Being part of a family means you miss them when you're gone."

"I've spent the majority of my life feeling disconnected from that. Constantly on the move. You know what they say about a rolling stone. I guess. I finally slowed enough in Hawk's Landing to finally gather some moss."

"You know, Rachel, that's not a bad thing. Like I said before, here is as good a place as any. The kids and I miss having you around. We got used to you being around in the short time you were here. It feels a bit empty now that you're gone." Rachel's mother exhaled slowly. "How's your search going? Any luck finding the answers you're looking for?"

"The address is for an abandoned building. I've got somebody who can hopefully shed some light on it. I'll probably have some direction to go from here within the next few days."

"And if you don't? If there's no answer? And this thing turns out to be a dead end? Then what?"

"I don't know. I guess I'll cross that bridge when I get to it."

"I saw Dalton Savage at the market the other day."

Hatch rolled her eyes and immediately knew the direction she was taking this conversation but played along anyway. "And how is Dalton doing these days?"

"He said to say hello. Told me he's tried to reach you a few times but that you haven't returned his call yet." Hatch's mother paused. "He asked me, if I ever reach you, to relay the message that he hopes you're well and to give him a call sometime to let him know how things are going."

"I know. I will. I've been meaning to call him. I just wanted to get things settled here first before I bother updating everybody on the nothingness that I've accomplished so far."

"You sound stressed."

"I'm just tired. Went for a long run earlier today."

"Well, get some rest. And know we're here for you whenever you need us."

"Is Jake there?"

"I'll get him." A few moments later she heard the boy's voice. "Hi."

"Hi, Jake. How are you holding up? How's your arm?"

"Healing. Doctor says I should have my cast off soon."

"Have you been training?" Hatch asked. She still owed the boy some additional martial arts lessons. But everything was on pause until she returned.

"Yeah. I've gotten better with my footwork, but they haven't let me spar yet. Not until I'm healed."

"There's a lot you can do in training without actually having to fight. Use this time to strategize, so the next time you face off with that Derrick Milton kid from your class you can surprise him." She hoped that by remembering his nemesis' name it would demonstrate to her nephew that she was truly thinking about him while away.

"It'd be better if you were here to teach me. Then I wouldn't have to go to the Flying Dragon anymore and I could just train with you."

"Someday. Hopefully soon. This is something I have to take care of. Once I do, I plan to come home to you guys."

"I'm not sure what it is you're doing out there but be careful. Because I'm not around to save you this time." Jake laughed at his own joke.

Hatch laughed with him, remembering the boy's bravery. "You remember that you're in charge while I'm gone? You take care of your sister and grandma for me. Can you do that?"

"Okay."

"I'll check in again soon. Gotta go."

With the conversation completed, Hatch felt conflicted. She was bound and determined to uncover the mystery surrounding her father's death, but to do so, she needed to leave behind, if only temporarily, a family who needed her. Her stomach rumbled loudly, distracting her from the call.

She looked at her watch. It was 6:55 PM. Hatch finished getting ready and slipped on her boots before stepping outside.

Hatch walked along the strip of rooms until she came to the last two units of the motel, the converted apartment home of Manuel and his family.

Hatch knocked on the door marked number twelve. She could smell the fragrant scent of garlic and onion. Her stomach rumbled once again. She suddenly realized she hadn't eaten lunch. After a hard jaunt up the base of Baylor Peak, her body craved for food.

The door opened and standing before her was the heavily bruised face of the teenage boy she'd saved earlier in the day.

The boy didn't smile. He dipped his head low, breaking eye contact with her as he stepped out of the way to let her inside.

NINE

HATCH ENTERED THE ROOM. The dividing wall which separated rooms eleven and twelve of the Moonbeam had been reconfigured, making a compact efficiency two-bedroom apartment. The room she'd entered had turned into a kitchen and dining area with a small living room nearest the door. A four-foot half-wall separated the kitchen space from the rest of the room. As small as it was, the apartment was immaculately clean.

"This is really impressive," Hatch said. "You did this work all by yourself?"

Manuel looked up from setting the table and gave a prideful smile. "I did most of the work. But had a little help from my son. My father was a carpenter by trade, and I learned a bit of it from him in my youth."

Xavier went about assisting his father by placing folded napkins by the plates and filling the water glasses set out. He quietly set about his chores. But one thing was for certain: He was not the one who invited her here. He wore his silent indignation on his sleeve for everyone to see, especially Hatch.

A woman came out of the bedroom wearing a blouse with a floral pattern. Her jet-black hair fell to the small of her back and she had the same deep brown complexion as her husband. She was attractive and had an air of natural elegance. Hatch guessed her to be in her mid-fifties but she didn't look a day over forty. She crossed the floor to Rachel and opened her arms wide.

She embraced Hatch with a brief hug. "Miss Hatch, I'm Camila. Xavier's mother. I know my husband already thanked you. But please allow me to as well." She released Hatch from the hug but rested her hands on Hatch's biceps a moment longer. "What you did for my thickheaded son is something I don't know if I'll ever be able to repay. But at least let us feed you well tonight."

"Whatever it is, it smells absolutely delicious." Hatch smiled, and let the woman lead her toward the table.

Camila released her guiding hand from Hatch and smiled at her. She then immediately went to the stove along the back wall and began tending to the contents simmering in a pan on the burner.

Hatch found it hard to believe she was standing in the same square footage of her room. Its arrangement was so uniquely different from room number three. Manuel had installed a full, albeit small, galley kitchen against the back wall with a four-burner stove and sink. The cabinets and counter space were excellently crafted.

"Can I get you something to drink, Miss Hatch?" Manuel asked.

"I'll have whatever you're having," she said with a smile. "And like I said before, people usually just call me Hatch."

She hated correcting the man, but it felt awkward to hear the *miss* title in front of her last name. It served as a reminder she was in her mid-thirties and still single and relatively alone in the world. In the same breath, her status suddenly called to mind a mental image of Dalton Savage. She dismissed it, figuring it was mostly likely due to the fact her mother had just mentioned him in their recent conversation. But deep inside, she knew there was something more to it. And if she were to be truly honest with herself, in the time since she left Hawk's Landing, she found her thoughts drift to the man more frequently than she'd ever care to admit.

Hatch played the mental game of what could have been or what might still be. She wondered if her potential chance at achieving normalcy in life rested with him. In the quiet moments of solitude, she allowed herself glimpses of a fantasy world in which she returned home to Hawk's Landing to live out her days with the man, taking on a parental role, or at least a full-time role of an aunt, for her niece and nephew. In this fantasy, she allowed herself to think of the possibility of having children of her own. Something she'd never really done before. Dalton Savage had accessed part of her she'd locked away. With him, her mind had begun to venture into uncharted territories.

She'd only felt something similar with one other, Alden Cruise, a Navy SEAL. But after being reassigned out to Coronado to join a West Coast team, things had fizzled. Dalton and Alden weren't much different, at least in their ability to handle situations. Hatch found it an increasingly rare trait to find a person who put aside his own well-being for the betterment of others. To be a risk taker but not a reckless one. A quality she'd come to love in both men.

Manuel poured a glass of red wine and handed it to Hatch. The bottle's label looked like a New Mexico license plate; red letters, SHI RAZ, set against a bright yellow background. "I hope you like red."

"I do. I don't think I've ever seen this brand before."

He topped off a glass and brought it to his wife in the kitchen. "This is local wine from Blue Teal Vineyards. And it's really good, in my opinion."

"I never thought about New Mexico being wine country."

"The Spaniards who settled New Mexico knew a thing or two about wine." Manuel let loose his infectious smile. "The climate's actually ideal in some parts of the state. Blue Teal has a shop in Las Cruces, but the wine is made up in Lordsburg. There's something like two-hundred acres of vineyard in the Pyramid Valley."

Hatch brought the stemmed glass to her lips and took a sip. She wasn't a wine snob and wouldn't know much difference from one blend to another. In her opinion, red was red and white was white. But one thing was certainly clear about this wine—it was delicious.

After serving his wife, Manuel walked back to the table and poured himself a glass.

His wife took a break from tending to the sizzling entrée in the pan to sip from her glass. She set it back down on the counter and turned to face Hatch. "Isn't it strange to call you by your last name? I've never heard that before. Is it common practice where you're from?"

Hatch thought about the question. It had become so common for her to present herself last name first, she never really gave it much thought. She had spent the majority of her adult life in the U.S. Army where her last name was affixed to the right side of her ACUs. Over the last fifteen years, she'd been referred to by her last name so commonly that Hatch felt out of sorts when people referred to her by her first name. Most of her military brethren probably couldn't even remember her first name if they' tried. Hell, she didn't even know if she would respond in a crowd if someone hollered out *Rachel*.

Hatch offered a conciliatory smile. "I spent a long time in the military. Everybody just called me by my last name. Now it's just how I introduce myself. Force of habit, I guess."

Camila laughed and then she gave a beautiful smile. Her supple, thin lips had a touch of lipstick for tonight's dining occasion. The peach coloring complemented her dark skin and darker hair. "Okay, Hatch. I'll call you that from now on. It feels like I'm in a James Bond movie." She giggled at her reference.

Hatch joined in the laughter.

Her broken-nosed son did not.

Manuel looked at the boy, who was still pouting silently. "Let's have a seat. Xavier, will you please serve us?"

The boy didn't argue at the direction given by his father but moved with a slight hesitancy which Hatch read as a quiet defiance. Xavier set about plating the food and then went around the table serving each person, starting with his father. He then moved to his mother and came to Hatch last. He set the plate down in front of her as if he were a waiter at a five-star restaurant. He didn't smile or speak. The boy returned to retrieve his food before taking his place at the small round table.

The' smell was aromatic. Hatch picked up a fork and knife and prepared to dig in, hoping to quench the rumble in her stomach, growing louder with each passing minute.

Manuel said, "Let's please join hands."

Hatch set the silverware down and paused. She wasn't wholly unfamiliar with the customary pre-meal observances and she could see from the variety of religious statues and paintings around the room that they were devout Christians. Hatch had been brought up in the Catholic church but after her father died, she'd distanced herself.

Hatch followed suit and extended her hand, joining her left with Camila as Xavier took her right hand. He did it in a way as though he was trying not to touch her but under his father's watchful eye, he had no other choice. Hatch felt his thumb graze the ridge of a puffy line of scar tissue extending just past her wrist toward the knife edge of her hand. The scar she hid from judgmental eyes.

Upon touching it, he looked down. Hatch watched him from the corner of her eye. He studied the scar and then looked up at Hatch.

His interest in Hatch was piqued. She thought her damaged and deformed arm would somehow humanize her in the boy's mind. Maybe with his fresh injuries he could now relate to her better. *Who knew?* But something seemed to change in the boy at that particular moment.

Manuel led them in a short prayer, thankful not only for the food, but for Hatch and the risk she'd taken in standing up for his son.

Hatch listened, grateful for the kind words but concerned that she'd done no such thing. It wasn't the time or the place to explain. Xavier was jumped. He was initiated. All she did was to lessen a brutal beating. Nothing more. Her intervention did little in the way of changing the course of the boy's life. Maybe because of her, the boy might have more problems. It definitely increased the likelihood of hers.

"Miss Hatch—sorry, Hatch. That's going to take me a bit to get used to." Camila smiled. "What brings you to our small town of Luna Vista?"

Manuel looked at his wife. "Camila, it's really not our place to ask such things. We are not nosy people."

"I wasn't being nosy. I was just asking. We don't get many visitors. Especially out-of-towners to stay at our motel." She took a sip of wine. "Sad, but most of our clientele come here for one night at a time. And getting payment from them is its own challenge."

"I don't mind the question at all. I'm here just following in my father's footsteps. He spent some time here years ago and I've always wanted to find out more about him. I found a letter and the return address was to this town. Well, actually the address said Las Cruces, but when I mapped the location, it was here in Luna Vista."

"That must've been a while back. Luna Vista now has its own zip code. We were just a blip on the map before, but our population is slowly growing. More so on the other side of town than ours." Camila shot a glance at her husband.

Obvious to Hatch from the exchanged looks, the location of the Moonbeam was an area of contention in their relationship. "About that. How does that happen? How does one side of a town get left behind while another side prospers?" Hatch asked.

"I guess you'd have to ask the police chief about that. All we worry about is keeping our business afloat," Manuel offered.

"Please don't take offense, but how do you survive if you have little in the way of paying customers?"

"No offense taken. It's a fair question. I'd be lying to you if I said it was easy. But we manage." Manuel cut one of the roasted green chilies and put a small forkful in his mouth. "When we have periods of days or weeks without income from the motel, I take odd jobs around town. I'm pretty handy."

"I can see that. What you've done here converting these two rooms into a beautiful apartment is nothing short of amazing. Maybe you missed your calling."

"Maybe I did. It's been my dream to refurbish this motel and make it a fun stop for people who want to embrace New Mexico and really experience the local flavor. I was hoping it would be different when we came here."

"My dad has big dreams, but they're not realistic." It was the first time Xavier had spoken since Hatch arrived. His mother cast him a sharp glance, but the boy ignored it and continued, "My parents are good people. Hard-working people. But this town doesn't value those things. To survive, you gotta go with the flow."

"Is that what you were doing today? Going with the flow?" Hatch asked.

"Lady, you don't know the first thing about what you thought you were doing today or thought you saw. Those people are my homies. They'd die for me. They'd take a bullet for me."

A flash of anger crossed Manuel's face.

Hatch looked at the boy. The damage to his face was now more pronounced, making his eyes look sunken underneath the deep, dark purple lines stretching all the way to the corners of both eyes. He looked like a football player who put on too much gameday black eye grease. "Doesn't look to me like they'd have your back. In fact, looks to me like they knocked you flat on it."

The boy didn't like the challenge. He began breathing deeply, his anger coming to the surface. But embarrassment accompanied the spiteful look in his eyes.

"I didn't need you. I was doing fine. I would've been okay. This is how we do it here. You have to prove you can take a beating." His voice lowered to a murmur. "Unless some random white lady steps in."

"You were nearly unconscious when I walked up. If they'd kept beating you, with the state you were in, I'm not so sure you wouldn't be dead." Hatch now leveled a narrowed glance at the boy. "So, I'm sorry for interrupting your early death. Wasn't like I went looking for trouble. But you guys aren't too quiet about how you do things here."

"You made a real mistake today. Those guys are angry. And they never forget."

Hatch could hear that the boy's warning wasn't made of false bravado but was done out of concern. The boy's external toughness and attitude quickly dissipated with a grip of his wrist by his father's hand.

Hatch gave a half-smile and said, "I've met tougher and survived."

The boy looked down at the scar on her hand and opened his mouth to speak but didn't.

Camila shot nervous glances around the table and was visibly uncomfortable with the direction the dinner conversation had taken. "Well, it's all over now. You've helped my son and hopefully those boys will leave him alone from now on."

Hatch said nothing and left the woman to believe whatever she wanted. Whether it was a lie she told herself because the truth was too difficult to accept or a naivety on behalf of the woman, Hatch didn't know. It was likely an easier pill to swallow, thinking her son was attacked by this crew and had no involvement himself.

Hatch filled the dead air that followed. "These things have a way of working themselves out." It was a strange thing to say, a vague and ambiguous response. But there was a truth to it. Much of the adversity she'd faced had a way of sorting itself out. Exactly how was another matter entirely.

Hatch filled her mouth with a bite of food. "These chilis are amazing!"

Manuel nodded. "Grown local. Fire roasted is the only way to properly enjoy them."

"There's a wonderful market in town." Camila gave a prideful smile. "This town really does have a lot to offer. Those chilis are delivered fresh daily. After they're fire roasted, you've got to freeze them if you're not going to eat them right away. We've got a freezer full of them. I can send some to you when you get back home."

"I'd like that," Hatch said. Then wondered when that would be.

Manuel jumped back in, talking excitedly about the cooking process. "The trick is to heat them so the skin blisters. Then cool them under water and peel the skin. What you're left with is that flavor you're tasting."

Hatch took another bite. Each mouthful was more enjoyable than its predecessor.

"If you want some real heat to those peppers, leave the membranes. That's the source of a chili's potency," Manuel added. "People think it's in the seeds, but that's not true."

"I remember hearing that before. We used capsicum spray in the military, more commonly known as pepper spray. I learned that the capsaicin oil used to make the spray burn didn't come from the seed like everybody thought but came from the pepper membrane." Hatch took a swig of water before grabbing her glass of wine. "These are pretty spicy."

"I hope it's not too spicy?" Camila asked.

"No. It's absolutely perfect. In fact, this is the best meal I've had in I don't know how long."

The woman looked absolutely pleased at that. Her gorgeous smile curled up again and the compliment seemed to wash away the tension created by her son's situation.

Hatch looked over at Manuel. He, too, seemed to calm. Over the next several minutes, they all ate silently.

Dinner ended. Hatch didn't count the number of refills of her wine glass, but it was now empty. Hatch was suddenly smacked with a wave of exhaustion. It was a combination of the drinks, the meal and her long day.

"I hope you won't think me rude. But I'm exhausted. I'm gonna turn in for the night," Hatch said. "I can't thank you enough for your hospitality."

"It was our pleasure, Hatch," said Camila.

Manuel said to Xavier, "Please walk Hatch to the door. And make sure you thank her."

The boy stood, setting his napkin beside his plate.

Hatch walked behind the boy. He opened the door and a cool blast of wind greeted her. As she stepped out, he whispered, "I think you should go. They're going to be mad. I wasn't kidding when I said that."

"And like I said, I can handle myself."

"They're connected. There's way more to this than you understand. You're in real danger, lady. There's no way out for me. But you can get in your car and drive away."

"I don't typically run from a fight."

The boy's eyes widened as much as the swelling would allow. "Listen, I'm sorry about my attitude tonight. I was just angry. But you interrupted something. I'm one of them now. And I don't want to be in a position where they tell me to do something bad to you."

"I hope it doesn't come to that."

"Hope doesn't matter here. It's the way things are. No changing it. You're in serious trouble. You won't get another pass from them. These guys don't fight fair."

Hatch tried to placate the boy's worry with a weak smile. "Neither do I."

TEN

HATCH DEBATED on making her way into town by foot or by car. Her legs ached slightly from yesterday's run and decided the exercise would do good to clear the lactic acid from her muscles. So, she laced up her sneakers and gave a slight stretch. Her back cracked in several places. Although the fight with the two thugs had been short, the explosive movements caused her muscles to be tighter than normal.

She took off from the motel and maintained a steady, but slower than usual pace. As Hatch pounded the pavement, she decided this morning she would continue her new routine of stopping by Harry's Diner for a bite to eat and some of his pot-burned coffee.

Arriving at her destination a short time later, she stopped for a moment outside the restaurant to stretch some more. In the cool morning air, she leaned to her side and saw the man Harry identified as the chief of police. He was working his way through the morning paper. In that moment, Hatch decided she would make this breakfast a business one.

She entered the warmth of the restaurant. Hatch walked over to the counter and took up the exact same seat she had taken the day before. The chief of police acknowledged her presence by turning away and giving her the cold shoulder.

"Good morning, Hatch," Harry said as he exited the kitchen and approached with a fresh pot of coffee.

"How's things, Harry?"

"Good, now that I see that you're still alive and kicking." He gave a wink before returning the pot to the burner.

The chief jostled the newspaper noisily as if trying to block out the friendly banter between the two. Hatch had learned how rapidly information flowed within this small town and assumed it likely the head law enforcement official had been made aware of her run-in with the local gang yesterday. For Hatch, the fact he didn't want to be involved spoke volumes.

"I'll take the same as yesterday, Harry. Thank you," Hatch said without looking at the menu.

"Sure thing." He smiled. "All that running you do must work up a heck of an appetite. Few people can take down my special the way you did and come back for seconds."

"I guess I'm blessed with a high metabolism."

"I guess so." Harry turned and made his way back to the kitchen to begin whipping up her order.

Hatch turned her body so the chief could feel her eyes upon him. He'd have to be the most oblivious man in the world not to notice she was staring a hole in the side of his head. But he continued to ignore her, retreating deeper into the fold of the newspaper.

With the paper still covering his face, the chief cleared his throat. "Are you going to sit there and stare at me all morning while I'm trying to read the paper? Or do you have something you'd like to say?"

"Well, pleasure to make your acquaintance, Chief. I'm Rachel Hatch." She stuck out her hand. The chief looked over at it but didn't accept it. Hatch left it out there and waited patiently, forcing the man to either blatantly disregard or accept her offer of cordiality.

He closed the paper with a grunt and set it beside his empty plate of food. He weakly shook her hand.

Hatch felt the man's hand in hers. It was moist with sweat. Beyond the dampness, she noted the softness of his skin. Definitely not the hand of a laborer. It had no trace of calluses, and by its smooth texture, Hatch deemed this man was one of privilege or at least had been in a position of such circumstance for a long time. You could tell a lot about a person by this subtle contact.

The short-lived handshake over, the chief leveled a serious gaze at the woman as if taking her in for the first time. "I assume you know who I am? I'm Chief Porter, and what is it that I can do for you this morning, young lady?"

"I'm not sure." Hatch answered honestly. She really didn't know what would come from a conversation with the man, but she really was dying to know how a department, small as it was, seemed to be turning a blind eye to what was happening in half of the town.

"You're interrupting my coffee and morning paper read with, what, small talk? I really don't have time for this."

"What exactly do you have time for, Chief?"

He turned on his stool, fully squaring his rotund frame to her. "What is that supposed to mean?"

"I'm just saying, what are you in a hurry to do today? Directing your officers to stop more people for running stop signs in Mayberry? Or has the gang problem finally caught your attention?"

"Gang problem? You been in Luna Vista—what—two days? And in that time, you think you understand things around here?" His jowls blotched to a soft pink. "You think you have the right to judge my town and the way I run it?"

"I'm not judging, Chief. I'm just stating the obvious. You'd have to be blind not to see what I see." Hatch remained stone faced. "Are you blind?"

His face, now fully reddened, made it readily apparent her words had struck a nerve. This was a man whose authority was not chal-lenged on a regular basis. Whether it was his status as chief or a deep-rooted personality trait, Hatch didn't know. But one thing was certain: She'd gotten his attention.

"I'm not blind to what goes on here. I'm doing the best I can with the staff I have and the resources made available to me." Porter angrily played with the folded newspaper. "Maybe it's something you have no experience with."

Hatch wanted to laugh. Especially after her last visit to Hawk's Landing where Dalton Savage managed his small and generally inept sheriff's department. With those limited resources, he was able to put together a large-scale federal case. She fought against her urge to spew forth her knowledge of how things work in a small town. But decided against it. Like arguing politics and religion, each side has their opinion and neither usually comes to some agreeable middle ground. Hatch bit her tongue and said, "Why don't you tell me how it works? Explain it to me how you have a small band of hoodlums that seem to run free in one portion of town. And you have another side of your town that remains untouched by crime."

The man picked up his porcelain mug. The dribbles of old coffee lined the side of the white porcelain. "It's complicated."

"Then uncomplicate it for me."

"What makes you think I need to spend any more of my time explaining anything to you? You're an outsider! You're just passing through, right? You'll be in and out of our town in a matter of days. Hopefully, less. We, in Luna Vista, have to live here long after you leave. So, I don't need your self-righteous judgments on how we do things. Nor do I need to explain a damn thing to the likes of you!"

She could see the man was preparing to leave, but he hadn't yet, and she decided to press further. "Just doesn't make sense to me."

"Not sure it needs to. Like I said, you're an outsider. Your opinion doesn't matter."

"You're right, I am an outsider, and maybe my opinion doesn't mean squat. But I've had the pleasure of meeting some good folk here in this town. And they apparently live on the wrong side. These are hard-working people with families. And not lifting a finger to keep them safe, to give them a sense of safety, is a major failing on your part."

"Well, thank you so much, Miss Hatch, for enlightening me on my community and the people I serve."

"It's just Hatch."

"Come again?"

"Never mind."

The man drained the remnants from his mug and placed it down noisily on the counter. He scooped up his paper, tucked it under his arm, and pushed himself away from the stool.

"Leaving so soon? We were just getting acquainted."

"Didn't you just advise me that I've got a town to protect? I guess I best get about doing it."

"Maybe you need some help?" Hatch gave a coy smile that only seemed to aggravate the man further.

"From what I hear, sounds like you've already done plenty. And if I were in your shoes, I'd probably be making arrangements to move along sooner rather than later."

"Is that a threat?"

"Not at all. Just a friendly bit of advice."

"I'll take that under advisement. Seeing as how you've been so welcoming to me thus far."

The man began to leave and headed toward the door when Hatch called to him, "You know, Chief? I've given it some thought. And I don't think I'm going to take your advice. I've just decided I'll stick around a little bit longer."

The man let out a low rumble. "Suit yourself." He shoved open the door, letting in a cold blast of wind. He disappeared from view as the door banged shut.

Harry walked up with a plate of food. He eyed the seat Chief Porter had recently vacated and then cocked an eyebrow at Hatch. "Now what'd you go and say to that crotchety bastard to make him run off like that?"

"Nothing that shouldn't have been said to him long ago."

"You seem to be picking fights everywhere you go."

Hatch gave a slight nod. "Afraid so. Force of habit, I guess."

Harry smiled broadly. "Well, I'm sure as hell happy you're here. This plates on me. And every other meal you want to have here. This town needs more people like you. Maybe things wouldn't have gotten so bad if we'd had them."

ELEVEN

HATCH LEFT the diner with a full stomach and the walk back to
the motel did wonders to assist in the digestion. She decided it was
early enough the gang bangers were probably still asleep and decided
to set out for the warehouse again. Hatch made quick work of the
drive to the outskirts of town to where the road branched off and ran
the quarter mile length up to the abandoned building. But this time
Hatch didn't drive past *no trespassing* signs and park over by the
shed. Instead, she pulled off the road before turning off the main
road. She tucked the Camry behind a thick overgrowth of spiny
shrubs and cacti before trekking down the arterial dirt road leading to
the warehouse.

Hatch adjusted the weapon tucked in the small of her back. After
crossing the main road, she looked back toward her rental car. It
wasn't completely hidden from view, but enough so she hoped it
wouldn't be noticed.

She didn't run. Still, her walking pace equaled most people's jog.
Her long legs covered the dirt path quickly. Cresting the small rise in
the land, Hatch had a visual of the front and side of the building.

From her vantage point, the Cadillac wasn't in sight. Nor any other vehicle for that matter.

Hatch was cautious by nature and slowed the pace of her approach. She knew that just because she didn't see a vehicle didn't mean somebody wasn't inside. The last thing Hatch wanted to do was get shot walking into the abandoned warehouse.

She crept up to the side of the building nearest her, opposite the shed she had parked behind the other day. All of the windows were boarded up but there was enough gapping between some of the boards for her to peer inside. Even though it was early in the day and a low ceiling of cloud cover cast the vast land in a grayish white, the interior was pitch dark. Hatch pulled a flashlight from her pocket, a small handheld Streamlight. She depressed the button on its base. The 1,000-lumen beam penetrated the dark and illuminated the inside.

It was clear, or at least as much as she could visually clear under the circumstances. She moved around to the front door and pulled the handle. It was locked.

A locked door was a mere inconvenience. After spending several years with people who sidestepped inconveniences like this on a daily basis, she'd become quite adept at disabling locking mechanisms. She popped the lock in less than thirty seconds. A moment later she was inside.

Hatch paused for a moment, taking in the space. She didn't activate her flashlight. Instead, she stood in the dark and allowed her eyes to slowly adjust to it. Now, being on the inside, the open slits along the boards covering the exterior windows added their slivers of light. After about a minute of standing completely still, her eyes adjusted to the darkness. The details of her surroundings came into focus as her natural night vision took hold. She preferred to navigate the space without wielding her flashlight. If she missed the arrival of the gang members, the light would put her at a disadvantage. They might see it before she heard them.

The warehouse looked to be roughly three thousand square feet. The majority of furnishings had been long since removed. The room in which she now stood was at one time some type of reception area. There was a couch, some chairs, and a coffee table in the center. Behind a dilapidated receptionist desk was a cracked door. Graffiti spray paint covered the walls.

Hatch walked to the cracked door and pushed against the warped wood. It resisted her efforts and creaked loudly. The lower hinge's pin was missing, and as she pressed, it separated from the frame and the door banged loudly against the concrete floor. A final shove freed the door with a terrible scraping sound like an amplified nail across a chalkboard.

This room had a dampness to it. A broken water pipe above her had a slow drip. Each droplet echoed in the openness. There were no windows in the room. Hatch pulled out her flashlight. The cone of light revealed the patches of laminate tile worn through to its bones.

It took her a second to piece together the room's layout. Hatch swept her flashlight and saw that the very back wall wasn't a wall but a pile of gravel. She walked down toward it to get a better look. Once close enough, she realized what she thought was gravel was ballistic mulch for a back stop. Hatch was standing in an indoor gun range.

She looked back toward the door and guessed the distance to be one hundred yards, give or take. She walked back to where she'd entered the room. Off to the left side were a line of training barricades stacked in neat rows. Wheels on the bottom platform enabled the user to adjust its position, similar to the ones used by police departments across the country during their firearms qualification. Mobile barricades provide practitioners an opportunity to shoot from various positions, simulating firing from cover. Something Hatch had done on numerous occasions, in both training and in the real world. After the injury to her right arm, she had to learn it all over again with her left. The result was that Hatch was now an ambidextrous shooter.

This was definitely an interesting place. The front lobby didn't look as though it was fit for a gun range. The ranges she'd spent time on didn't typically have a lounge area. Although, just like cigar aficionados, there were gun enthusiasts who'd probably like nothing more than to sit and talk guns with their fellow marksmen. Personally, Hatch wasn't much for talking about things like that. She was more of a doer.

She scanned the floor and the walls, looking for anything that could be used to identify what was once here, a business card or a flyer of some sort. Hatch didn't find anything except a couple of spent shell casings of different calibers, proving a variety of different weapons had been fired here. It was unknown to her whether the casings were left behind by the gang bangers or their predecessors.

A perfect hideout, Hatch thought. For a gang to have a clubhouse in the front and indoor gun range in the back seemed like a winning combination. Hatch had witnessed firsthand the sophistication of gangs during her time as an MP. Larger gangs like the Bloods and Crips saw the benefit of properly training their young foot soldiers. And who better than the U.S. military?

One of her first cases as an investigator with CID while stationed at Fort Bragg had exposed her to the gang influence. A group of soldiers had siphoned shipments of guns from the armory. When Hatch broke the case wide open, she learned these soldiers were tied to a Blood set out of L.A. and they had been shipping the weapons out to California using an extensive network. It had been an eye-opening experience for Hatch.

Remembering what Gabe had said during their brief exchange, she wondered if these Outlaws had been responsible for the crate of weapons stolen from the gun shop. She decided to go back out to the lounge area and dig around a bit.

She worked the door back into its hinge and then exited the indoor range and entered the first room. Hatch began a methodical search. The poorly maintained room was cluttered with trash. Visually dividing it into quadrants helped focus her attention to details, although she wasn't exactly sure what she was looking for. But for the moment she treated it as though the room was a crime scene. And somewhere in it was the needle in the haystack.

She began her search on the far-right corner. Hatch moved along an invisible grid pattern she'd created in her mind. The ground was littered with fast food containers and empty bottles of booze. As slovenly as this crew was, she also deemed them to be resourceful. A portable generator, most likely stolen, was set in the corner of the room. A space heater, lamp, and stereo were plugged in. Heat, light, and music—a crude but base level of creature comfort.

The first quarter of the room didn't yield any results, minus the roaches that scurried away as she cleared her way through the filth. Moving toward the center of the room where the couches and small table were located, Hatch noted the burnt remnants of smoked marijuana. A piece of mirrored glass had been set on the table, and she surmised the white powder to most likely be cocaine.

Although her primary role had been as an interrogator during her time when she was attached to a Special Forces unit, she'd been raised to never stand by idle and to make herself useful. Making work is how her father phrased it. So, when one of her team's high value target extractions didn't result in a target being acquired, Hatch would assist in secondary searches. Evidence and information gathered were for intel. Instead of standing by twiddling her thumbs, Hatch learned the finer art of searching. What she found was that hiding spots could be anywhere and desperate people were nothing if not creative.

She pushed the table aside, giving her room to search the couch. A line on the floor's dust indicated the table leg's original position and would make it easy for her to return things to the way they had been. The whole room was coated in a thin layer of dirt and dust blown in through the cracks in the windows. Hatch made a mental note to clear any obvious signs of her presence before departing. She didn't need anybody thinking Goldilocks had been inside.

Hatch lifted the couch cushion on the right side. Springs poked through in several spots along the torn and tattered frame. The couch's soft leather had given way too many years of use and was now a faded tan with little remnants of its original dark brown luster. She was careful when she moved the cushions, ensuring there were no needles. She didn't need to get poked. No telling who'd graced these couches over the years. She imagined others, transient homeless people, had found their way in here a time or two. And with that came a high probability that some wares had been left behind.

She lifted the second of the cushions. Hatch immediately noticed the boxed spring was covered by a board. She worked her fingers to the lip of the inch-thick plywood and lifted. Underneath was a cache of weapons. A shotgun and numerous handguns were strewn about the makeshift treasure chest.

Hatch thought about writing down all of the serial numbers and checking them against the gun owner's database to see if these were the ones which had been stolen. But after her recent conversation with Chief Porter, she deemed it a wasted venture. Plus, she'd have a hard time explaining what she was doing rummaging around the abandoned warehouse.

So, Hatch came up with a different plan of action. She figured maybe there was a way to level the playing field with these Outlaws. She pulled the weapons out one at a time and laid them on the floor in front of the couch. There was a total of one shotgun and five handguns, all Smith & Wesson M&P—the same make and model as the ones stolen from the gun store. Enough firepower to wreak havoc on a small town like Luna Vista.

Hatch took the first pistol. She released the magazine and pulled back the slide, rendering the weapon safe. Hatch then set about breaking the gun down into its parts with purposeful diligence.

She worked the firing pin and pocketed it. A gun without a firing pin was useless. If nothing else, she'd disable their functionality. It'd be her gift to the town and give her some peace of mind. She would render the guns inoperable but put them back together the way they looked when she had first arrived. If by chance the time ever presented itself and the gang decided to come after her, Hatch would have an advantage.

Breaking down a weapon and removing the firing pin wasn't all that complicated, but it was somewhat time-consuming. With the first pin pocketed and the weapon reassembled, she picked up the next gun. Hatch repeated the process.

As she extracted the firing pin from the second gun, she heard the pop and snap of tires over the rocky dirt followed by a low rumble of bass. A vehicle was approaching. Company had arrived earlier than expected.

Hatch quickly reassembled the second weapon and began putting the guns back into the couch's exposed cavity. She then placed the piece of wood on top followed by the couch cushion. Hatch slid the table back into place and swept away the track mark on the floor.

The car was close now. Too close for her to safely exit. With no avenue of escape, Hatch took the only option available and moved quickly toward the door access to the indoor range. If worst came to worst, a soundproof room in which to engage a room full of gang bangers wouldn't be a bad thing. But her goal right now was not to fight. She was here for another purpose and getting into a gun battle with the local gang would only expedite the timeline which she could spend within the borders of Luna Vista. And effectively cut short any chance of locating information about her father. She couldn't risk it.

With the room assembled the way it was before she'd arrived, Hatch quickly moved to the damaged door separating the two rooms. Working against the door's stubborn hinge, she shouldered her way into the back room and reset the door back in place. Hatch closed her eyes for a ten count and then opened them, effectively speeding up her visual adjustment to the darkness.

She tucked herself behind the cluster of barricades and then bent into a low crouch facing the closed door. Hatch freed the weapon from the small of her back and held it steady at the low ready. With the door's damaged hinge, there'd be no way to sneak up on her. And the delay in their ability to quickly enter would give her the drop if needed.

Loud muffled voices filled the silence as the front door opened and closed. By the sheer clamor of their entry, it was obvious they didn't expect anyone to be inside. Hatch relaxed a bit.

There would be no lingering odor of her, either. Hatch never wore perfume. The only bit of fragrance was that of whatever soap she used to clean up. Today it was the generic paper-wrapped small rectangular bar provided by the motel.

Now it was a waiting game. Hatch needed to patiently wait to see if they would enter her space and force her hand.

Time passed as the minutes ticked by. She finally assumed nobody was coming in and therefore Hatch slowly crept out from behind her barricade closer to the door.

She stood on the hinge side of the door and listened. The talking on the other side of the door became clear. The conversation was heated, and she immediately recognized the voice to which it belonged.

"How many times do I gotta tell you guys? When they say move a product, you move the damn product! Is it really that hard?" Macho asked.

"They gave us some real pure shit. I actually cut it three times before baggin' it up. Broke it down real nice and then I sent it to my guy in Las Cruces. Not my fault he's not moving quick enough." The man speaking had a thick, throaty voice. She didn't recognize it, but seeing as how Macho was leading the conversation, she assumed it was most likely one of the two men she had knocked out on the previous day.

"I should have the cash back by the end of the day. I've gotta make my run later. When are you supposed to meet with the Savages?"

"It was supposed to be an hour ago. So, you understand my problem now? I'm late on my end because your people aren't comin' through on yours. We're middlemen here. You feel me? We might be higher up on the food chain, but we're still low enough that they can cut us free at any time. We're expendable. Don't forget that. I don't want that. I kind of like our life. I like the money. I like the way things work around here. The only way it continues is if we keep holding up our end of things."

"I'll see what I can do, Macho. Just chill for a minute, man."

"I'm not going to chill! Not until I have the money. And you better get the count right because if I'm going to be late, then I'm gonna come correct. I'm not going to be shortchanging them. I'm not going to stiff them one dollar. You count every penny of what comes back to you and make sure it's right. If it's not, you fix it. If you can't fix it, then you put your own money in and make it right. Understood?"

Hatch couldn't hear the response. It was more of a grumble, but it seemed like Macho's message was being received.

"What about that bitch from yesterday? How are you planning to deal with her?" Hatch recognized the man by the screechy crackle in his voice. It belonged to the one she had cracked in the chin with her elbow strike. She noticed that today his voice carried a little lisp. She took pleasure in the sound of it.

"No need to worry about her now. I got something planned for her ass, but business first. You know how we do. We handle the business end of things before we get to partake in the fun side of our profession," Macho said.

A rumble of laughter followed like the cackle of a pack of hyenas circling their prey. Then she heard a new voice. One she now knew better than the others.

"Why we gotta do anything about her? Maybe she's going to be out of town soon. Like you said, hurting a person like that—an outsider white girl—could mean serious heat."

"Look at you, sticking up for your superhero. But she ain't here now to protect you from another ass whipping if you open your mouth again. Remember, you're new to this. Just because you survived your initiation doesn't mean you've proven shit to me," Psycho said.

"Enough!" Macho boomed. "You two sound ridiculous. For one, we'll do her as soon as we're done with the business side. If I say something, it's as good as law. And two, X, you make a good point about bringing the heat. So, like I said the other day, ain't nothing comin' back on us when we do."

"Understood." The boy's voice was soft, barely audible through the door.

Hatch respected the kid for sticking his neck out for her in a room full of thugs. The teen showed some real moxie.

Whatever they had planned seemed to be on hold for the time being, at least until they sorted out whatever business arrangement they had worked out with the Savages. Whoever they were, apparently, they were above the Outlaws in the pecking order.

Hatch wasn't here to solve Luna Vista's gang problem. She was here for one purpose and one purpose only—to find out who killed her father. As of right now, she was no closer to that answer than she was when she first arrived. But to turn a blind eye to those in need was in direct contradiction to who she was at the core.

The skunked odor of marijuana seeped in from the crack underneath the door and unbearably loud music drowned out any ability to hear any further conversation between the men. Hatch decided to move back to the barricade and wait them out.

She found the gang's behavior a bit ironic. For all the hot-headed talk about their business and getting their money, they certainly took time out of their busy schedule to get high. If and when things escalated to the point where they came for her, they'd most likely be under the influence. At least it would increase her odds of survival.

Right now, all she needed to do was wait out the group of stoned thugs until they left. Hatch's body prickled with goosebumps and she shivered. The space heater hooked up to the generator in the other room provided zero warmth for the room that she was in. As she sat on the cold concrete floor and rested her back against a barricade, she put her mind somewhere else. And in the quiet isolation, she thought of Dalton.

TWELVE

A LITTLE LESS THAN half an hour passed before the group decided to depart. Hatch heard the front door bang shut. She then did a slow count to ten before pulling open the finicky door separating the two rooms. She welcomed the lingering heat of the room. The air was thick with the hazy cloud of marijuana.

Hatch moved quickly to the window and peered through the slats. The Cadillac wasn't the only vehicle. Today there were two additional cars parked in the dirt lot. Macho entered the Caddy alone and pulled away first.

She watched as Xavier got into a purple Dodge Charger with Blaze. They drove off a moment later.

Psycho sat in his car a little bit longer. He lit a cigarette. Hatch took pleasure in watching the man rub the bottom of his chin and wince. Whatever damage she'd done was lasting.

With Psycho alone, Hatch considered taking the initiative. But to do so would only draw more attention and escalate whatever plan they had in store for her.

She wanted them to remain off balance and underestimate her. If she went on the offensive now, it would totally give away her ability. In lieu of action, Hatch waited.

It wasn't long until the brake lights of his Honda CRX illuminated. A minute later, the vehicle was rolling slowly down the arterial passage that led back to the main road, the same road where her vehicle was still parked by the shrubs.

Once Psycho's car was out of visual range, she exited the building and began a slow jog down toward the road. Hatch wanted to make sure as she made her way she wasn't caught in the rearview mirror of the thug. This was an unforeseen opportunity to get a deeper look at the gang's network. Hatch made a mental note to come back and finish dismantling the weapons.

In less than three minutes, her trek back to her car was complete. She entered the partially hidden Camry. She pulled out, making a U-turn and headed back toward Luna Vista. Hatch was only a few minutes behind the Honda.

Her interest piqued by the conversation she'd eavesdropped on, Hatch accelerated the rental car. Going fifteen miles an hour over the speed limit, she tried to make up the gap in distance between her and Psycho's car.

Within a few minutes, she saw the vehicle a couple blocks ahead of her stopped at a red light. Hatch slowed to maintain a safe distance.

Traffic was light in Luna Vista, but there was enough that pausing briefly along the side of the road allowed for a large SUV to merge from a side street. The bulky vehicle was positioned in front of her and provided exactly the kind of concealment she needed. It enabled her to maintain eyes on the Honda, but the SUV obscured her enough that she most likely would be able to avoid detection.

Psycho didn't stop anywhere along the way. He drove straight through Luna Vista and continued west on Highway 70 toward Las Cruces.

Once inside the city limits of the larger city. Psycho dog-legged his movements through the grid pattern of streets until he came to a stop at a Valero gas station on Elks Drive. He pulled the Honda into a spot on the far side of the station's service center. He didn't cut the motor and instead sat idling.

Hatch drove further down the street and pulled into a Walgreens parking lot across the intersection to North Main Street. She parked facing away from the Valero and used her side and rearview mirror to keep her eyes on the target. The waiting game continued.

Conducting surveillance as a civilian was far different than when she'd been an investigator. Those operations required her to photograph and document as many details as possible. But now she was free to act more naturally. There would be no reports. No supervisor oversight. No courts. This was strictly an information gathering mission, a much simpler process. To what end, she still did not know.

Psycho waited in the Valero with the car running for nearly half an hour before a blue Mazda with heavy tints pulled into the spot to the left of his. Hatch watched through the side mirror. As soon as it entered the lot, Psycho perked up and flicked his cigarette butt out the window onto the ground beside his car. Based on his change in behavior, she assumed this was who he'd come to see.

After a little delay, Psycho exited his vehicle and climbed into the passenger seat of the Mazda. He remained inside the car for only a minute or two before reappearing. She couldn't see who was in the driver's seat or if there were any passengers. The tints were definitely illegal.

When Psycho exited the car, he had something in his hand. She couldn't see exactly what but based on the conversation at the warehouse, it was most likely the money.

Back in his car, Psycho sat in his vehicle and lit a cigarette as the Mazda pulled out and departed the same way it had come. Psycho did not leave immediately. He continued to sit and finish his cigarette over the course of the next five minutes. When the butt flicked out the window, he slowly backed the Honda out and drove toward the highway.

Hatch let him move down the road a bit, assuming he would most likely be heading back to Luna Vista. Once Psycho's Honda was swallowed by the traffic of the bigger city, and Hatch felt that there was adequate distance between them, she picked up her loose tail.

Hatch followed the Honda back into Luna Vista. He wasn't headed back to the abandoned warehouse. Instead, he drove in a different direction. Hatch had run through it on her way into Harry's Diner. It was a rundown neighborhood.

Psycho turned left by a broken-down school bus and then an immediate right. Most of the residences were duplexes. It looked like a military compound, something Hatch was familiar with. She thought about the town's proximity to White Sands and wondered if this had at one point been used as off-base housing. A lot of small towns are born in the sprawl that surrounds military training sites and installations.

He pulled the Honda up the short driveway of a small one-level ranch-style house. He parked partially on the grass, or what could be interpreted as grass. It was a red-brown dirt with patches of weeds and debris. Several beer cans and bottles were strewn about the land-scape. Whoever owned the property cared little for curb appeal.

Psycho had the package in his hand when he walked from the car, the same one she saw him with at the gas station. He quickly walked inside. Hatch watched from down the street. Surveillance on a residential road was harder to mask, and she knew sitting in a running car outside a stranger's house could draw some unwanted attention. She had gathered quite a bit of intel today and figured, with Psycho out of sight, she would head back to the motel and get a fresh start tomorrow.

As Hatch prepared to drive off, she saw a vehicle pull up along the curb in front of the house Psycho had entered. A younger female, in her late teens or early twenties, exited the passenger side. She turned and had a small verbal exchange that was well out of earshot of Hatch. The girl then walked to the door Psycho had entered only minutes before. The car pulled away from the curb and drove off as the door to the ranch-style house opened. A second later, the girl, dressed in a purple puffy coat and black mini skirt, disappeared inside.

Hatch waited a moment before driving away.

THIRTEEN

SUNLIGHT SLIPPED in through the crack between the curtains. Light struck Hatch's closed eyelids, causing her to stir. She was grateful for nature's alarm clock. Always an early riser, the military solidified the morning person. The Army's old ad saying "do more before 9 AM than most people will do all day" had proven true. She recalled numerous occasions when she was up before 4 AM and hit the ground running. Sometimes those mornings would stretch into days. But even on the more benign ones, she did more in those first hours of being awake than many would do in a full day's work. It was the simple beauty of the military machine. Lying in bed now, she missed her former life. Hatch ran her hand over the scars that had forever changed her course. She allowed her pity party to end and decided to realign herself to a new purpose.

Hatch's life was wholly different than it had once been. In the early morning swath of sunlight that fell upon her sheets, she thought of her young niece and how she crawled into bed with her. Daphne, sweet Daphne, who in her simple childlike way had reconnected Hatch with a sense of humanity. A piece of her she'd lost somewhere along the way. She recalled the last conversation she'd had with the girl. And her promise to return home as soon as she finished what she was doing. Hatch felt her life had been repurposed. Instead of fighting the world's problems, she now dealt with her own, different but equally challenging. In truth, this new direction was harder than anything she'd faced before. Raising her sister's family in the wake of her death was a daunting task, and one that was currently being handled by her mother. New Mexico wasn't an escape of her duties. It was a calling. Hatch knew she would be forever divided if she didn't bring closure to her father's mysterious death.

Hatch pushed the thought from her mind and focused on the task at hand. But before she'd begin her newfound hobby of studying the local gang, she began her day with her Luna Vista morning routine, a jog through town and breakfast at Harry's. She was becoming quite fond of both the food and the man who served it. There was something about him she liked: a good-natured way about him. It wasn't only the delicious food he provided, or the snarky banter. Harry had an intangible quality. He was a throwback to the people she'd known during her growing up in Hawk's Landing. Small-town wisdom oozed from the man. Maybe his long time spent in the foodservice industry gave him some gift of understanding people. Made sense to Hatch. By all accounts, waiting on people from behind the diner counter for years on end and the constant exchange and observation of people seemed to heighten some innate ability to spew forth the profound. Like a sage master who was able to channel his observations into teachable moments. Hatch enjoyed the brief but meaningful conversations they had together since she arrived in town.

She got herself ready and headed out the door. Hatch added a new accessory to her attire, the Sig Sauer. It was tucked neatly into her tight-fitting jogging pants. The bulk of it felt a little bit strange without a holster properly securing it. But the lycra material provided a good balance of tightness with stretchability along her waistline and snugged the weapon in place. She did a couple of jumping jacks to both warm up her muscles and check the gun's stability. Hatch deemed it secure enough to stay in place. She didn't plan on breaking any land speed records this morning. It was a short jog, only a couple miles, and enough to loosen up her legs and clear her mind for whatever the day had in store for her. Closing the door to her motel room, Hatch took a lungful of the dry New Mexico air and set out on her run.

Hatch arrived at the diner four minutes slower than she had on the previous day. A layer of smokey steam filled the cool air surrounding her. Unlike the previous mornings, the Luna Vista's Chief of Police wasn't sitting in his usual spot at the counter. In fact, he wasn't in the restaurant at all. Hatch found this amusing and hoped the reason he wasn't comfortable sitting at his usual spot was because he feared she would come and spoil his morning routine. Hatch fancied herself a good read of people. And what she read in the manner and tone of Chief Porter was less than desirable. She was sorely disappointed in his lack of interest in protecting the good people on the poorer side of town.

She conducted a quick cooldown stretch. Hatch pressed the ball of her foot against the low concrete lip of the brick exterior, loosening her calves before stepping inside.

Harry's face brightened into a wide smile. His greeting was much different than it had been on the first day she'd entered the diner. The skeptical glower he greeted her with on that day had completely dissipated. But she hadn't taken offense then and knew its reason. She and Harry were people cut from a similar cloth. Warming up to people took some time. It wasn't that Hatch was cold or uncaring. Her emotions remained in check until she fully trusted somebody, and even then, she typically held back. Over the course of her life, her trust had been tested, and few people had earned hers.

"Good morning, Hatch."

"Morning, Harry. Nice to see you this morning." She eyed the chief's seat. "I see that you're missing a customer this morning. That's a shame." Hatch added an overacted frown.

Harry laughed. "Oh yeah, I noticed that, too. Strange, he came and got his order to go today. I can't imagine why."

"That is strange." Hatch played along with the schtick as she took up her stool.

"You got quite a way about you. Anyone who's able to make Porter nervous and feel out of place has a rare talent. I'd like to keep you around here to ward off all the other evil spirits."

"So, you consider the chief an evil spirit?" Hatch offered with a laugh.

"I didn't say it. You did." Harry winked.

"And you didn't disagree."

"Now, I don't like going around badmouthing somebody behind their back. It's not my way. I'm the kind of guy that if I got something to say, I'll say it to your face. But let's just say, it's nice to have a little break from the man this morning."

Hatch bellied up to the counter. Her new and temporary routine. Routine was something she made a conscious effort to avoid. Because with it came predictability. Hatch didn't plan on staying here long enough for it to be an issue. And therefore, she allowed herself a deviation from her rigidity. These mornings with Harry gave her a sense of comfort and connectedness. Hatch took a moment to fiddle with the plastic-coated one-page menu, as if she was going to order something new.

"What's it going to be this morning? Gonna try one of my other specialties?"

"You know what, Harry? I like a little adventure, but not in my breakfast." She slipped the menu back into place between a napkin dispenser and a bottle of ketchup. "Once I find something I like, I stick with it. So, hit me up again with the Luna Vista Special."

He smiled, and without being asked, filled her cup with coffee from a fresh pot. Drips fell to the coffeemaker's burner plate, creating a sizzling sound as the dark liquid quickly evaporated. Harry set the pot back into its cradle.

Hatch forewent the cream and sugar, enjoying the bitterness. The pot itself seemed to have created its own unique taste, like a cast iron pan that retained the flavor of previous meals. It was hard to define, but in the few days she'd had Harry's coffee, she'd definitely come to enjoy it. Better yet, she actually looked forward to it. Looking forward to anything was a big step for Hatch. Looking into her father's past had her twisted in a knot of uncharted territory. Ever since separating from the Army, she was left adrift in a limbo state. Sipping her coffee and taking each moment as it came, she sought to find her balance.

Harry returned with her breakfast. "Ya know, for somebody as—please don't take this the wrong way—for somebody with your physique, my food doesn't seem to have much of an impact on you."

"My physique?"

Harry threw his hands up. "I didn't mean any offense. I'm just saying you seem very fit. Look around, you're not my typical customer." He leaned in, resting his elbows on the counter. "I mean, hell, I think I've added twenty pounds to every resident of this town. But you come in here, the spitting image of health, and you're taking my biggest menu item in stride."

"My stomach is like Teflon." Hatch slapped her abs for effect. "Plus, doesn't hurt that I ran here."

"Whatever you're doing seems to be working. Maybe I should start earning my meals." The diner owner slapped at his gut and gave a hearty laugh.

"I bet you could hold your own back in the day, Harry."

"I don't like to toot my own horn. But toot, toot."

Hatch smiled and took a split second to size the man up. "What'd you do before all this? Before you settled into the diner?"

"I was an ironworker. Mostly commercial projects. Did that for about twenty years. But the body can only take so much before it starts telling you to move on. My last job had me in Albuquerque. Moved down here with my wife looking for a simpler life. The diner thing just fell into my lap. The previous owner died, and his family no longer lived here. They sold it for a song. And this has been my life ever since. I guess I've always been a fan of food." He again tapped his belly for good measure. "I figured how hard could it be? I started as a breakfast and lunch spot. But I added a dinner menu a couple years back. Now I feel as though I pretty much live here."

"And your wife? She likes it here in Luna Vista?"

His smile faded. "She passed a few years back. But she did."

"I'm sorry to hear that."

Harry gave a dismissive shrug. "One thing's for certain, all of us eventually get off this ride called life. And my Jenny made a good run of it. She was a beautiful creature, both inside and out. I guess heaven needed another angel. Cancer took her from me."

Hatch caught some movement out of the corner of her eye and turned to see a girl standing on the sidewalk in front of the diner. Hatch recognized her as the same girl from last night. The one she'd seen get out of the car and enter Psycho's house, or whatever that place was. Most likely a stash house. Smart gangs had multiple locations scattered about to effectively misdirect law enforcement.

The girl was in the same clothes she'd been in the night before. The purple coat and mini skirt looked like odd attire in the early morning. The girl had a slight stagger to her walk. She was cold. It was apparent from the way she hugged herself and rubbed the sleeves of her coat. She stood near the entrance to Harry's diner but didn't enter. Hatch assumed she was attempting to warm herself by the heat escaping from it.

Hatch felt sorry for her. She got up from her stool. "Could you keep this warm for me?" Hatch slid her plate toward Harry.

Harry walked the plate into the kitchen area and placed it under the orange glow of a warming lamp.

Hatch then walked to the door and opened it.

The girl jumped back like she was a dog left out in a thunderstorm.

"Are you okay?" Hatch asked softly.

The girl eyed Hatch coldly. Her eyes held a visible skepticism. The mistrust was most likely a byproduct of her circumstance. The question coupled with the genuine concern in Hatch's tone seemed to throw the girl and momentarily stall her ability to answer.

She stepped back from Hatch. "I'm fine. Just a little cold is all."

"Why don't you come inside and warm up?" Hatch gestured to the diner.

The girl was in the same clothes as last night, but her face was not in the same condition. She had a bruise underneath her right eye and her lip was swollen to the size of a golf ball.

"I don't think that's such a good idea. I was just trying to warm up a little bit. No need to bother with me," the girl said without making eye contact.

"It's really no bother. I just sat down to eat myself. Food's pretty good here. I don't know if you've ever had it before?"

"I have." The battered girl paused. "It's been a while, but yeah I used to eat here quite a bit when I was younger."

"Well, Harry's great. Makes a mean breakfast plate. Why don't you come in and keep me company a little bit?"

"I don't have any money to waste on breakfast. Don't worry about me. I'll be fine. I'll just keep moving."

Hatch knew the mentality. Although they came from different worlds, the girl's "keep moving" comment reminded Hatch of the comment she'd made to her mom during their phone conversation. A rolling stone gathers no moss. From the observations Hatch gathered about the girl's situation, the moss she was so desperate to avoid was most likely guilt. Perpetually moving forward probably kept her from thinking too much about last night. Or whatever she'd done in her past.

Hatch knew a thing or two about past lives, and how they grabbed hold. Ever since leaving the Army, Hatch worked hard to distance herself from hers. She'd desperately sought to find a new direction, a new purpose. Maybe all this girl needed was a new start. If *the girl was standing at a proverbial fork in the road, Hatch could do something to shift her in the right direction.* If nothing else, a good meal would give her a better start to her day and provide a slight reprieve from the cold New Mexico air.

"I'm fixing to head back inside now. I'll be ordering another one of those Luna Vista breakfast specials Harry makes. I'd hate to try to eat two of those on my own. One's enough to basically feed me for a day. So, it'll be there if you want." Hatch didn't want to force the girl. No need to pull her by the arm. She didn't say anything more and let the open invitation linger as she turned and reentered the diner.

Hatch returned to her stool at the counter.

Harry peeked out from the kitchen. A moment later, he brought her the warmed plate of food. Using an oven mitt to set it down, he said, "Watch your hands. That plate's hot."

Steam rose from the meal in front of her. The marvelous scents floated up to Hatch's nose. She took a moment to savor it. Peppers and onions mixed with the smell of the extra crispy bacon. The cayenne pepper used to season the home fries caused her mouth to water. "Hey, Harry, how about another order of the same?"

Harry gave her a double take. "You gotta be kidding me. I mean, I'm impressed that you can take down one plate. But two? I don't think a lumberjack can do that kind of eating."

Hatch just smiled. "I'll take two."

He looked out toward the pane of glass and the girl visible through it. Harry leaned in, pressing his thick forearms onto the counter in front of him. His face grew serious. "She's not worth it."

"I haven't made my mind up about that yet. Maybe after a little bit of food and conversation I'll be able to agree or disagree with you. One thing's for certain, I never judge a book by its cover." Hatch subconsciously rubbed the scar hidden underneath the long sleeve windbreaker she wore and felt the ripple of the scar tissue wind its way around her arm, up toward her shoulder. She thought about how many had judged her and judged incorrectly.

Harry argued his point no further and retreated back into the kitchen area, but not before topping off her coffee.

As Hatch took a sip, she heard the door's bell announce the arrival of a new patron. She waited. Moments later, Hatch felt the coolness of the air still surrounding the girl's clothing and body as she took a seat beside her. Harry looked up from the little opening in the kitchen. A non-verbal exchange took place between the diner owner and the girl. The girl broke eye contact first and started playing with the zipper of her purple coat.

"Glad you took me up on my offer," Hatch whispered.

The girl shrugged and continued to play with the zipper. "Who's dumb enough to pass on free breakfast? I'm certainly in no position to look a gift horse in the mouth."

"Regardless of your reason, I'm glad you did."

"Harry doesn't like me here. He says it's bad for business." She flicked her eyes in the man's direction. "He doesn't like the look of somebody like me inside his restaurant."

Hatch thought about calling Harry over to discuss this—make a point of treating each customer as an equal but thought better of it. Not the time or place to do so. In her short stay in Luna Vista, she'd only come in contact with a handful of people whom she connected with. Harry was on a very short list. So, she decided not to offend the man who'd been so kind to her.

Hatch looked around the interior of the restaurant and saw a booth in the back corner partially obscured by a coat rack and the high-back booth seat. She looked at the girl and said, "Would you feel more comfortable if we take our breakfast over there?"

"Sure. You're buying. That means you're in charge."

Hatch grabbed her plate. The oval-shaped porcelain plate retained the heat, and the warmth permeated her skin. Hatch walked briskly to the booth and set her plate down.

The girl sat as Hatch went back to her spot at the counter and grabbed her cup of coffee. Harry acknowledged their relocation with a slight nod.

Hatch took up her position in the cushioned seat of the booth and looked at the girl across from her as she sipped her coffee. She decided to wait until the girl's food arrived to begin devouring her plate. It felt wrong to start in the presence of a girl who looked so hungry.

"Tell me a little bit about yourself. Are you from Luna Vista?"

"Born and raised. Trust me. It's not something to brag about."

"My name's Rachel, but people call me Hatch."

"Why? Strange nickname." The girl's voice had a crackle to it like that of a long-term smoker or somebody just coming down with a touch of bronchitis.

"Hatch is my last name. And the job—people would refer to me by it. So, I guess it just kind of stuck."

This answer sufficed. The girl shrugged. "Okay—Hatch."

The girl let go of her zipper and edged toward eye contact with Hatch. Her shoulders dropped as she said, "Well, my name's Wendy." It was as if her name was synonymous with shame.

"All right, Wendy. It's nice to officially make your acquaintance."

It wasn't long before Harry arrived with another steaming plate of identical portion size to the one in front of Hatch. He slid the plate down in front of the girl with less care than Hatch had seen in the way he delivered her meal. But nonetheless, regardless of Harry's opinion of the girl, breakfast was served.

Harry looked down at the girl and poured her a cup of coffee without waiting for her permission. He leveled a steely gaze and said, "It's been a while, Gwendolyn. I haven't seen you in a bit."

The girl lifted her head slightly, but not all the way. She restrained herself from making full eye contact with him and murmured, "Well, at least now you know I'm not dead."

Harry turned and started to walk away. "I'll make sure to tell your mother that," he said with a gruff grunt. He then returned to the kitchen to attend whatever was on the griddle.

Hatch raised an eyebrow. "Thought you said your name was Wendy?"

"It is—well sort of—it's my nickname. Gwendolyn's my real name but only my uncle still calls me by it."

"Harry's your uncle?" Hatch asked.

"He is my mother's brother. But they haven't seen each other in quite a while."

"Does your mother still live here, in Luna Vista?"

"No. She ran out on me. Last I heard she was in Albuquerque. But that was a few years ago. She bolted on me the day after my sixteenth birthday. Hell of a gift, right? She told me she was fed up with me and the choices I was making. So, she went off to make her own series of bad choices—most of which involved meth. Harry took me in. He was *unprepared to take on the responsibility of raising a teenage girl*. And voila—I learned to fend for myself."

Hatch decided not to press any further about her family tree, fearing the story was more depressing and more tragic than she really wanted to hear during her morning breakfast. Hatch was a big believer in focusing on the here and now. Not on things that could not be changed. "If you don't mind me asking, how old are you, Wendy?"

"I'm nineteen."

"What happened to your face?"

"Sheesh, I didn't know I was going to get the third-degree. I thought it was just some offering of kindness. A meal because you felt sorry for me."

"Everything comes with a price. Mine is a relatively simple one. Conversation. You eat and we talk. I think it's a fair trade. And from the looks of the beating you took—a far better one than you received last night."

The girl shoveled a spoonful of the spicy home fries and scrambled egg into her mouth. Wendy ate as if it was the first real food she had put inside her in a while. The girl had a ravenous appetite. Hatch waited as the girl swallowed.

Hatch was accustomed to the quick consumption of food trained into her by the Army. She learned that every meal was a gift and every opportunity to eat needs to be done as quickly as possible to prepare for whatever comes next. There was no time to sit and sip. No time to slowly enjoy each morsel. It was about getting enough energy so you'd be ready to perform at a moment's notice. Food was fuel. After being out for over a year, she continued to treat meals with the same regard.

Hatch joined Wendy in the rapid consumption of their plated breakfast. It was as if they were in some type of competition at a county fair's pie eating contest.

Hatch forced herself to slow down and decided to re-engage the girl now that the food had reached her stomach. In doing so, hopefully it would remove some of the girl's angst.

"How about it? What happened?"

The girl sipped at the hot coffee but the warm mug on her lip caused her to wince as she did so. Wendy swallowed hard and cleared her throat. "It's nothing. Just things happen, ya know?"

"It doesn't have to be that way."

"What are you going to do about it? Beat him up?"

"Already did," Hatch said with a smile and took a sip from her mug, draining the last bit of the coffee and resting her fork back on the center of her now empty plate.

The girl's face brightened for the first time since Hatch had encountered the teen. Wendy looked genuinely happy, that Christmas-morning-found-the-presents-under-the-tree kind of happy. "That was all he complained about last night. I assumed his busted jaw was from some rival gang. He never said anything about a girl."

"Makes sense he wouldn't."

"But it was you?"

"I don't like to brag, but he had it coming."

"You don't have to tell me that twice." She rubbed her cheekbone.

Hatch was quiet for a moment before speaking again. She could see from the vacant look that the girl was momentarily transported back in time to whatever awfulness happened to her. She could only imagine the highlight reel of abuse that Psycho, and men like him, had given this girl over the years.

"It's a dangerous line of work you're in," Hatch offered.

"Yeah, well, I'm pretty tough."

A false bravado resonated in her voice. Hatch heard it but decided not to address it. "I agree. I can see that about you. Still doesn't mean it's not dangerous. You seem like a smart girl."

"I know what comes next. You're going to tell me to go get a real job. After the track record I've accumulated here in this little town, I'm all used up." Tears started to well up in the girl's eyes. "Nineteen and I'm all used up." Her hand went back to the zipper of her purple coat.

"How about you get yourself cleaned up and we can have this conversation again? A few good meals and a hot shower. After a little time away from the people who did that to your face, then you can tell me what kind of life you want to have."

Wendy looked down at her coffee. No longer cold and hungry, she was already in a better way than she had been when she'd first come in. Hatch's offer was hopefully being considered by the stubborn teen.

Hatch hadn't initially intended to be Wendy's saving grace. She selfishly hoped to gather some intel on the gang while giving this girl a hot meal and a temporary break from the harshness of the street life. But after hearing her story, there was no way she could walk away from her in good conscience.

If Wendy wanted to redirect the course of her life, then Hatch wanted to help. And if in the course of doing so, Wendy felt so inclined to share some things about the gang, then so be it. The girl's well-being took priority.

Hatch waited for the girl to formulate her answer. Patience was a key ingredient in any interrogation. A person's innate need to fill the emptiness of silence with words sometimes coerced a person's willingness to confess. Or in the case of Wendy, agree with Hatch's offer.

Several minutes passed. The girl finished the last bit of food and carefully wiped her lips, avoiding the swollen cracked lump.

Wendy set the napkin down and looked at Hatch with as much confidence as she could muster. "Okay. What did you have in mind?"

"I'm staying at the Moonbeam. There's a bunch of empty rooms. Tell you what, I'll put you up for a couple of days. Watch TV, shower, eat and sleep. And when you're feeling up to it, you and I will talk. Maybe I can help you figure something out that's a better option than the path you're on now."

"Why would you do that for me?"

"Good people get themselves into bad positions. I'll help because it's the right thing to do. So, let me."

This time the girl's willpower to hold back the reservoir of tears broke and a solitary tear rolled from the corner of her eye, across the bruise, along her upper cheekbone, and down her face. "I'll do it."

FOURTEEN

HATCH WALKED into the main office of the motel. Manuel exited from the back room with a stack of neatly folded white towels. He smiled at her.

"What can I do for you?"

"Manuel, I'd like to rent another room."

He frowned slightly. "Is there something wrong with number three? I can take a look. If it's the heat or water supply, I can get it fixed up for you. It can be a bit temperamental."

"No. It's not that at all. I have a new guest and I'd like to put her up for a night or two. Next door to me. In room two, if it's available?"

Manuel looked past Hatch and out through the window at the young girl seated in the passenger seat of Hatch's Camry. He then looked back at Hatch. "I've seen her around. She's not going to be a problem, is she?"

"No. I'll vouch for her." Hatch cast a glance at the girl fiddling with her coat. "This kid just needs a little bit of a break to get herself back on her feet." Hatch watched as Manuel processed the statement. She knew a man born from hardship, a self-created entrepreneur, would find some resonance in that. Everybody needs a little help now and again.

"Are you still paying in cash?" he asked.

Hatch nodded as she retrieved her wallet. "How about we start with two nights. I'll figure out where things go from there." She unfolded her wallet and set out four crisp twenty-dollar bills.

Manuel didn't bother offering the guest sign-in sheet. He slid the money off the table and exchanged it for a key with a red diamond-shaped plastic identifier.

Hatch took the keychain embossed with a bold number two in faded gold lettering. She thanked Manuel and exited the office.

She walked directly over to the room and opened the door. Hatch waved her hand to the young streetwalker, Wendy, signaling her room was ready. The teen exited the car and hesitantly followed Hatch inside.

"Cleaner than I thought it would be," the girl said.

"Manuel and his wife take real pride in this place. For a small motel, in the middle of nowhere, he treats it as if it's the Ritz-Carlton."

"Hey, I'm sorry for being such an ass earlier. I-It's just that people don't typically show me the kindness you did back there. The kindness you're showing me now. I guess it caught me off guard. Sorry."

"There's absolutely no reason for you to be sorry. Hell, I'd be a little nervous too if some stranger came up and offered to put me up in a motel, especially after some of the things that you've been through. I want to thank you for trusting me enough to give it a shot. Any leap of faith requires a moment of hesitation. Because once we step off that invisible ledge, we don't know where we're going to land. Maybe this is the beginning of something really good for you. Seems to me like you're long overdue."

The girl just dipped her head low, looking at her feet. Hatch knew that look. The self-loathing doesn't go away immediately. Anger one feels toward themselves when they're in a situation like hers doesn't just dissipate from one act of kindness. Life isn't a Hall-mark movie.

Wendy didn't feel deserving of such kindness, but either way, Hatch was committed to putting forth the effort with her in the hopes something would take. If nothing else, she would get cleaned up enough to possibly win back some of Harry's trust. And then maybe the old diner owner could take the reins for a bit and give her the home life she deserved.

Hatch said none of this to the girl. Those predictions, spoken or otherwise, in circumstances as volatile as this, could be as detrimental as strong-arming the girl. So, she did her best not to preach the dreams of a better life and instead decided to give the girl some space.

"I'm going to head out for a little bit. Once you get some rest, I'll pick up some food from the diner. Do you have a meal preference?"

The girl shook her head slowly from side to side. "Anything is fine."

"Okay. When I come back, I'll try not to bother you if you're sleeping. I can always grab a key if you don't answer. I'll leave the food on the table."

"Don't worry about waking me. It's fine. Really. Feel free to wake me up. I wouldn't mind the company."

"I'll see you later then."

Hatch walked out and closed the door behind her. She heard the latch of the deadbolt slam into place and the dangling chain lock rattle against the door. *Good*, thought Hatch. At least she was taking some precautions. Not that anyone would know she was there. But Hatch felt better about leaving, knowing the girl had secured herself inside.

Hatch got back in the beige Camry and pulled out of the lot.

It wasn't a long drive. She pulled into a similar position where she was parked the night before. This time, in the daylight, also meant she was easier to spot. Hatch was careful. She made sure she was farther down the road and tucked neatly behind an oversized pickup. Parking in a residential area, in front of a home where the resident, if home, wouldn't recognize her, could be problematic. Hatch didn't want to draw unwanted attention from the neighbor. They could call a police officer to investigate. Although she was less concerned about that based on the attitude displayed by the chief of police. But unwanted attention was unwanted attention and Hatch liked to remain off the radar. This was just a surveillance op. She wanted to see if she could figure out a little bit more about the location and the comings and goings of the gang.

Psycho's Honda didn't appear to have moved from its parked position. The front wheels were still on the patchy grass yard. Beer bottles and trash littered the area around it. But there was one glaring difference. Today, two black motorcycles with leather saddlebags were parked in the driveway. Hatch assumed this must be the men Macho referenced during his tongue lashing dished out in the abandoned warehouse.

She was tempted to exit her vehicle and snoop about but immediately thought better of it. Bad enough she was already on the gang's radar. Even though they were a local crew, small as they were, it was still dangerous business. She didn't need to make her way up their food chain and draw attention from whomever it was they'd aligned themselves with. Hatch, never afraid of a fight, had picked hers, and it was with the Outlaws. Not whoever they were working with. She also didn't like to engage until she had a good understanding of the odds.

About a half-hour passed. Every time a vehicle drove down the street, Hatch pretended to be fiddling on her phone. At one point, when a dog walker approached, she held her phone to her ear and pretended to be quietly engaged in a conversation. An effective ruse of disarming any nosy neighbors. She learned in her many years of investigations that hiding in plain sight sometimes only took one or two layers of deception before people wrote you off as being normal. For as much as she hated them, cell phones had become an amazing impromptu disguise kit.

Fifteen more minutes ticked by. Then the door to the ranch-style house opened and two men exited. They didn't look anything like the Outlaws. Both men had long hair. They had on the traditional biker garb. Even in the cold weather they wore short sleeve black T-shirts and leather vests with tasseled ends. Hatch was too far away to read the rockers, the identifier of a motorcycle gang.

The door to the house closed and the two bikers got on their choppers. One of them had something in his hand. It looked like an overstuffed manilla envelope. He slipped it into his saddlebag on the right side of the motorcycle.

Hatch was intrigued. *Was it the cash they'd discussed?* she thought. It was the most probable guess. She then wondered if Psycho had done his job and counted it to ensure its accuracy. She had no reason to believe he wouldn't but thought it funny if he happened to slip up. It might bring a hasty end to Luna Vista's Outlaw problem.

They walked their bikes backward onto the street. The rev of the engines was deafening as the two drove off. Luckily, they departed in the opposite direction from Hatch's position.

She debated sticking around to keep an eye on Psycho but decided to give the bikers a loose tail. If nothing else, maybe she'd be able to identify their rocker. Armed with the knowledge of their actual gang affiliation, she might be inclined to call Dalton Savage and have him run it through the system. Even Hawk's Landing had access to national and international law enforcement databases. Technology had connected the police from around the globe. Whether she would actually call Dalton was still up for debate. She knew the man well enough that he'd get suspicious if she were asking about a motorcycle gang. And the last thing she wanted was for her hometown sheriff to call in the cavalry down here.

Hatch drove down the street after giving the motorcycles a decent head start. As the Camry passed Psycho's parked Honda, the front door to the house opened a crack. Standing in its threshold was Psycho himself. Hatch was uncharacteristically unprepared for his surprise exit.

She made eye contact. She saw in his eyes a pure and utter hatred. Hatch was familiar with it. She'd known the rage of men. The majority of her adult life had been in battle with such people. She also knew that once bloodlust—that overwhelming desire—took hold, rationality went out the window.

She turned away and faced forward, accelerating away from the house. Too late. Psycho was already on the move. He ran toward the Honda at a dead sprint. The man's cornrows were no longer braided tightly against his scalp. His hair, which looked more like a clown wig, bounced wildly as he ran. He was wearing the same hooded sweatshirt and jeans he'd worn last night.

Hatch watched him in her rearview mirror as he jumped into the car. Backing out wildly onto the grass, he did a wild K-turn, swinging the vehicle onto the street behind her. His Honda cried out as it accelerated. She could hear the roar of his engine over her own even with the windows closed.

The Honda gained incrementally on Hatch's rental. *This isn't good*, she thought. All she'd sought to do was gather some more intelligence and formulate a plan of action. Now, Murphy's Law kicked in and Psycho was hot on her tail. Her plan to pursue the bikers was now abandoned. With this maniac behind her, she knew she needed to clear this residential area and create some distance. Her mind ran a mental map of the area. She then thought of the open road between Luna Vista and Las Cruces and headed for it. Hatch took a left turn at a high rate of speed, and she watched as the two motorcycles disappeared from sight.

With every turn she made, Psycho continued to keep the pressure on. He wasn't a great driver, but his reckless abandon seemed to keep an invisible tether to her. She watched as he fishtailed around a corner. Although the man's pursuit driving skills were amateur, he was relentless. One thing was certain: He was definitely not giving up the chase.

Hatch gained a little bit of distance when her pursuer lost control and sideswiped a parked minivan. The Camry's RPMs were pegged as she headed toward the edge of town. She wondered where Officer Cartwright was right now. She'd blown just about every light and stop sign in town. Yet, she hadn't seen one of Luna Vista's police officers. Hatch planned to bring up this point of contention some other time. Right now, her entire purpose was focused on evading the man in the Honda. She needed to create enough distance and, hopefully, at some point, shake him completely.

She passed by the sign rooted at the town line. It was a picturesque rendering of the town at sunset. The sky a fire red with the Organ Mountains set in the backdrop. The paint was faded now. The sand-infused wind had seen to that, but the faded caption was still legible. *Leaving so soon? We'll miss you.* Hatch would have laughed at the irony had she not been engaged in a high-speed chase with a madman.

Hatch gunned the gas once she hit the open expanse of road at the town's end. It was like a scene from *Mad Max*. The roadway was surrounded by dry desert landscape on both sides. The cracked pavement was covered in windswept dust, adding to the desolate feel. In the distance was the cityscape of Las Cruces. At least now she was away from the residential area of Luna Vista, should this chase break bad. Hatch didn't need the watchful eyes of its citizenry on her.

She weighed her options. Drive into the larger city and hope to lose the man in the more densely populated area's traffic flow. Or deviate her course and head off to a more remote area. The speed at which Hatch contemplated life and death decisions rivaled a layperson's ability to add sugar to their coffee.

Hatch chose option two.

She jammed the brakes and took a hard right onto a side road leading north. Hatch accelerated, kicking up a vortex of dust in her wake.

Psycho followed.

The road seemed to be devoid of human life. No town or indication of one anywhere in the distance. As she crested a slight rise in the road, Hatch saw a rundown gas station about a quarter mile up on the right. A sign hung from its last remaining bolt. The windows to the two-pump station's store were boarded up.

Hatch checked her rearview mirror. With the distance she'd added between her Camry and Psycho's Honda coupled with the endless swirl of dust, she hoped she could tuck in behind the building and ditch him. She redlined the Camry.

She whipped the sedan hard to the right and fishtailed as she rounded the station's abandoned store. If nothing else, she'd be able to position herself and prepare for the man.

Hatch didn't have much time. She heard the roar of the Honda's engine as soon as she slammed to a stop just beyond the backside of the building. She made a hasty exit.

A rusted and rotted out dumpster was set near the corner of the building. Hatch ran to it. She took up a prone position and lay on the dirt ground, wedging herself into a spot where she could see but not be seen.

Hatch drew her weapon with her left hand and was aiming out from underneath the metal dumpster. She waited.

The halting tires spit rock and gravel as the Honda came to an abrupt stop just past the pump area.

Hatch prepared her mind, taking in three combat breaths, in for a two count and out for a three. The ability of operators to prepare for the unforeseeable made them formidable adversaries. And Hatch was as formidable as they came. In this interim before battle, she made a mental checklist of potential what if's, and what she'd do so that if and when they came to fruition, she would be able to act more quickly.

She hoped she didn't have to use the gun in her hand. Not that he didn't likely deserve it. Her thoughts on the matter were more in line with self-preservation than some altruistic concept of right and wrong. Shooting the man would only cause problems.

Hatch lay in wait. It wasn't long before she heard the Honda's door slam. The crunch of his feet was loud on the dirt-covered ground. His plan of attack seemed to be similar to his approach the other day. He intended to intimidate through loud aggressive actions. He hadn't learned his lesson. So, Hatch would have to re-teach it now.

Psycho's arms flailed the same way they had the other day. The only difference was this time a gun was in his right hand. He waved the pistol about and screamed, "You should've left when you had a chance. Now you ain't ever gonna leave this town. I'm gonna put a bullet in your head!"

Hatch said nothing. She made no noise at all. She didn't move, didn't whimper. She was a rock. Her eyes focused intently on the man, keeping him in the front sight picture of her Sig Sauer. The pad of her index finger rested on the crescent trigger of the gun. There was no indexing in a situation like this. There'd be no commands to halt or drop the weapon. She wasn't law enforcement anymore. She was a survivor.

Psycho stepped closer. He edged closer to the dumpster.

The silence must be unnerving him, she thought. Hatch noticed a hesitancy to his movement now as he worked his way closer.

The man's eyes were wide and jumped around wildly as the wind blew through his puffy hair. He flailed his gun, pointing it in every direction but Hatch's. He was a combination of scared and angry. And as he got close enough, Hatch could see he was trembling. For all the macho bravado and noisy threats he'd made, the man was terrified. Hatch smiled at this observation. Then she thought of Wendy's face. And how scared the nineteen-year-old girl must've been last night when this thug used her as his personal punching bag.

He wasn't as stupid as she'd thought. Hatch half assumed the man would rush blindly forward. But apparently once he realized she wasn't huddled in a corner crying or begging for his mercy, he slowed his progression and then stopped altogether.

At this point, the man was less than fifteen feet away from her. With each step closer, more of her target area disappeared. All she could see now was the area from his kneecaps down to his feet. The rest of his body was obscured because of his proximity. Hatch adjusted her point of aim.

The man began making his taunts again. Hatch didn't pay attention to the words. Her ears were focused on listening for passing motorists. She heard nothing but the howl of the wind as it zigzagged relentlessly in the open space.

Hatch took a deep breath and exhaled slowly.

Bang!

It was loud. The fact that her weapon was positioned underneath the gapped space between the bottom of the rusted dumpster and the ground meant the sound of the bullet's release dramatically increased. The explosive release resonated through the metal like an amplifier. It took a few seconds for her ears to recover. Once they did, she heard the screaming from the man on the other side of the dumpster.

The bullet struck its mark. Exactly where she intended it to go. The man's left foot. The round entered the instep just past his big toe. Hatch knew the bullet tore through the gang banger's flesh and bone as it ripped through the midsection of his foot. Painful, but not life-threatening. A wound capable of leaving a permanent limp. Maybe enough lasting discomfort to give him pause every time he stepped forward to intimidate some innocent person in the future.

Hatch remained still and continued to lay in the same position. She watched him, his entire body in full view. He had collapsed in an awkward fashion, lying on his side. He reached down to his blood covered foot. The red pool saturated the dirt, turning it a dark brown. Hatch scanned the ground around him. It took her a moment before she saw what she was looking for. The gun had been thrown. The injection of pain and the shock of the gunshot apparently scrambled any thoughts he had of using the weapon. It was some thirty feet away from him. Not that it would matter much had it been closer. The man was rolling on the ground and cursing angrily.

Hatch pushed herself up from the ground. There was a split second where she lost visual contact with the injured man while traversing her barrier. She quickly came out from around the dumpster to see him in the same pained position. Hatch didn't immediately go to him. Instead, she fanned out wide and worked herself in the direction of where the gun rested. She then stepped on it and temporarily secured it underfoot. She maintained her point of aim on the man. He finally took notice of her.

"You crazy bitch! We're gonna hurt you so bad you'll be beggin' us to kill you. It's going to be slow and painful. Gonna take you days to die! You just mark my words."

"That's a lot of tough talk from a man who doesn't have a weapon in his hand." She nudged her gun in his direction. "But does have one pointed at his head."

It was at this moment that he seemed to come to the realization that she was standing on his gun. Whatever his plans or intentions were prior to this moment, they seemed to completely fall apart. His face went white with shock.

"You're bleeding pretty good. I'd be thinking of getting to a doctor instead of making death threats."

"That's because you shot me!"

"I did shoot you. And I'm really trying hard not to do it again, but you're making it more difficult than I thought. So, please don't give me another reason to pull the trigger. The next time I'll be aiming a little higher."

The man spat at her. It made a frothy splat on the ground near his head. This time, no vengeful words followed.

"You're starting to lose some blood. Going to need somebody to take a look at that."

"Why don't you just shoot me and get it over with?"

"Now what would be the fun in that?" Hatch asked with a smile. "But I'll tell you this— I'm not going anywhere soon. So, when you see me around town, I suggest you walk the other way. Or there's going to be a round three between you and me. And if one and two are any indication, you're not gonna come out on top."

Psycho looked back at his bleeding foot. "So, what? You're just gonna leave me here?"

And with that, Hatch had a thought. And the thought made her smile. She picked up the gun from under her foot and tucked the Smith & Wesson into the right side of her waistband. She put the Sig Sauer back on her left side.

Hatch walked over to the Honda. It was still running. She turned the ignition and removed the keys.

She dropped the keys into her front pocket and slid out her pocketknife. She flicked it open. She started going from tire to tire, driving the sharp blade into each of the rubber Firestone tires. A loud whoosh of air released and the vehicle sank. Hatch worked her way around from the driver's side, to the backend, and then back up to the front. In a matter of seconds, all four tires of the Honda were completely deflated.

Hatch looked at the man as she passed by and got into her Camry.

Hatch pulled the Camry around the building, stopping briefly near the injured man, she lowered her window and said, "Have a nice walk back."

FIFTEEN

HATCH DROVE BACK INTO TOWN. She took her time, wanting to retrace her exact steps. She drove by the street with the house where Psycho had met with the bikers. Stopping down the street, she saw there were no cars or motorcycles in the driveway. Hatch decided to let things cool off and didn't risk exposing herself any further for the moment. She decided to make good on her promise to Wendy and swing by the diner to pick up some food.

She pulled to a stop in front and saw Harry through the window. Hatch stepped inside the diner.

"Back again so soon?" Harry asked.

"I'm just picking up a to-go order." Hatch walked over to the counter and took a seat.

"Let me guess—"

"You don't have to. You already know who it's for." Hatch picked up the menu in front of her. She ordered a couple of cold cut sandwiches.

"You want a cup of coffee while you wait?" Harry asked.

She nodded. A piping hot mug was in front of her a second later.

It didn't take long for Harry to whip up the sandwiches. He

added a couple apples and three bags of sour cream and onion Ruffles to the order. "These were always her favorite chips as a kid," he said stuffing everything into an oversized brown paper bag and setting it down in front of Hatch.

"Ya know, Harry? She still is." Hatch took out her wallet.

"Still is what?"

"A kid." Hatch saw the man's cheeks flush as she opened the wallet. "How much?"

"You know my policy with you. It's on the house."

"Harry, if you keep being so charitable to me, you're gonna go out of business. I really don't mind paying for my food. Especially since I've become a frequent flyer to your establishment."

"I told you. You don't have to pay while you are visiting." Harry looked at the brown bag on the counter. "But this time it's on the house for her."

Hatch nodded and took the bag in hand. "I'll let her know."

"You don't have to. I'm not looking for her thanks."

Hatch started to leave but realized he wasn't done talking. She turned back to face him. He had a sad look in his eyes, uncharacteristic of the man she'd come to know over the past few days of their daily banter exchanged over breakfast.

"I love that girl. I truly do. When she came into my life, I mean really came into my life, a few years back, I wasn't in a good place. It hadn't been very long since my wife passed and I wasn't in a spot where I felt I could be of any good to anybody. Then I get a troubled sixteen-year-old girl dumped on my doorstep. Her mother, my sister, just up and abandoned her daughter. Who does that to their only child? Just gives up and leaves? My sister left me holding the ball. Although, the problem was, I dropped it. I'll be the first to admit that I was no good in the time following my wife's death. Plus, I was totally out of my element, never having any children of my own."

"It's a two-way street. The burden can't squarely rest on your shoulders. Wendy has to meet you halfway. You can't constantly chase someone who doesn't want your affection or help." Hatch thought of her mother. And how, at eighteen, she left and never looked back. She'd effectively turned away from her family and isolated herself, starting a new life in the Army and all that came with it. Now, fifteen years later, Hatch was just starting to reconnect with her mother and niece and nephew. Hatch knew she was just as much at fault for letting things fall apart, and the blame was to be shared equally. So yeah, Hatch understood better than Harry would ever know.

"I wasn't in a place to help then, but maybe now I can do something. Ya know, be more involved this time around. That's if she'll let me."

"Tell you what—she's definitely a hard case and she's in a tough spot right now. I put her up at the Moonbeam so I could keep an eye on her and give her a break from the street life. How about we give her a couple days to rest and recuperate? Once her head clears a bit from the fog of whatever she's been through, I'll mention what you said about giving it another go. I won't press. I won't force her. She's a grown girl who's fended for herself for a while. But I will let her know that your mind is open to it—as well as to possibly rekindling whatever sense of family you guys once had."

"You're a good person, Hatch."

"You are, too." She wasn't great at accepting compliments. Plus, she wondered if the kindhearted diner owner would think the same if he knew she'd just shot a man. *If Harry knew the number of the things she did while in service to the country, or in service to her code of honor, would he still think she was a good person?*

Hatch offered a weak smile and said, "I'll see you tomorrow, Harry." She turned with the sack of food and headed for the door.

Standing outside on the sidewalk in front of the diner, she scanned the area. Her threat receptors were on high alert after her most recent altercation. Nothing stood out on her radar. As she made her way back to her Camry, the front door of the Vista Gun shop opened and standing in the threshold of it was Gabe Smith. He waved with a big shit-eating grin on his face.

Without an invitation, the man hustled across the not so busy street to where she stood.

"Rachel—sorry, Hatch. Hey, just wanted to say hello. See how you were doing. You never came back to talk with my father." The man fumbled with his words like a lunatic fresh out of the asylum. He seemed almost giddy to see her, and the warmth of his reception made Hatch feel slightly awkward.

"Speaking of your dad, is he around?" Hatch felt like she'd just given a cold shoulder to his greeting and returned it with her best rendition of Joe Friday's *just the facts*. Realizing this, she reconciled by softening her response. "Sorry. I just haven't had a chance to make it back yet and chat with him. But if he's around now, I'll be right back. I've just got to run to the motel to drop something off first."

Gabe shook his head. "He's not around. But I'd be happy to close up shop for a bit and show you around town."

Hatch thought about blowing the man off. Then she remembered his kindness had provided her the gun she'd used to stop a recent threat. Without it, the outcome could have been far different. She decided not to offend Gabe any further. "Sounds good. I can meet you back here in a little bit."

"Don't bother. I'll get things locked up and pick you up. What room are you staying in?"

"Number three."

"See you soon." Gabe walked across the street, barely paying attention to any potential traffic.

Hatch was struck with a sudden wave of dread. He was picking her up and taking her on a tour of the town. Food would probably be involved. *Did Gabe just ask me out on a date?*

This town had proven itself truly strange. She'd only been here a couple days. And in that time, she'd been in a fight, stumbled across a gang problem, and been in a shooting. Now, she was possibly being asked on a date by a man, who didn't know a thing about her. The strangest part about it was that she had accepted.

"I'll see you in about a half hour," Gabe hollered from across the street and then disappeared back inside the gun store.

Hatch tossed her sack of sandwiches on the passenger seat and sped back toward the motel.

HATCH KNOCKED on door number two. The deadbolt retracted and the chain lock went limp, signified by its jingling on the other side of the door. It opened slowly to a wet-haired Wendy. The girl stood in the doorway wrapped in a towel. She was already looking a little better than she had when Hatch left her earlier.

Hatch extended her hand. In it was the bag of food. "Compliments of your uncle. Harry whipped up a couple sandwiches. They're cold cuts, so you can just stick them in that mini fridge over there and eat them whenever you want."

Wendy took the paper sack and peered inside. Seeing the chips on top, she smiled. The weakness of the smile was either due to her tentativeness at accepting the gift from her uncle or the pain of her damaged lip. "Thank you. You really didn't have to do this. I don't want you troubling yourself over me."

"No trouble at all. Get some rest. I'll let you get back to whatever it is you're doing. I'm happy to see you're taking my advice and relaxing a little bit. I won't bother you again today, but if you want, I'll stop by in the morning. I've become quite addicted to Harry's breakfast. If you're interested, I'd be happy to have the company."

"Sure. If I'm up, I'll go with you."

The answer made Hatch feel a sense of hope. The girl's responsiveness was as genuine as much as it was surprising. "I won't even make you run." Hatch chuckled at her weak attempt at a joke.

Hatch turned and walked next door to her room. She heard Wendy close and latch hers as she entered.

Hatch sat on the edge of her bed and thought about changing into something nicer than her current attire. Not that she had a large selection of wardrobe options, but she had borrowed a few things from her sister's closet before leaving Hawk's Landing. After a short deliberation, ironically longer than her decision to shoot the man in his foot, Hatch decided against changing her outfit. Getting dressed up, even casually, made the idea of this upcoming outing into a date. What if she'd read Gabe wrong? She was a master at detecting deception. But when it came to relationships, she was a fish out of water. Besides, she wasn't in Luna Vista to start a relationship. She found some middle ground and took a moment to wash her face and add an extra layer of deodorant.

She had started to doze off when she heard a knock, Hatch got up from her nearly supine position on the bed and walked to the door. She looked out the peephole to see Gabe Smith standing in a fishbowl created by the concave lens.

SIXTEEN

THE CHEVY TAHOE'S vent pushed warm air through a clipped-on air freshener, giving Gabe's SUV a minty fresh smell. It combined with the distinct odor of gun lubricant which permeated the interior.

"Ya know, I've already taken a drive through this neighborhood. Funny story. I was actually only in this area for less than a few minutes before I was pulled over by one of your local cops."

Gabe smiled sheepishly. "Yeah. Makes sense. The town works hard to protect this side of Luna Vista."

"Why isn't the other side worth protection? I'd think you'd be up in arms about it. Your gun shop is right at the dividing line. The invisible barrier that separates the seedier side of town from this, obviously more affluent, section."

"It's complicated."

"Maybe you could uncomplicate it for me."

The man breathed out, making a sound like a deflating balloon. His shoulders slumped a fraction of an inch as he continued to drive. "I don't know what I can really tell you. It probably won't make any sense once I do."

"Try me."

Gabe glanced at her out of the corner of his eye. "It's just that there have been some alliances made. Basically, a pact that keeps trouble out of this area."

"In exchange for what?"

Gabe was silent.

Hatch continued to press. "It sounds like an unfair pact if you ask me. For whatever reason. To allow an arrangement that subjects one side of town to criminals who, from what I see, run unchecked. And this side, protected under a dome of police protection, remains unscathed and turns a blind eye to it.

"It's not just Chief Porter. The town council is involved. And, like I said, it's complicated." He now turned his head toward her. "I don't expect you to understand. Hell, there are days I don't understand it myself. But then I think back to how it was before the arrangement. We had a real problem years back. Luna Vista was a throwback to the Wild West. For lack of a better example, it made the violence of Albuquerque look like Disney World in comparison."

"So, things were bad and the town elders struck a deal with the criminals? Hey, guys, you commit crimes over here and we'll do nothing as long as you leave us good, rich folk alone?" Hatch clenched her fists, trying to temper her rising anger.

"I know how this sounds. Believe me, I do. But you've got to understand how bad it was. We were scared."

"I've been in a lot of places. And have seen a lot of things. Alliances with evil never hold."

The man huffed. "We're a small town with a limited law enforcement presence. At best, we have twelve officers. Four of those are part-time employees. One of them actually works as a grocer for his regular full-time employment. Effectively, we've got eight police officers out working the streets. Spread over a twenty-four-hour day, that leaves us with just one officer on patrol per shift, maybe two at best. To say we're ill-equipped to handle a large-scale criminal operation would be the understatement of the century."

"I've seen smaller departments handle bigger problems," Hatch interrupted. Her mind immediately went to the four-man sheriff's office of Hawk's Landing. And the man at the helm, Dalton Savage.

Gabe gave an involuntary roll of his eyes. "We've asked for federal and state assistance. But for whatever reason, we never got it. We couldn't afford to bulk up our own ranks. The budget doesn't allow for it. And the state police's jurisdiction ends just outside of the town. We are an island unto ourselves and left here to police our own. If you had been here several years ago, you would understand why we did it. And see that this arrangement enabled us to turn this town around."

"Or at least half of it," Hatch said under her breath, but loud enough for Gabe to hear.

"I get it. You're an outsider. You see these nice houses in this neighborhood while you're staying over at the Moonbeam. I know it looks bad. But you've got to believe me, it was for the best."

Hatch didn't respond. It was apparent to her Gabe's opinion on the subject was unwavering.

"At least let me show you the bed-and-breakfast I told you about. I'd like to take you for a bite to eat, too. There's this great little bistro nearby."

"The food at Harry's has been plenty fine for me," Hatch said.

"I get it. I know what you're saying. Those people are worth protecting. I agree with you. You're getting me all wrong on this. Like you said, my gun shop is right there on the invisible border. And we've had our problems, too. I told you about the stolen guns. Theft of a firearm is a serious thing."

Hatch thought about the stashed guns she'd found in the compartment of the couch at the abandoned warehouse. After finding the secondary location where Psycho had met with the bikers, she assumed there were probably others scattered about the small town or neighboring area. She wondered how many of those guns she tried to disable came from the store. Hatch debated telling Gabe but couldn't do it without him asking too many questions about how she knew and where she found them. Plus, after all his talk of this secret pact, she wasn't sure where his allegiance lay.

Gabe filled the silence between them. "If you just tried for a second to see things from my perspective, you might begin to understand why the town did what they did."

"You can take me to all the fancy bistros in the area. It won't change my opinion. I can't see why this town is so afraid to handle the Outlaws. There are enough cops to handle a small gang problem. If not, I'm sure mutual aid from outside jurisdictions would assist."

"You think this is because of the Outlaws?" Gabe laughed. "I mean, sure they're a problem. But they're more of a nuisance compared to the real threat. The reason behind the pact."

She thought about the two bikers and knew before he spoke who he was referring to.

"Every time the Outlaws get snatched up for whatever crime they've committed, they're back out on the street the next day. Scary to think about. But most of their crimes were relatively petty. Although, we did have a shooting recently. Happened just before you arrived in town. And I know for a fact the police are working hard to solve that crime."

Hatch's eyes widened at this information. Nobody had spoken about the shooting to her. Not Harry or Manuel. Maybe it was due to her status as an outsider. "Any leads? I'm assuming it was the gang. Doesn't seem like a long list of suspects."

"I'm not privy to the case specifics. But from what I hear, the kid was killed on his way to his tutor's house. And from what I understand, there were no witnesses."

"You said, kid. How old?" Hatch asked.

"Fifteen."

Hatch felt a knot bunch in her stomach. She thought of Xavier Fuentes. "A fifteen-year-old boy was shot dead and yet the short-staffed law enforcement agency working to solve this horrendous crime still has time to pull people over for rolling a stop sign? Doesn't seem to me that Chief Porter's made this crime his top priority."

"You ask a lot of questions."

"It was my job. And yeah, maybe I do ask a lot of questions. But that's because these questions deserve answers. If not for me, then for the victim and his family."

"That's where my father's been going. Right now, he's at another closed session town council meeting. Much of what's being discussed is this case. A lot of people want answers. We might be a small town, but we're not idiots. Everybody assumed the shooter was one of the Outlaws, but nobody has come forward as a witness. Doesn't sound like there is much in the way of evidence. So, without any support from the community, the case is stalling out. We're left to conjecture and assumption."

"What was the boy shot with?"

"Shotgun. He was shot in the small of his back. If he had survived, he would've been crippled for life."

She thought about the first time she'd seen the Outlaws. On her first day in town when she'd done a recon of the abandoned warehouse. Hatch remembered the one they'd called Blaze. He'd been carrying a shotgun when he'd entered the warehouse. She was suddenly filled with a palpable anger. The shotgun hidden in the couch seat had undoubtedly been the one used to end the fifteen-year-old's life.

"The kid who was shot wasn't a troublemaker. From what I hear, he wasn't involved in anything gang related. The kid's name was Juan and worked as a bagger at the grocery store here in town."

"Some kid was gunned down on his way to his tutor and you don't see the error in your town's ways? This alliance is just as responsible for the death of that boy as the person who pulled the trigger."

Gabe slowed the Tahoe as if Hatch's biting comment shut down his ability to move the vehicle forward. It was like progressing any further would've been misconstrued as dismissing its significance.

"It's tragic. It truly is. But you've got to believe me. This is the first major incident of its kind since this agreement was put into place. The town's leadership is truly up in arms about it, questioning if it was a mistake."

"I think that question has been answered. And answered very loudly. Any pact which allows a gang to run free, for whatever purpose it serves, is foolhardy at best. The death of that teenager should affirm its failure to achieve whatever balance it formerly served." Hatch breathed deeply, working without success to calm herself. "That means it's time we take off the gloves and deliver a heavy counter strike. At least that's the way we do things where I come from."

"You're in Luna Vista. And if you can't tell, things are much different here."

"I can clearly see that."

"Listen, Hatch, I don't want you to get me wrong on this. That poor boy's death was an absolute tragedy. I'm keeping my fingers crossed Chief Porter and the members of the town council can come to some resolution with regards to this unbalanced alliance and bring those responsible to justice, but—"

"But what?"

"But this also isn't your fight."

"What if I make it mine?" Hatch folded her arms.

"You seem like a good person with a good heart. You weren't born and raised here. It was an absolute disaster area before it had gotten better. And it really had gotten better. The town isn't perfect by any means. And you've clearly noted its disparity between the two ends. But the crimes were minimal compared to what it used to be. Sure, we knew there were some drugs being sold. And the things that go hand in hand with it, like prostitution. But nobody had been killed. There were a couple acts of violence but no death. So, yeah, we made an agreement. And yeah, it may seem to an outsider like yourself like absolute insanity. But I'm telling you, it really did work. It really made things a whole lot better."

Hatch looked at the man. He had pulled over to the right side of the road and now had a pleading look in his eyes.

The man was handsome. That fact was undeniable, even if part of her was turned off to him because of his association with this side of the town. And his stubborn defense of the illogical manner in which it was run. Turning a blind eye to injustice which ultimately resulted in the death of a young hard-working boy tainted him.

"Tell you what. Let's get a bite to eat. You can pitch me on what you think we as a town should do. Convince me." The dimples of his cheeks deepened as he gave a tight-lipped smile. "You talked about taking the gloves off. But we're a town that's had them on for so long I don't think we even remember another way of doing things. We need somebody like you to show us the way."

Hatch was surprised at his redirection. A minute ago, he was defending the town council's choice. And now he was opening his mind to the suggestion of an alternative path.

His smile remained fixed. "How about it, Hatch? Let's temporarily bury the hatchet and have a little meal. During which you lay it out for me. Give me a plan of attack. Something I can take to the town council. Help me convince people like my father to get on board to do the right thing. Because honestly, that's all we've ever tried to do here. We tried to fight back and it didn't work. So, we made an alliance, as sketchy as it may seem to you. It did work for a time, but I can see that was a mistake. Would you be willing to do that? To help us?"

"If you're truly looking for my insight, I'll provide it. I've been in towns like this one before, stateside and overseas, that made fragile alliances with the wrong people. As a result, bad things happen to good people. Just like it did here in Luna Vista." She eyed the man, weighing her next words carefully. "Yes. I'd be willing to help in any way that I can."

The man lifted his foot off the brake and the Tahoe began to roll forward. "Thank you," he said.

"Don't thank me yet. You don't know what you're asking for."

He only drove for a couple more blocks before he pulled down Main Street. A far different ambiance than the one where she had spent her mornings. This was a cutout from a Hallmark movie. The only thing it was missing would have been cobblestone streets with horse-drawn carriages. But each of the storefronts were neatly decorated for the winter season, and she saw people walking along carrying cups of coffee. It was literally like being transported into an entirely different world. If she'd been blindfolded for the drive, Hatch wouldn't have believed she was still in Luna Vista.

Gabe pulled to a stop. He parked along the street in an angled space in front of a place called Maggie's Bistro. The shit-eating grin was back when he turned to face her. "Shall we break some bread? And maybe have a temporary truce?"

He did have a disarming charm to him. Had she not been engaged in a heated debate about the balance of life and death—of right and wrong—and the apparent moral ambiguity of the town's leadership, she might've found herself attracted to him. But Hatch's guard was definitely up now. And although she returned the smile, she did it hesitantly.

"You're in for a real treat."

"I don't know. I've gotten quite accustomed to Harry's cooking," Hatch said.

He laughed out loud. "Keep it up and we'll probably be rolling you out of this town."

The two exited the vehicle and entered the bistro. There was a hum to it. The noisy laughter of people enjoying an early evening meal. Glasses of wine graced some of the tables. After the start to her day, a little food and drink seemed like a nice change of pace.

SEVENTEEN

HATCH LET the conversation she'd had with Gabe Smith marinate. During their time together at Maggie's Bistro, the gun shop owner's son spent the majority of it in endless explanation of what life was like in Luna Vista before the pact was made. And went back to defending the reasons for making a deal with the devil. Gabe said the original agreement had been made with a motorcycle club but now extended to small-time gangsters under their protection, such as the Outlaws. He admitted it was much better before the Outlaws were given any power. The bikers were more organized and didn't like unnecessary attention. Their lower level counterparts were the polar opposite and had caused a rift among the members of the town council and their decision to continue to extend the courtesy. The dead teen made it impossible for them to look away from the fact that whatever they thought they had gained had been lost.

Although the conversation was a rehash of his weak attempt at validating the town's inability to control a monster they had created, Hatch managed to enjoy a glass of wine with him. The food was surprisingly good, but she never intended to mention this to Harry.

She felt, in some strange way, that she had just had an affair with a plate of food, cheating on Harry's Diner with Maggie's Bistro.

Hatch was aware Luna Vista wasn't her town. Everybody she'd met during her short visit had made sure of reminding her of that. And without much subtlety. They were all right, but she was slowly developing a sense of connection, most notably with Manuel and his family. Harry and his estranged niece were a close second. Regardless, Hatch was now connected. And unlike the town council, she didn't turn a blind eye to injustice.

Gabe drove the Tahoe through the invisible barrier into the unprotected side of town.

"Is there a time that would be best to stop by tomorrow so I could speak with your father?" Hatch asked.

"How about you plan on stopping by at ten? It's right after we open shop. He's usually always there at that point. He likes to do a once over of the inventory before leaving it in my care. I'll relay our discussion and some of the insight you provided on how to better deal with the situation at hand. Maybe you two will have more to talk about than the history of the abandoned warehouse."

"Hopefully he's as open-minded as you." She let the compliment hang in the air. Hatch could see by the man's coloration in his cheeks that it had registered. It was awkward for her, and she immediately wished she could retract it. Gabe had asked her on, for lack of better terms, a date. And now she had served up a compliment at its conclusion. She hoped he hadn't misconstrued it as some type of subtle flirtation because it was never intended as such. Plus, there was no chance at starting any type of relationship with him. As soon as she had what she needed from his father, Hatch would be moving on. The conversation tomorrow morning with Gabe's father would hopefully provide enough of a lead to provide her with some progress on her quest for answers about her father's death. And with it, some closure. Then, maybe, she could return to Hawk's Landing, and the family she had left behind.

As they approached the street, more of a dirt path than a roadway, which led to the motel, she heard a loud roar of a fire engine. The noise was immediately drowned out by sirens. By all accounts, a strange sound for this side of the town. Hatch searched in the direction from which the sound came and realized it was up ahead. In the direction they were heading. Just above the rise in road, she saw thick black smoke rise up into the early night sky.

Hatch's heart skipped a beat, and she looked over at Gabe. "Step on it!" she said.

Without protest, the man pressed the accelerator pedal to the floor and the car's engine roared to life.

They rounded the rise and came down the bend. Hatch looked on in horror as the sight confirmed her worst fear. The Moonbeam Motel was ablaze.

Gabe pulled the Tahoe up and stopped ten feet shy of a fire truck. There were several police cars scattered about the unpaved lot of the motel. A deluge of water rained down from the deck gun atop the large fire engine. Hatch's rental car was parked between the engine and the portion of the motel engulfed in flames. It took her a moment to evaluate the scene. The burning room was hers. She shielded her eyes and looked more carefully at the burning structure. She was wrong. The source of the fire hadn't come from her room. Its epicenter was next door. In room number two.

The room, temporarily home to Wendy, was fully engulfed. Roaring flames flickered and pushed their way out from the window, fighting against the downpour of water with an equal ferocity.

Hatch got out of the car and started running. She heard Gabe call to her, but Hatch was focused on the scene in front of her and tuned his words out completely.

She zigzagged through the myriad of personnel working to battle the blaze, desperately searching the crowd, small as it was and mostly consisting of uniformed personnel, looking for any sign of Manuel and his family. She let out a sigh of relief upon seeing all three members of the Fuentes family seated on the back end of an ambulance, shrouded in blankets and surrounded by several emergency medical personnel tending to their needs. From the distance, she thought the darkened marks on their faces was soot from the fire, but as she got closer, Hatch could see their faces weren't covered in ash, but bruises and blood. Manuel and Camila had been badly beaten.

Hatch ran to them. In unison, the three looked up at her. Reading them, she saw a combination of worry and utter sadness in the two adults. But in Xavier's eyes, she saw something entirely different. Anger.

"Thank God you're alive. What happened?" Hatch asked. She posed the question to the group but directed her attention to Manuel.

"I don't know. The fire alarm in room one went off. We have an interconnected alarm system, so I heard it immediately. I stepped outside and there was fire everywhere. I thought it was coming from your room. I was worried, and I ran to help. Camila came with me." He coughed uncontrollably for several seconds.

"What happened to your face?" Hatch asked.

Manuel didn't answer and looked down.

"Who did this to you?" Hatch asked angrily.

Xavier narrowed his eyes and spat on the dirt-covered ground near her feet. "You did," he said with disgust.

Hatch hadn't expected that from the boy. She hadn't expected to hear that kind of accusation, and it momentarily staggered her. She looked at him with a concern. "What do you mean?" Although, she could read well enough between the lines to infer the answer.

"You brought this trouble here! If you'd just have minded your own damn business the other day, none of this would've happened! I told you to leave. I warned you something bad was going to happen."

Half listening to the angry teen's tongue lashing, she scanned the area and realized there was no sign of Wendy. She looked back at the fire. The battle to get it under control was still underway.

She ran toward the burning room. A few feet from the door, somebody stepped in front of her. The unforeseen collision sent a tingle down her damaged right arm, and she looked at the man who had caused it.

Officer Cartwright restrained her, firmly gripping her by the arms. "You can't go in there. You'll be dead. It's fully engulfed."

The same cop who pulled her over for running a stop sign was now gripping her tightly and holding her back. She thought about knocking the man aside. It wouldn't have taken much. He was already slightly off balance from their collision. But she immediately realized the futility of such action. And deep down she knew he was right.

She realized in that moment, if Wendy had been inside, there was no way she'd survived. And Hatch's entry would only add to the fire's body count.

Hatch ripped herself free from the man and turned away. She started walking back toward Manuel. Xavier still held his contemptuous glare. She stopped in her tracks. Hatch was suddenly torn between the burning room number two and the angry teen. Both were people she'd tried to help. One dead and the other hated her. In the chaos of the moment with the building still crackling with fire, she evaluated the family who had welcomed her into their home. Camila cast her head down. The beating this family had endured on her behalf sickened Hatch.

They had undoubtedly come for Hatch and in return killed Wendy.

Hatch couldn't help but hate herself. She walked out toward the far end of the lot and away from the judgmental eyes of Xavier and the acrid smell. Beyond the flicker of fire and the flashing strobe of the police cars, Hatch found herself in darkness, emotional as much as physical. She was filled with a desperate need to find those responsible. Whoever it was, she was going to make damn sure they paid in full.

One thing was for certain: The town of Luna Vista would no longer have an outlaw problem. The Outlaws were about to have a Hatch problem.

She felt the weight of the pistol resting at the small of her back. It called to her, pleading with her to take action, to finish what she'd started. Listening to the crackle of the burning room, she wished she had taken the second shot on the man at the broken-down gas station. Hatch wished she had put a bullet through Psycho's skull, ending him right then and there.

Hatch knew better than to second-guess the decision. Hell, there'd be plenty of time for that later. There always was. Every battle had its lulls, and during those times, soldiers took stock of the decisions made in those split seconds of chaos. A burdensome weight each soldier shouldered for a lifetime after. Hatch knew, without a doubt, this would be one of those moments. Her time in Luna Vista added to her battle scars, both internal and external.

She stood there, in the dark, a moment longer, surveying the carnage. She'd done some arson investigations during her time in CID. The aftermath was devastating to the human body. Once the fire was doused, there would be a recovery effort. Hatch couldn't imagine seeing the girl who she'd tried to save from the streets. Then she thought of Harry. *My God. Harry's niece was gone*, she thought. The same day the man had opened his heart to the idea of reconnecting with his estranged Wendy, the door was now closed forever. A lifetime would be left to ponder what could have been.

There was a black cloud over this town, as deep and dark as the one now covering the sky above the Moonbeam Motel.

Things weren't great before she'd arrived in Luna Vista. The dead teen spoke volumes to that. But she'd definitely fueled things. In effect, Hatch had torn off a Band-Aid on a much bigger problem and exposed the wound. Its effect was oozing out into every fabric of these people's lives. And right now, bathed in the orange hue of the burning motel, she couldn't help but feel responsible.

The only thing she could do from this point on would be to make things right. Find who did this and make them pay.

A touch on her shoulder snapped her from her train of thought. Fury bubbling inside her, she turned with a clenched fist and almost punched the man. The same man who had just taken her to an early dinner. The man who, by all accounts, was charming and kind. Hatch worked to soothe her raw nerves.

"Are you okay?" he asked quietly, just loud enough to be heard over the'commotion around them.

"No. I'm not."

And then she heard a sound off in the distance by a dark cluster of twisted Juniper trees. The rumble of a motorcycle and the silhouetted figure of a man with long hair. Hatch squinted and stepped closer. His face came into view, illuminated by the embers of a cigarette hanging from his lips. His beard was thick and black. What stood out about his features was the half-moon scar extending from the edge of his beard up and around his left eyebrow. Hatch never got a clear look at the men from the night before and couldn't tell if it was one of the men she'd seen leaving after the exchange with Psycho. But in her world, there was no such thing as coincidence. And the sight of this biker was far too coincidental. He straddled the black motorcycle less than thirty feet away from where Hatch stood. She began moving toward him.

His headlight kicked on, momentarily blinding her. Rage was visible on her face as she began to run at a dead sprint, barreling forward. Her right hand shielded the light from her eyes while her left held firm the pistol tucked in the small of her back. She pulled it out. She didn't want to display it until the last possible moment. She thought about the cops nearby, but Hatch dismissed reason. In a rare moment, she felt herself operating solely on anger. Once close enough, she had every intention of firing a round into the person she deemed responsible for this fire. She'd deal with the fallout after-ward. Vengeance fueled her now.

The biker registered her fast approach. He revved the engine and popped it into gear. With a slight fishtail, the motorcycle sped away. Hatch pulled the weapon from the small of her back and took aim. Finger on the trigger, the thought of Daphne's face flashed before her. *Pull the trigger and you'll likely never see the little girl again.* It was the single thought halting her from killing the man.

No matter how damaged the justice system was in Luna Vista, if she shot a man dead in front of a group of cops, life as she knew it would end. And true justice, for Wendy and Manuel's family, would never be served.

Hatch didn't lower the weapon. She stood poised in an isosceles shooter's stance with feet spread just beyond shoulder width. Her finger continued to rest on the trigger. Her mind had made the decision not to fire, but her body resisted.

As she looked down the front sight at the back of the biker, Hatch was able to make out the club name on the top rocker. Savage Renegades, the name of the motorcycle club would forever be etched in her mind. Until she crossed it out.

As Hatch watched the motorcycle fleeing, she stowed the weapon back into place and ensured it was covered by her shirt.

She turned and started walking back toward the flickering blue and red strobes. The fire was smoldering. A uniquely distinct odor accompanied the burning wood, metal, and glass. It was a smell unlike all others. She'd smelled it on her own body years ago while serving overseas. The smell of burned flesh. She immediately knew its source. The thought of it sickened her.

She couldn't escape the smell. It brought her back to her own pain. Then she thought of Wendy. Hatch, said a silent prayer the smoke had taken her first or that she was asleep when it happened, and there was no pain in her death. But Hatch lived in a world of real things and death typically didn't come pain-free. In her experience, it was an ugly thing.

Thinking about Wendy trapped in that room, her last moments surrounded by fire, confined and desperate, Hatch hunched and vomited on the ground in front of her.

She felt a pat on the small of her back between her shoulder blades. Hatch turned, expecting to see the face of Gabe Smith. To her surprise, it was Officer Cartwright at her side.

"You okay? Do you need some medical attention?" he asked with genuine concern.

She stood, wiping the dangling bit of spit from her lips on her sleeve. "No. I don't need medical attention. What I need is for you to tell me every damn thing that's going on in the godforsaken town! Starting with that biker gang."

Cartwright stepped back but said nothing.

"You still think that other side of town is the only one worth protecting?" Hatch fumed. The anger in her voice gave way to the palpable rage bubbling its way to the surface.

His shoulders went slack and his face offered no resistance to the charge. "I'm as fed up as you."

"Then prove it. Do something about it. Or at the very least, help me do what nobody around here seems capable of doing."

"This isn't the Wild West. We don't just hunt down bad people and string 'em up."

"Maybe it's time you should. Send the message to that biker gang. Luna Vista is no longer under their control."

"I know you're upset."

"You have no idea," Hatch said.

Hatch walked away and back toward Manuel and his family.

She felt Xavier's anger wash over her. His eyes still daggers. She moved alongside and took a knee in front of Manuel. Hatch laid a hand on his shoulder. "I'm so sorry that this happened. I promise I'm not leaving here until I find out who did this. And make it right."

"It's too dangerous," he said.

Camila reached out and touched Hatch on the shoulder. "Listen, Hatch, we appreciate everything you've done or tried to do for our son, but you can see these are bad people. They will stop at nothing." She whimpered between deep sobs.

"Neither do I. They've crossed the line with me. I can't allow them any safe passage. It's a code I have. Something I've always honored. I can't leave until justice is served."

Manuel sat up and dug into his pocket. He pulled out his keychain. Taking one of the keys off, he handed it to Hatch. It was a key to a Ford. She furrowed her brow.

"Looks like your car is going to be out of commission for a while." Manuel said.

Hatch looked over at the front end of the rental. It had taken some heavy damage being so close to the fire.

"You can drive my pickup while you're here."

"I can't. I don't know what to say. Manuel, I really can't take your vehicle."

"I insist. I'll just use my wife's Toyota if I need to. You drive the Ford." Manuel shot a glance at his son. "I've been saving it for Xavier. Planned on giving it to him for his sixteenth birthday. But he's gotta earn that still."

Xavier rolled his eyes and turned away with folded arms.

Hatch took the key and pocketed it. She stood and looked down at the family. "I'm sorry this happened to you. I truly am. When I intervened, I never intended for any of this to come back on you or your motel. And for that, I'm truly sorry."

Manuel didn't answer. He just looked off toward the charred midsection of his motel.

She walked away and back toward the cop. He turned as she approached.

"Has anybody told Harry yet?" Hatch asked.

The cop looked confused. "Not sure what you mean."

"The girl inside that room is his niece."

Cartwright's eyes went wide. "Wendy? But why was she—"

"I was trying to help her out. I put her up in the room next to mine. I wanted to let her get some rest. Take a few days away from whatever it was she was involved with."

Cartwright looked back at the damaged structure. "I knew her," he said softly.

"Somebody must've thought I was there."

Hatch took a moment to process what she'd just said. Without saying another word, she walked directly back to Xavier.

She grabbed the boy by the shoulder and led him away from his parents.

Out of earshot, Hatch leaned in close and in a hushed, angry whisper said, "How the hell did they know about room number two?"

He looked scared and tried to wriggle free from her grip, but she held it firm. "I don't know what you're talking about."

"Yes, you do. Why did they torch room number two?"

"Because I told them! I told them you were staying in number two."

"Why would you tell them that?"

The boy's eyes started to swell up with tears. "Because I knew you weren't. I knew you were in number three. I figured your car was parked there near enough. I told them the wrong room—and you seem like you can handle yourself—and figured you could escape when the alarm went off."

"You didn't know about the girl in room two?"

"No. You gotta believe me. I never ever would've told them if I'd known. I was really trying to help you. Keep you safe. At least give you a fighting chance. There's no stopping them!" A tear fell from his eye and rolled down his cheek.

Hatch released the grip on his shoulders and the boy began to sob uncontrollably.

"My parents did. That's why they're all banged up. They tried to stop them."

She softened her tone and saw in the boy's sadness that it was the truth. He wasn't lying. He didn't know about Wendy. The anger she'd seen earlier was a combination of guilt and remorse.

"I know what you did was to protect me. And I thank you for that," Hatch said. "I know you also harbor some anger and hatred toward me for intervening the other day. And I understand that as well. I'm sorry that I intervened. Actually, come to think of it, I'm not. Those guys need to be taught a real lesson."

"You shot him in the foot," Xavier said with a loud sniffle.

Hatch had almost forgotten that in the chaos of the fire.

"I did. Apparently, I should have killed him."

"He was really angry. Like crazy angry, ya know? I've never seen him like that before. And trust me when I say this, I've seen him very angry. He was talking about all sorts of crazy things, but Macho came up with the plan. He and Blaze carried it out."

"What about the man on the motorcycle?"

The boy hesitated. He actually looked to where the motorcycle had been earlier just to make sure it wasn't still there. "He's more dangerous than all the Outlaws combined. Heard stories about him. Crazy shit. Stuff that makes Psycho look like a puppy dog."

"Does this dangerous man have a name?"

The boy shrugged and wiped his nose. "I don't know his real name. They call him Mongoose."

"And why was Mongoose here tonight?"

"He was sent to make sure it was done right. And now that he knows you're not dead, there's going to be problems. Big ones for us. But especially for you."

"I can handle myself."

"You don't understand. They know we didn't get the right room. Since we failed, they're going to come for you, lady. And these guys operate on a totally different level. They make us look like a kindergarten class in comparison. These are really bad people. There's a reason they've kept this town scared for as long as I can remember. It was way worse before. Why don't you take my dad's truck and just run? Get out of here while you can. They're gonna kill you."

She messed his hair with her hand and tried to give as confident a smile as she could muster. "Not if I kill them first."

Hatch escorted Xavier back to his parents. The daggers he looked at her with earlier were gone. The only thing in his eyes was sadness.

Hatch planned to satiate the despondency she felt with vengeance.

But first she had to tell Harry about Wendy.

EIGHTEEN

HATCH FELT STAYING at the Moonbeam beyond this point would be a bad choice. So, she opted for isolation and drove out of town. The rundown gas station where she'd shot Psycho in the foot seemed as good a place as any for her to rest and collect herself. Comfort wasn't a major concern, as she knew well enough that sleep would not come easily.

Hatch parked the Ford pickup around the backside of the building. She wanted to remain out of eyesight of any motorists traversing the roadway. She cut the engine. It sputtered once and then went silent. The only noise was the whip of the wind as it swirled around her. The dusty swirls and desolate landscape reminded Hatch of time in the Army. She allowed the sound of the gusts to soothe her.

Looking at her watch, she'd only been asleep for a few hours. More than enough rest to regroup, both physically and mentally, from what she had witnessed the night before. Her mind was now cleared and ready to handle the tasks ahead. Sun penetrated the dust-covered windshield. The warmth of it took some of the chill out of the air. She rubbed her eyes and adjusted to the light.

It was early. Her routine morning start at Harry's would be a challenging one at best. She'd driven to the diner last night, but it had already closed. Hatch realized she didn't know anything else about him. Not where he lived or his phone number. She had decided to wait until morning to try again.

Hatch drove the short distance back into town. The truck's heat was on and it made a loud, rattling sound. As she passed the street leading to the motel, Hatch swore she could still smell the burnt remnants of room number two.

She arrived at the diner a few minutes later. Today, Chief Porter was back in his usual spot. Maybe he assumed the fire from last night would send her running. A thought made more probable when she entered. The chief of police spun in his stool and gave a look of surprise. He caught himself and immediately returned to his paper and began his daily routine of ignoring her.

Harry didn't look his usual chipper self. He was not bright-eyed and excited to see her as he had been in days past. Hatch took up her post on the stool next to Porter, who grunted and closed his newspaper. The rotund chief stood and walked out without saying a word. Hatch did nothing to encourage him otherwise. She didn't want to speak to the man. And was concerned about what would come out of her mouth if she did.

Harry grabbed the coffee pot and approached. Routine being a person's best friend in time of distress. She knew this better than most. *Stay the course. Keep the routine. Push back against the rising tide of pain.*

He poured the cup, more sloppily than he had on prior occasions. The dark roast dribbled onto the counter. She saw the man's eyes were glossy. The lids were puffy and red. It was plainly obvious the news had been delivered. The tragic death of his niece had reached his ears before she was able to deliver it herself. Then she thought about it. She was by all accounts an outsider. Maybe it was better it came by way of a close friend of the family, somebody he trusted and had known for a long time. She wondered who the bearer of such grim and disturbing news had been. Cartwright? She thought better of it. In a small town like Luna Vista, the message was most likely delivered by Porter himself. Regardless of who carried the message, it had been delivered.

"Harry, how are you holding up?"

The man shook his face from side to side. His loose jowls quivered, and he made a whimpering sound. He was on the verge of breaking down.

"I'm so sorry," Hatch said. She meant it. Though words couldn't convey it, she felt the loss of Wendy as if she had known her for many years. More so than loss, Hatch felt an overwhelming sense of guilt. She was the one who'd brought her in and, knowingly or not, placed her in harm's way. She had taken the teen girl out of the proverbial frying pan of her crappy life and thrown her into the fire of Hatch's. In her reckless need to help, she had effectively brought about the demise of a young girl at a crossroads in her life. Hatch bore this quietly, unable to confide her pain to the uncle who was dealing with an entirely different set of guilt. He would forever question everything he had done prior to the day she walked out of his life. Questions without answers. The torment of the dead's decisions on the living.

Hatch had wallowed in death's unanswered riddles. Her father's death was at the forefront. The answers she sought brought her here. *And what if there were none to be had?* she thought. *What then?*

"Are you gonna do your usual today, Hatch?" Harry asked, putting on his best face.

"I thought maybe I'd just sit here with you this morning. I'm not much for eating today," she said. "Coffee is good enough. And if you don't want to talk, I understand, but I want to just be here for you. To listen to you if you do."

The man's face twisted. She could see he was fighting back against the emotional tidal wave seeking to burst forth. A tough man, not accustomed to sharing his emotions, this was a daunting task. But somehow Harry regained his composure. He did something she hadn't seen him do before. He grabbed a cup from under the counter, filled it with piping hot coffee, and then walked around, joining Hatch on an adjacent stool. He bellied up to the counter and took a sip from the steaming cup.

His face red and his eyes still puffy, he said, "Ya know, when I found out, I was devastated." He paused and took another sip. "But you know the first thing I thought of when they told me?"

Hatch shook her head, allowing the man to continue uninterrupted.

"It was about this time, when Wendy was ten years old. We had this great big willow tree in our backyard. She was always a high energy kid and used to love to climb it whenever she would come over. Before her mother had fallen into drugs, she used to bring her over on Sundays after church. Every time, rain or shine, Wendy would go out to that willow and climb. Her mom would tell me that I needed to cut the low branches so she wouldn't be able to. But gosh, she loved it and I couldn't imagine taking that away from her. One day, she fell out of it and broke her arm. Of course, I was to blame, right?"

Hatch encouraged him with a smile.

"You'd think I would've taken the hint and cut the branches. But I just couldn't bring myself to do it. If you saw her face after climbing to the top, you'd understand." He took another sip. "To make a long story longer, about a week after Wendy got her cast off, she was over visiting with her mom. I looked out my window to see that crazy girl climbing the same tree. I mean, she had just broken her forearm a few months prior, and here she was scampering back up like a squirrel. And sure enough, I watched as she fell all the way back down to the bottom. Broke her arm in the same place." He laughed out loud at the conclusion of the story, but with the laugh came a choked cough and a teardrop. It rolled down his cheek and fell into his steaming cup of coffee. He drank both the coffee and the tear, swallowing back the pain.

Hatch joined in the laughter. She knew the importance of

keeping these kinds of memories. Hatch was grateful to the man for the story.

Hatch took from that story something that may or may not have been intended in the man's telling. Wendy was a stubborn ass, even at age ten she was making her own decisions and apparently bad ones at that. Then repeating the same bad decision after a horrendous outcome. She liked her fearlessness. In some ways, it reminded Hatch of herself. Hatch thought of the ten-year-old falling from the tree. She then thought of those who'd cut her life short nine years later. Feeling the human connection to the girl, beyond that established in their limited interaction, Hatch was reaffirmed in her decision to seek vengeance for her death.

"Harry, I want you to know that whoever did this to your niece is going to answer for what they did."

The remnants of the smile formed from retelling the willow tree memory faded completely. His head began to slowly shake back and forth as he looked into his nearly empty cup of coffee as if examining it for the words. "She's not coming back, Hatch. Nothing you do will change that."

Hatch knew the truth in the man's statement. It didn't change the fact that she was unable to stand by and let what happened to Wendy go unpunished. To do that, to stand idly by in the face of evil, is to silently condone it. The very core of who she was sought justice, but all she offered the man in return was a simple, "I know."

The two finished the rest of their coffee in silence, but Harry seemed genuinely grateful for the company. She waited for him to talk. And was there for him in the event he wanted to share more. He didn't, and time slowly passed with little else said.

A few customers meandered in. Harry looked pleased to have the opportunity to busy himself with the chores of cooking, cleaning, and clearing tables.

Hatch had somewhere to be. She hoped it would temporarily lift the fog of last night by preoccupying her mind. The clock on the wall said it was only 9 AM and Gabe told her the shop didn't open until 10. She swiveled in her seat and looked out the window.

Gabe and an older man with a thick head of snow-white hair, who she assumed to be the elder Smith, were raising the steel security gate in front of the main entrance. Both men then went inside.

Harry was busy and she could see he no longer needed her company, at least for the moment. Hatch drained the last sip from her cup and nodded at Harry, who was already moving toward a booth with his order pad in hand.

As Hatch made her way to the door, Harry quietly called out, "Thank you for stopping by this morning. And thank you for what you tried to do for my Wendy."

"Don't mention it. Harry, you're a good man." Hatch pushed her way out the door as a cold blast of wind kicked up. It was blowing wildly, throwing dust. A storm was brewing, both inside Hatch and in the world around her.

Hatch hustled across the two-lane road to the gun shop catty corner across the street. The sign on the door was still flipped to the closed position. Knowing both men were inside, she knocked on the glass door anyway.

A few seconds later, she saw Gabe approach. He unlatched the door's lock and pushed it open. Gabe's face was different this morning. No shit-eating grin. His manner was anything but welcoming to Hatch, opposite to his demeanor yesterday during their tour around the fancier part of Luna Vista.

"Good morning, Gabe. I know you said ten, but I was in the area and figured I'd stop by."

"It's definitely morning, but I'm not sure how good it is," he snarked. Gabe then looked over his shoulder toward the rear of the store. "I mentioned to my dad that you'd be stopping by. But, to be honest, he really doesn't want to see you."

"I guess the conversation you had with him about taking back the town didn't go over well?"

"After leaving the motel, I spoke with him. He was more than agitated."

"Rightfully so. Another member of your town was murdered. I would think everybody in this town would be agitated. This is the second murder in less than a week. First the teen and now Wendy. This whole town should be lining up outside the police station and protesting the lack of justice."

"No. He's agitated at you."

Hatch was confused. "Me? What did I do? I was trying to help."

"Exactly. This alliance, this thing we had, was fragile at best. Everybody walked a fine line. I'll admit it wasn't easy, but we did it. Then you show up out of the blue. A couple days into your visit and all hell broke loose. You've pissed in the wind. And look at the fallout."

"You think I'm the problem?" Hatch seethed. "Anybody who agreed to that alliance with the bikers is to blame. They let those people run around with impunity. Your town fed that beast. The dead boy should have been your wakeup call. The fact that another person had to die and you're still not pointing the finger in the right direction is insanity."

"So you say," Gabe mumbled.

"Alliances, like the one made here, can only remain in balance for a short period of time. Then they implode."

"Your opinion has been noted. Doesn't change the fact that my father's not much inclined to talk to you today."

"Too bad. Because I'm not leaving until he does." Hatch folded her arms angrily.

At that, the white-haired older man came out from the back room. "My son's right. Don't have much to say to the likes of you. I think you've done enough damage for now," Wilbur Smith said gruffly. "If I give you the information you've been looking for, will you take it and leave this town?"

"That's the plan," Hatch lied. "Then I assume you knew my father? And you know why I'm here?"

"I didn't know him personally, but I can point you in the direction of a man who does. Heed my word, the quicker you leave, the quicker our town goes back to normal. It's that simple. You may not agree with our way of life here or in the things we've done to keep the status quo. But that's just it. It's our life, not yours. The faster you get back to wherever it is you came from and leave us be, the better off for all concerned." The man stuck out his hand. A business card was balanced between Wilbur's thick, stubby thumb and index finger.

Hatch plucked it out of his grip. She flipped it over. On the back of the card was a name and an address.

"Who's this?"

"It's what you've been looking for. It's the person that can answer your questions."

Hatch looked at the card in her hand. She was momentarily transfixed by the name on it. Even though she didn't recognize it, the sight of it in her hand meant she was closer to finding out about her father. The address was somewhere in town. She remembered seeing the street name during her drive with Gabe.

She had what she came to Luna Vista for. In her hand was the first step in answering the questions haunting her. But holding the card in her hand and knowing what it signified didn't give her any sense of peace. Maybe if she had received this information a few days ago, she might've already been on her way. Wendy would still be alive, if not forever, then at least for the time being. Hatch's trouble with the Outlaws and their biker counterparts, the Savage Renegades, would be nonexistent. Before she could follow the lead this card potentially provided, Hatch had to close out a few things first.

Having just spoken to Harry and seeing firsthand the sadness and damage Wendy's death had caused and learning of the young teen who was gunned down, she knew she couldn't leave in good conscience. Not without handling some unfinished business.

Hatch stuck the card in her pocket. She said nothing to either man as she strode out the door.

NINETEEN

HATCH STOOD outside the gun store. There was a commotion to her left, and she watched as a media van zoomed past. She saw the source of the frenzy. Chief Porter stood on the steps with another man she didn't recognize. He was the approximate age and size of the chief, but slightly better dressed, presumably a senior member of the town council. The two were poised on the front steps of the police department/town hall building addressing a small entourage of newscasters. If Hatch had to guess, it was most likely in regard to last night's fire.

Reporters were firing questions at the men, looking for their soundbite to this tragic event. The burning death of a nineteen-year-old girl was bound to draw attention. Hatch watched the chief, his face solemn, as he went about describing the events. From her distance she couldn't hear him, but she knew enough about the man, and this town's secret, that much of the retelling lacked critical details. Many pieces of this particular puzzle were undoubtedly being left out. Wendy's death would be described as a tragic accident.

Hatch, disgusted at the thought of it, had a sour taste of bile in her mouth coinciding with her rising anger. She headed toward the media circus, and in particular, the man it surrounded. As she crossed the side street separating the gun shop from the town hall, a uniformed officer stepped out from a cruiser parked along the curb. Her vision was tunnel focused on the man on the steps. Her intent, not completely planned, was to, if nothing else, disrupt the lies the chief was spouting. All she needed to do was plant the seed about a young girl who wasn't killed accidentally. Hatch wanted them to know it had been done intentionally and by a group of criminals this town had silently endorsed.

If she was able to get the attention of the news, then with it, a federal, or at the very least, a statewide investigation would follow. It might be enough to shut down what was going on in the town of Luna Vista.

The officer stepped out into her path, almost causing Hatch to barrel through him. She stopped before doing so. It was Officer Cartwright. She glared at him. "You're like a bad penny. You keep showing up."

"The same could be said for you." He cocked his head and offered a friendly smile. "I can see it in your eyes, you're going to do something really stupid. Not sure what exactly, but I can assure you, nothing good will come from it."

"Nothing too crazy. I just plan to let the media in on the town's little secret."

"Didn't look that way to me. Looked like you were going to walk right up on those steps and lay out the chief."

Hatch opened her hand. She hadn't, until that moment, realized her fist was balled. The raw nerve of Wendy's death was still exposed, causing her to uncharacteristically lose her control. *But Cartwright, the observant young cop, had seen it and intervened on her behalf,* she thought. "I honestly don't know what I was going to do, but I'm grateful you stopped me."

He raised his eyebrows and seemed surprised at her comment. She hadn't been openly warm to him during their few exchanges. She'd made him the whipping boy of the department since first meeting him during the traffic stop. He was perceptive and intelligent. He'd proven that during the traffic stop, and she had witnessed his diligence at the scene of last night's fire. By all accounts, Hatch regarded him as a good police officer.

"Are you running security for him? Keeping the angry citizens back?" she asked sarcastically as she surveyed the semicircle of reporters and noted none of the citizens of Luna Vista were present.

Hatch knew from her experience with the media that they would use a tight angle and make it seem as though there was more fanfare. She wasn't sure whether the lack of public interest was intentionally hushed or commonplace because of the fear blanketing the small town. Who knew what backlash would result if Joe Schmo was given the spotlight? A Q&A session taken out of context with one of the town residents could potentially expose the secret. That would be fraught with negative consequences.

"No. I was actually just heading to my car after grabbing a cup of coffee from Harry's. I saw you charging forward and thought it might be a good idea for me to step in," he said with a boyish charm. "For all parties concerned."

"Thanks for looking out," Hatch said. She turned to walk away, and he reached out and gripped her shoulder, similar to the way he did at the fire, gentle and firm at the same time. Even though she knew he couldn't feel the scar tissue under her thick sweatshirt, the proximity of his hand caused her to reel back slightly. Her subconscious attempt to mask the disfigured appendage.

"Where are you heading off to right now?" Cartwright asked.

Hatch thought about the business card with the name and address stuffed in her pocket. Then she thought about Wendy and the Fuentes family and said, "I'm really not sure." Giving it further thought, she said, "Why? Do you have somewhere you need to be?"

"Not particularly. I was gonna drive back to the scene from last night. I like to look at things again in the daylight. Maybe there's something I missed."

"Care for some company?" Hatch wasn't sure how she'd be

received, asking such a question under the circumstances, and in close proximity to the chief, who obviously did not like her presence in town.

"Actually, I'd like that very much."

"You're sure about this? Your chief isn't very fond of me. He might have a problem with me riding along with you."

Cartwright turned slightly and shot a glance at the portly figure-head of the Luna Vista Police Department. "Oh, I think my chief has much bigger things to concern himself with today than worrying about what I'm doing."

With that, he went over to his cruiser, a black and white Crown Victoria. He unlocked the passenger door, removed his patrol bag and stowed it in the trunk, making room for Hatch.

The two entered the car. Cartwright pulled forward, leaving the chief to spin his lies to the media circus. The reporters had no way of knowing they were standing at the invisible dividing line of Luna Vista.

The Crown Vic made quick work of the drive to the outskirts of town, where the Moonbeam Motel sat, now adorned with a burned scar right in the middle of the row of rooms. Like the one on her ravaged arm. Hatch knew, better than most, that scars heal. With any luck, and Manuel's determined and hard-working nature, the motel would be back up in working order in no time.

TWENTY

THEY PULLED up to the motel. A tattered bit of yellow police tape flapped in the breeze. It was caught on a jagged piece of room number two's door frame. Hatch surveyed the aftermath. It was far different in the daylight than when it was fully engulfed in flames during the previous night. The smell lingered in the air, penetrating the closed windows of the cruiser where she sat still.

Cartwright turned to her. "The scene is no longer active. They wrapped things up last night. You're welcome to check it out with me, if you want."

"Did the fire marshal send an arson investigator?"

Cartwright nodded. "He came out last night. I was the last one here. I got relieved early this morning."

"And you're already back?"

"Small town. We've had some big crimes in the past few days. So, not much in the way of sleep." The man yawned as if to punctuate his fatigue. "But I volunteered to take the morning shift."

Hatch understood the demand of the job well enough. His decision to volunteer and to return to the scene spoke volumes of the young cop's dedication.

"If the scene has been cleared, then, yeah, I wouldn't mind walking it again with you."

"I'm not sure what I hope to find, if anything, but in my limited experience, I've learned that sometimes it's good to look at things with fresh eyes, ya know? To see it from a different perspective. Maybe get a different take on something that was missed or misinterpreted under the stress and chaos of an active scene."

Hatch was impressed that the patrolman would think in these terms. She couldn't help but think his talent was being wasted here. That tenacity would be better served in a bigger city, like Las Cruces or maybe Albuquerque, where there was a high demand for officers like him. Cops who would go the extra mile and put forth the legwork to see a case through. Not everybody who wore the badge had the same persistence and drive.

Then again, maybe Officer Cartwright was exactly what the town of Luna Vista needed. With him at the helm of a department like this, Hatch envisioned him turning things around. He could usher in a changing of the guard, an obviously necessary one. But as the long shelf life of small-town chiefs go, and Cartwright's relative youth, it might be awhile before that would come to fruition.

Hatch pulled the handle of the door and stepped out into the cold air. The smell was much clearer now, but a gust sent the odor hurtling into her nostrils. She could taste the char of the room as she faced it. She could taste something else in it but didn't want to let her mind drift too far to the image in her head. It came with a wave of guilt.

Knowing what the room contained, Hatch suddenly didn't know if she was strong enough to face it. Pushing past her resistance, she edged forward. Each step forward was done with forced mental effort. Hatch absorbed the scene, taking it in inch by inch as they approached. Cartwright matched her step for step, moving in tandem like a military procession to a slow drumbeat.

Neither spoke. It was another thing Hatch had come to appreciate in the young officer. Small talk, especially at a crime scene, distracted from the focus needed to see everything, smell everything, and mentally assimilate the evidentiary pieces of the puzzle. Cartwright received another check in her book.

They now stood only a few feet from the walkway in front of the long row of interconnected motel rooms. Hatch's rental car had been badly damaged during the fire. The front end was singed black and the front windshield had folded inward, melting to the dashboard. The front tires were flat and the car dipped forward, lowering it onto the curbing. Seeing the car in the daylight, Hatch was grateful for the truck Manuel had lent her.

There was no sign of the Fuentes family. She assumed they were staying elsewhere after last night's violent encounter. Maybe they had family or friends in the area to put them up. It would be an ugly irony if they had ended up at the bed and breakfast Gabe had pushed her to stay at. The smoke damage to the adjacent rooms would make it some time before they would be livable. Hatch was secretly grateful for not having to face them again so soon. The damaged face of Manuel and his wife was hard enough to see last night. She didn't need the reminder of the pain she had caused them.

"What do you think?" Cartwright asked.

"When I got here last night, I noticed that the window was broken and the bottom pane was shattered," Hatch said.

"I saw that, too, but I just figured maybe with the heat, the pressure popped the pane." Cartwright shrugged. "Fire investigation isn't really my area of expertise."

Hatch nodded absently and walked onto the sidewalk. She crouched low, in front of the windowsill and then she turned back toward Cartwright. "You're not wrong. It is a possibility in fires. Structures shift when they burn. Under the intense heat produced, windows can give way. If the window had shattered, due to the room's internal pressure, as you suggested, then we would see glass on the outside. Here, in the general area of where I am." Hatch pointed to the ground around her feet.

Cartwright moved alongside her and crouched down. His knee

gently grazed Hatch's as he maintained a wobbly balance, teetering on the balls of his feet. He looked down at the area Hatch had indicated. "I'm not seeing anything. No big pieces of glass. There were a lot of firemen on scene. It's possible somebody may have kicked it aside. Hell, I might've."

Hatch listened to the man's attempted explanation for the missing glass and then said, "Hold on a second. I just had a thought."

She stood up and walked down the strip of rooms, passing the burned entrance to number two and continuing on past the main office. She rounded the back of the motel and came to the area where only a few days before she had first encountered the Outlaws. She stood in the same spot where she'd rendered both men unconscious. Hatch was at ground zero for where this all began.

Hatch looked up at the small un-openable window to the bathroom resting above the tub and shower area. This decorative window had been designed with the sole purpose of letting natural light through the frosted pane of glass.

Cartwright caught up to her and looked up at what she was staring at. "Well, I'll be damned. I definitely didn't notice that last night."

The bathroom window to room number two was shattered. Hatch did a cursory sweep of the ground beneath it. Again, there was no glass on the dirt-covered ground.

Hatch turned to Cartwright. "There's no glass here either. Just like the front. And that's because the windows weren't broken from the inside. It wasn't a causative effect of the heat and fire. Or even Wendy in some desperate attempt to escape. These windows were broken from the outside."

Cartwright's mouth hung open.

"But I'm nothing if not thorough, so let's look inside to be sure."

Back in front of room number two, Hatch found herself pausing by the open space where the door used to be.

She peered inside. The light of day pushed her shadow in, but Hatch's feet remained rooted. Cartwright stood by her side and she took a step to the right, letting him lead the way. Something Hatch typically didn't do. She always prided herself on being the first in, whenever possible. There was something about having the early eyes on a scene, but she knew the reason for her hesitation today.

The truest definition of strength was knowing what lay ahead, whether the dangers were of a physical or mental nature and forging a path regardless. Hatch exhaled slowly and stepped inside the room.

The charred walls' paint was blistered and peeled back to reveal the bones of the room. Her attention was immediately drawn to a dark spot on the carpeting between the bed and door. Hatch knew what it was before her brain fully comprehended the sight before her.

At first glance it looked like Rorschach painting. Hatch's eyes traced the blurred and imperfect edges, piecing together the image. Wendy's burned body had left an imprint. The shadowy form became clearer. The dying girl's arm had been outstretched toward the door. Hatch envisioned the girl's last moments in this hellish room. Wendy was awake when they had come, or at the very least was awakened by the attack. Any thought of a quick and painless death dissipated at the sight of the shadowed stain on the floor in front of her.

Wendy had been trapped in the room. Most likely she had hit the floor and attempted to make her way to the door. The smoke or fire had rendered her unable to breathe, and therefore unable to move. She was probably blinded by the heat of the engulfed room. Her outstretched arm reached for salvation, the door, and never found it. The twisted shape of the girl's last moments was now burned into Hatch's mind as they'd been burned into the motel floor.

Hatch found herself at a loss. She'd even momentarily stopped breathing, her body's autonomic system on pause. Like kickstarting an old motorcycle, she inhaled deeply and everything came into focus once again as the whirlwind of thoughts lingered.

Hatch could feel the eyes of Cartwright on her and she righted herself, clearing her mind as best she could.

On the table, she noticed an interesting pattern on the burnt wood. A glossy sheen coated it. "Here it is," she said, breaking the silence.

Cartwright came close and looked around her at the table. "What's that?"

At first glance, it looked as though someone had spilled a glass of water on the burned table and then frozen it.

"That's the glass from the windowpane. It melted it to the table-top. Forensics would have to do a comparative analysis to verify this. Not sure your chief is going to dig for answers."

"I doubt it. I overheard talk it was being listed as accidental with the cause to be determined."

"Do you want to know what really happened here?"

Cartwright looked her in the eyes. "Absolutely."

"I would put my money on the fact that when the glass was broken, it landed here on the table. When the fire took hold of the room and the heat and flames worked their way around the space, the heat melted it, sealing it to the table. I'm a big believer in being thorough. Let's just check the backside window to confirm."

With that, Hatch moved toward the bathroom, carefully stepping over the shadowed spot on the ground, the final resting place of nineteen-year-old Wendy. The bathroom's door was damaged and half unhinged. She slid inside.

The porcelain tub and sink had fared better than the main space's furnishings. There were heavy burn marks on the inside of the room, If Wendy had been able to make it in here through the gauntlet of fire, she could have run the tub and stayed somewhat protected by the water. But even that would've been only a temporary solution. With a fire as intense as this one, the water would eventually come to a boil. The end result would have been equally awful.

In the tub was a similar melted glass pattern to the one on the table. She turned to Cartwright. "I guess we have our answer."

"I heard the arson investigator say something about it being related to faulty wiring. Blaming the motel's condition as the possible cause."

"And you believed it?"

Cartwright shook his head. "No, I didn't. But as I've come to find out lately, it doesn't matter what I believe or think because not much is going to happen. The chief is working on damage control now. I'm sure if we were to watch the newscast later, we would get a totally different picture than what you're painting."

"This was no accident. The breaks in the window were the access point for whatever accelerant they threw in here. Most likely some type of Molotov cocktail. They attacked from both sides of the room, effectively cutting off any chance of escape."

"If she'd made it into this room, she could've kept the door shut and run the shower full blast. Maybe she could have created a layer of protection until help arrived."

"They cut that off as well."

Hatch looked back into the main room at the bit of shadowed outstretched arm peeking out from beyond the end of the bed. "She never had a chance."

Cartwright was silent.

"What are you going to do about it, now that you know?" Hatch asked.

"There's not an easy answer. I'm not scared of standing up to them, if that's what you're thinking. But what do we have to go on? I'm not an expert, in any way, shape or form, but I would imagine that most likely any bit of tangible DNA on whatever was thrown in here burned up in the fire."

Hatch nodded.

"So, where does that leave me?"

"They didn't come for her," Hatch said softly.

His face contorted in confusion. "What are you saying?"

"They came for me."

"Who did?"

"I know it was Blaze and Psycho. The Outlaws carried it out. But the shot caller was higher up in the pecking order. I know you said you didn't see him last night, but there was a biker watching. Ugly guy with a nasty scar across half his face."

Cartwright broke eye contact with Hatch. It was subtle, but enough for her to recognize he knew exactly who she was talking about.

Hatch pressed, "Heard of the Savage Renegades?"

"Trust me, if I could do something about them, I would," Cartwright offered.

"Jurisdiction problem?"

"It's more than that. I can't even get support from my own department to take the gloves off and go after these local thugs. But the motorcycle crew? They're in a whole different playing field. And yes, jurisdictionally speaking, they are out of bounds for me."

"Well, they're not outside of mine."

"Hatch, I get it. You're a tough lady. I can see that. Hell, I know that. But you can't take these guys on alone. They're killers. This crew is filled with some nasty people. And somehow, they're protected. I hate to say it, but they're untouchable."

"Nobody's untouchable." Hatch folded her arms and squared herself to him. "All I need to know is where they are. Tell me where they hang out, and I'll take it from there."

"I don't think this is something you should do on your own."

"You're free to come," Hatch offered.

Cartwright hesitated and broke eye contact.

"It's okay. I'm used to going things alone."

TWENTY-ONE

FOLLOWING CARTWRIGHT'S DIRECTIONS, Hatch drove to the Savage Renegades' clubhouse. She was surprised to find it located on the same road as the abandoned gas station where she'd squared off with Psycho, putting a bullet in his foot.

It was ten miles farther down the road from the gas station. Hatch had slept in Manuel's truck only a few minutes' ride from where the scarred biker had undoubtedly returned to.

Hatch was armed with two guns now. The Sig gifted to her by Gabe and the Smith & Wesson M&P she'd acquired after shooting the gang banger. Hatch was surprised the gun owner hadn't requested she return the pistol, especially after the cold shoulder she'd received earlier in the morning from Gabe and his father. Maybe deep down he was still concerned for her safety.

Hatch wasn't exactly sure of the plan, but sometimes the best way to handle a problem was head on. One thing was for certain, they'd never expect her to walk through the front door of their clubhouse.

She had a singular purpose. Find the guy with the scar, the one from the motel last night. What would come from it was still as unpredictable as the sandstorms that blew through these desert plains.

Hatch turned into the dirt lot of the clubhouse. It was undeniable she was in the right spot. Ten-plus motorcycles were parked out front in a line. The building's structure was unique, as if an auto body shop and Wild West saloon had a baby. The exterior of the structure was paneled wood with a long plank porch. At the far end was a metal rollup access door, to what Hatch could only assume was some makeshift motorcycle repair area. One large man stood outside, guarding the main entrance.

Hatch pulled Manuel's Ford to a stop alongside the last chopper in line, only leaving a small gap between the driver's side door and the matte black of the fuel tank. She knew the care and adoration these men held for their bikes. And so, Hatch took extra care to open the door with as much force as possible.

The impact would have been much louder, but the wind muted the clang of metal on metal. The bike wobbled but didn't collapse. Part of her had envisioned a domino effect of falling bikes. There'd be time to try again when she departed. The edge of her door had left a healthy dent on the Harley-Davidson, scratching the black paint and exposing its undercoating. If this was the only damage she did to the Savage Renegades, they could consider themselves lucky.

Staring at the club's bouncer, Hatch's lack of a plan weighed heavy. She'd arrived, fresh from the scene of the girl's death, and was running on vengeful rage, teetering on the border of lunacy. Worst of all, she knew it. But she was still in that motel room seeing the charred remnants of where the young girl took her last breath. The stink of it saturated every thread of her sweatshirt.

No clear-headed approach today. All she thought about was walking through those front doors and the look on those bastards' faces when they saw her standing there, unafraid.

The large man standing in front of the door didn't wear a cut, the leather vest denoting he hadn't risen to the rank of Prospect. He was an uninitiated member of the gang tasked with things like guarding a door in the cold New Mexico wind.

Unlike the men she had seen before, his hair was short, and his beard consisted of patchy, disconnected stubble. He was young, maybe in his early twenties, but one thing stood out about the guard...he was big. Hatch guessed him at 6'3" and put his weight at roughly two-hundred-fifty pounds. From the tightly fitted shirt, it appeared the majority of his bulk was muscle. His left arm was wrapped in a full sleeve tattoo. A colorful image of a snake and a naked woman were intertwined in some demented perversion of the Garden of Eden extending up his forearm to the middle of his bicep before disappearing into his shirt sleeve.

She thought about her own tattoo on her damaged right arm. Its words no longer legible, twisted amid the web of scar tissue. To the untrained eye, the difference between Hatch and the muscle-bound man would make it seem the odds weren't in her favor. But Hatch saw a deeper layer of difference. She was battle-tested, and the man with the pristine tattoo was not.

"Where d'ya think you're going, babe?"

"Babe? Now, that's something I haven't been called in a very long time." Hatch gave a coy smile. "You guys serve beer, right?"

"Sure do. To members." He made an overt act of sizing her up and down. "And from the look of it, you're not fitting the bill."

"I guess you're not either," Hatch shot back. "Is that why they have you standing out here?"

"You got a smart mouth. How about I shut it for you?"

Hatch laughed softly, which only seemed to enrage the man further. "How about you just step aside, so I don't have to embarrass you in front of your club."

"Embarrass me? Lady, I don't know who you think you're talking to, but this here club is run by the Savage Renegades. And like I said, it's for members only."

"They don't like you enough to let you go inside? Or maybe you get to lick their boots and keep their motorcycles safe." Hatch thumbed in the direction of the truck. "Which, by the way, you've done a shitty job so far. There's a hell of a dent in the far one. But I'm sure they won't care."

The big man's jaw clenched tight and the points of his eyebrows met in the middle of his face, contorted in anger.

Action versus reaction. Hatch decided not to wait for the man to move. He stood rigid. The tension in his muscles would make him slower. Unbeknownst to the man, she was poised, ready to spring like a rattlesnake.

Hatch stepped off to the side, quickly kicking downward at a forty-five-degree angle. The bottom of her boot struck hard, impacting the outside of the man's knee. The blow took the man's balance, immediately buckling the leg and causing him to lean in her direction. She met his descending torso, slamming her forearm across the side of his neck. The momentum of his massive body's fall added to the devastation of the strike. Hatch delivered it with surgical precision along the vagus nerve.

The large man went limp and flopped onto the porch like a dead fish being tossed from a net. He lay unmoving on the ground. Hatch knew his current condition was only temporary but with enough lasting power to give her easy access through the front door. Embarrassment would be the least of his worries when he woke.

Hatch shoved open the door to the clubhouse.

The interior was darker than she'd expected. Some of the gray afternoon light entered the space, but most of the windows were either covered in black paint or obscured by posters. It smelled of stale beer and body odor.

Hatch stepped inside and let the door shut behind her with a bang.

In her quick count, she tallied nine men in the room. Each were dressed in similar garb, wearing leather vests adorned with a variety of patches. She evaluated them, but none seemed as big as the man in front. Unfortunately, they looked far more menacing. These men were battle-hardened. Visible scars and tattoos of the prison variety decorated their flesh from their fingertips to their skulls.

All eyes were now on Hatch, who stood in the doorway as still as if a mannequin on display.

She looked at each of the faces, searching for the distinguishing half-moon scar. Even in the dark of this dingy clubhouse, she'd be able to identify him easily.

In the back corner, by a narrow, dimly lit hallway was a table. Seated facing her was the man she sought. Next to him was another biker, an older man with long, curly salt and pepper hair. This man gave Hatch a smirk, as if amused by her dramatic entry. He then settled back in his chair. Although the older biker looked ravaged by years of abuse and rough living, he seemed to have an air of superiority the others lacked. Hatch deemed him to be their leader. The scarred man seated to the right was his soldier.

"You seem a little lost," the older biker said. His voice was gruff and raspy.

Hatch guessed by the sound of it he was at least a pack-a-day smoker, maybe two. Longevity wasn't something guys like these worried about. She figured the Savage Renegades didn't have much in the way of healthcare plans. Retirement in a crew like this was death. By the looks of the older biker, he was ancient by gang standards and had probably outlived numerous minions and enemies alike.

"I'm here for him." Hatch pointed to the man next to him. The man with the scar.

Hatch's eyes adjusted to the dismal lighting and she was able to make out a small patch just above the scarred man's nametag. Mongoose had a One-Percenter patch. Hatch knew the significance. It was originally used to mark a member of a motorcycle club who'd killed somebody. Nowadays, the patch was a symbol of biker gangs considered outlaws. Hatch noticed the leader didn't have the same patch, meaning Mongoose was a dangerous man.

Hatch was a One-Percenter, too, although she didn't need a patch on a vest to tell the world about it. Keeping that secret to herself gave her an advantage.

Mongoose said nothing. Hatch calling him out in front of his boss and crew had no effect. His face was emotionless. She quickly surmised this was a man not easily intimidated. She imagined numerous enemies had posed similar threats, and with undoubtedly more intimidating messengers than Hatch, standing there in her jeans and sweatshirt. Being a woman must've minimized the impact of her words to this group.

The biker leader laughed. As if waiting for his cue, the rest of the crew followed. "Oh, is that all?" The laughter was now uproarious among the group.

Hatch's face was deadpan as she stared at the man. "No. That's not all. Today's the last day the Savage Renegades come into Luna Vista. The town is now officially off-limits to you."

The laughter continued. Its volume rising.

"You've got some nerve coming in here, into my club, and running your mouth the way you just did!"

Hatch scanned the room. This time she was picking out targets. She thought about the two guns tucked at her back. She had more than enough rounds for the number of adversaries she was facing. The problem lay with her ability to engage them quickly enough, should it come to that.

This situation could quickly go from bad to worse. From the look in the biker leader's eyes, it was beginning to lean in that direction. Not that Hatch had delusions the MC club would accept her terms of turning in one of their own and walking away from the town they controlled. She expected to be met with challenge. In fact, Hatch banked on it.

She gained access with relative ease but getting out would be a whole different set of problems. Her eyes adjusted to her dimly lit surroundings and she saw the biker leader more clearly, including his nametag, Cain. She wondered what a man did to earn the biblical brother slayer's moniker, but doubted she'd ever get the opportunity to ask.

Cain cut his mock laughter off and the others followed suit. The room was plunged into silence and the man's eyes were deadly serious. "I think it's best you leave," he said in an icy rasp.

Hatch remained unmoved, though her left hand had slid closer to the rear of her hip line. Her thumb now touched the outside of her sweatshirt. Under it, she could feel the butt of the pistol. "I told you what I wanted. And I'm not leaving until I get it," Hatch said with a similar iciness.

Cain looked around the room and said, "Did I hear this lady correctly? Or am I losing my mind?"

"You've got to be wondering how crazy I am to walk into your clubhouse and make these demands. Maybe you should think twice before you dismiss me."

Cain leaned and whispered something in the ear of Mongoose, the club's one-percenter. Hatch moved her hand closer to her gun, hoping the biker nearest her didn't notice the subtle movement. Her hand was now underneath the sweatshirt and her index finger crept toward the trigger housing of the Sig. Millimeter by millimeter, she worked her hand along the pistol's rough grip until she could gain full purchase. The web of her hand pressed firmly into the dovetail of the grip, where the frame met the slide.

Just as she was about to pull the semi-automatic pistol from her backside, something caught her eye in the narrow hallway. A well-dressed man exited from what appeared to be a bathroom and approached the table with Cain and Mongoose. Seeing Hatch, he paused and did a double take, and then looked at the horde of bikers.

Hatch recognized the man, although she didn't know his name. She had seen him earlier, standing next to Chief Porter during the press conference. The pasty complexion of the man's round face spotted in a blotchy red.

Hatch looked back at the table and realized there were three beers set around it with one in front of an empty chair. *How did I miss that?* Hatch was angry at herself for the slip up. Eleven men to contend with, nine bikers in the room, one unconscious out front, and now a senior member of the town's council. Things just went from bad to worse.

She heard something from behind her. Hatch recognized it as the door opening. She spun to see the angry uninitiated member of the club. The debilitating effects of her blow had worn off quicker than she'd expected. The bulk of the man was silhouetted by the light of day flooding in behind him.

Hatch pulled the weapon free. Just as it cleared her sweatshirt, the man's fist, already in motion, came crashing down on the left side of her head near the temple. It was a staggering blow. Not unaccustomed to taking a punch, Hatch fought to remain on her feet. But the impact dazed her, buckling her knees and causing her to lose focus. The gun was still in hand, but she was knocked off balance and her eyes were temporarily blurred.

She heard a commotion around her, but in her dizzy state, Hatch couldn't pinpoint the direction. The next strike came from another direction. And wasn't done with a fist. Wood from a chair leg shattered over the top of her head.

Hatch fell flat. Nearing a state of unconsciousness, she pulled the trigger, blindly firing as she tasted the blood in her mouth. She got off two shots before a heavy boot crashed down on her left hand. It was followed by a searing pain as the gun was ripped free from her grip. She felt her index finger snap and knew it was broken.

She fought her right arm back toward the other gun, Psycho's Smith and Wesson. An onslaught of blows rained down on her from all sides. It was a blur of feet and fists. At one point she felt the heavy weight of glass break over the back of her skull. Her mind raced as she slipped in and out of consciousness.

Pinned by the weight of several men, Hatch could barely breathe.

The last words she heard before she gave way to darkness were, "Not here. Take her to the spot and get rid of her."

TWENTY-TWO

A LOUD BANG woke her as the side of her swollen head slammed into something sharp. It took Hatch a second to connect the pieces. Her mind replayed the moments before everything went dark.

She fluttered her eyelids, trying to clear them and regain her visual acuity. A dark shape in front of her came into view. She realized she was staring at the bottom hinge of a seatback. The metal lip protruding out must've been what she'd banged her head on. It still stung, but she figured it was more a result of the terrible beating she'd endured at the hands of the Savage Renegades MC Club.

Hatch was mad at herself for not taking a different approach in dealing with the gang. Her rage at the sight of Wendy's darkened stain on room two's carpet had catapulted her forward. Her mind was now clear, and so was her plan. First things first, Hatch needed to get herself out of her current situation.

She surveyed her surroundings. The hinge was connected to the worn leather driver's seat of a pickup truck. She was staring up at a single row bench seat. Working her head around, Hatch recognized it. She was stuffed behind the seat in the storage area of Manuel's old Ford pickup. The truck he'd lent her. First the man's motel, and now his truck. She had a large debt to repay to him. Hatch just hoped she'd live long enough to make good on it.

She lay silent on the formed rhino-lined floorboard. The older model truck was loud, providing its own barrier of white noise. In the short time she'd used it, Hatch had learned the quirky rattle and hum of the engine. The Ford was on its last leg, a few years of light driving left before it ended in a scrap heap. Manuel had most likely put in some sweat equity to keep it running.

She was grateful for the cab's loud rumble. It would mask her movement as Hatch worked to figure out the bindings wrapped around her body.

Her wrists were pinned behind her back. The cord was wrapped tight, but not so much that she couldn't wiggle them. Hatch manipulated her fingers and twisted the palms of her hands inward as if in prayer. Pressing her fingers together, she pushed against the restraints with her wrists. It stretched under her exertion. They'd bound her with some type of bungee cord. *Amateurs*, she thought. Her feet were bound at the ankles in similar fashion.

Never bind somebody in something with any give, if you expect them to remain secured. During Hatch's experience in the Army's Survival, Evasion, Resistance, Escape school, more commonly known as SERE, she'd learned how to escape a variety of situations. Ones much more challenging than her current circumstance. The bindings she was trained to defeat were best done right, with interlocking knots, so the more somebody struggled, the more it would bite into their wrists. Wrapping her in bungee cords did little in the way of that. In fact, when she flexed and pushed against the cords, she felt a little bit of give. And with that, she began the process of wriggling her way out of them.

She focused on her wrists first. By folding her right hand inward and slipping a finger inside one of the gaps it created, Hatch was able to incrementally widen the gap. She continued to wiggle her hand until it came free. Her skin burned from the friction of the cord's nylon coating, but it was a minor price to pay. Once the one hand was free, the cord's tension went slack and she freed the other hand. The index finger on her left hand was definitely broken when they'd stepped on it. Free of the restraint, she felt its painful throb.

Hatch paused with her hands behind her back. From her current position, she didn't have a visual of the driver. She remained still. The truck continued on without a change in pace. Satisfied the first phase of her planned escape had gone unnoticed, Hatch slowly scrunched down toward her ankles. With her hands free, it didn't take long to undo the knot securing them. She then draped the cord loosely over her ankles so it would look as though they were still tied.

She resumed her original position and tucked her hands underneath her buttocks. The truck rumbled forward. And Hatch waited for her opportunity.

Angling herself back slightly, Hatch was able to get a view of one of her captors. The man in the front passenger seat was definitely a biker, but not the one she'd hoped to see. This man's greasy hair was pulled back into a loose ponytail. It exposed his face and she was disappointed it was not the one-percenter. In her current position, she was unable to see the driver, but as she thought on it, she doubted Cain would send his number one to do cleanup detail. Tasks like this would be left to underlings. No need to risk exposing his number one man to this type of work.

The truck shook violently. Hatch banged her head against the hinge again, reopening a gash on her forehead. Blood dripped down into the outside corner of her face, stinging her left eye. She blinked rapidly to clear it and dipped her head, wiping it on her shoulder.

The shaking continued, amplified by the truck's worn out shocks. The driver and passenger seemed to be getting their share of it, too, expressing their displeasure in the form of an endless stream of profanities.

Every jostled movement caused by the truck seemed to find a way of highlighting one of her recent injuries inflicted by the savage beating she'd endured in the clubhouse. She was lucky to have survived it. After an attack like that, some people never wake up.

She'd need a bit of time to fully recover from the damage she sustained, but for now it would have to wait. It wasn't the first time she had to complete a mission after taking a hit, and if current circumstance was an indication of her future, it wouldn't be her last.

"I think this is good enough. Stop here," the passenger said, raising his voice over the clamor of the truck.

"Maybe there's time to have a little fun with her first," the driver offered. His accent on the word fun.

"You heard Cain. No screwing this up. We're supposed to make this look like an accident. Her body can't come back on the club."

"But look at her back. She's a sweet piece of ass. Who's gonna know if we have our way with her first?" the driver pleaded.

A loud slap followed. And the truck swerved in reaction to it.

"What the hell?" the driver yelled.

"Are you an idiot?" the passenger asked. "DNA, man, don't you watch those crime shows? If they find your DNA in that girl right there, we're done for. What comes back on us, comes back on the club. She ain't worth it."

"You're right, I suppose. Just thinking it'd be fun, is all," the driver whined.

"I want to be rid of this bitch as quick as possible."

Hatch felt the vehicle slow to a stop. A moment later, she heard the ratcheted click of the parking brake. The engine, in neutral, remained running.

"Let's pull her out my side. Then we'll shove her in behind the wheel and roll her down the hill," the driver said with an excited giddiness.

"I don't know why they just didn't follow us down here with the van. It would make this a hell of a lot quicker. Plus, we wouldn't have to walk all the way back to the road."

The driver groaned. "Ya know, you're a real dumb ass for somebody who just lectured me about DNA. If there are two sets of tire tracks coming off the road down to this spot, it's going to raise questions. If the only tracks are made by the truck she's in, then it'll look like she just drove off the road and crashed into the ravine. Stuff like that happens all the time. No big deal. The troopers will think she either fell asleep at the wheel or was blinded by a sandstorm. Either way, it'll be an open and shut case."

"I just don't feel like walking a mile and a half back to the road to get picked up."

"When you're in charge, you can make the decisions. But since you ain't, we're following orders. The walk back ain't gonna kill you. And if we do this thing right, it'll get us our patch. We'll be freakin' one-percenters, brotha." The driver slapped the other man's shoulder.

"Hell yeah."

With that, both men opened the doors, letting in a blast of wind and dust.

Hatch kept her eyes closed and prepared herself for the next phase. While the men wasted time with their mindless banter, she had taken the bungee cord used to bind her wrists and balled it up in her right hand. She listened for the sounds of the seat's release latch.

The back of the bench seat lurched forward as the rear compartment access door opened. Her body remained slumped as if she were still unconscious.

Hatch felt one of the men pawing at her. He gripped her underneath her armpits, scooping up her torso. He began yanking her out. Hatch did her best not to wince or react to the pain of the movement. Her broken index finger dragged under the weight of her body, twisting it violently. Hatch stayed in character, playing the unconscious victim. Her head drooped chin down and was slammed against the hard metal edge of the cab door.

As her body reached the halfway mark of the forced extraction, she felt the second man's hands slide under her lower back and thighs in a cradling carry. Hatch was nearly out of the vehicle now. Her knees broke the plane of the truck, and she bent them. Planting the bottoms of her feet on the bottom lip of the cab's frame, she pressed down with all her strength and launched back into the men holding her.

The bikers were wholly unprepared for the sudden explosive burst, the force of which knocked both men backwards. Her upper body struck the driver with the most kinetic energy. Feeling her back on his chest, Hatch arched back with her head. The base of her skull struck the driver in the bridge of his nose. He immediately let go, dropping her.

Hatch hit the ground and rolled sideways. She sprung to her feet with the bungee cord held tight in her right hand. The driver was on the ground, clutching his bloodied face. Hatch squared to the pony-tailed passenger. He stepped forward. Hatch, less than three feet away, fired a kick into his soft midsection. The man doubled over but didn't fall.

In one swift move, Hatch lunged forward, moving to the rear of the hunched man. The bungee cord was still in her right hand, and she quickly threw it around the man's neck. Catching the other end with her left, the pain was excruciating but Hatch pushed it from her mind and held tight.

The man grasped at his throat. Hatch yanked back on the bungee cord. The biker staggered back as she shifted her body and cinched down, using her right forearm to lock the makeshift noose into place. He began to flail wildly. Hatch hooked her right ankle in front of his left foot. She swept his leg out from under him and torqued her hip for added effect.

The ponytailed man fell face first to the ground, sending a plume of dirt into the air. Hatch landed on top and drove her knee into the center of his spine. Pressing down and pinning him, she yanked back and simultaneously twisted her right elbow. A loud snap accompanied the break she felt. The body under her went limp.

She released the dead biker, letting go of the cord as she stood. The driver had recovered from the initial effects of his broken nose. Without warning, he launched forward with a knife. It was a big knife, the blade at least six to eight inches long. And it was clear he planned to plunge it deep into Hatch.

The man was sloppy, and he swung the blade in wide, uncontrolled arcs. Hatch backed away in a zigzag pattern and turned the backs of her forearms out toward her assailant. Better to get cut on the non-vital part of the arm, should he manage to land the blade.

He shoved the knife forward like a swashbuckler looking to end the battle in one fell swoop. Hatch dodged, sidestepping the blow. It slipped past, just barely missing her midsection. The knife point snagged the pocket of her sweatshirt, tearing it open.

He had overcommitted on his efforts, and in doing so, it put him off balance. Hatch seized the opportunity, trapping him at the elbow in an armlock. Hatch slammed her head down on the shorter man, aiming for the broken nose. The biker, who only minutes before had been intent on raping the unconscious Hatch, let out an agonizing scream.

With the man's arm still locked in place at the elbow joint, Hatch pushed up against it with her left forearm while pulling down in the opposite direction with her right hand. The pop was sickening. The volume of the man's shrieking tripled as he dropped the knife. She gave him no opportunity to plead for mercy or tap out. In real world combat, the more damage she inflicted increased her likelihood of survival.

The man reached for his lame right arm as blood continued to flow from his twice-shattered nose. Wobbly and weak, the would-be-rapist was now on the verge of collapse. Hatch stepped back, keeping a firm grip on the wrist of his injured arm. She twisted his palm inward and applied pressure to the back of his hand. The man yelped as the pain drove him to his knees.

Hatch swung her knee upward. Still maintaining her grip on the wrist, the hard bone of her kneecap smacked into the man's temple. She felt him go limp. It wasn't a blow meant to kill him, but delivered with forceful devastation, it rendered him unconscious. Hatch released her grip and the driver slumped to his left.

Time was of the essence. She heard their conversation before they came to a stop. These two bikers were expected to be back on the main road for their pickup. Based on the plan and factoring in the mile-plus walk back, she had to move quickly before their people started to worry and reinforcements arrived.

Hatch went over to the dead man and released the cord from his neck. She then set about using it to secure the unconscious man. She would not make the same mistake they had in their binding job.

The unconscious man was shorter than Hatch by a few inches, but he had a thick, stocky frame. His limp body made moving him difficult, but even with her damaged body and broken finger, she managed. She shoved him up into the driver's seat of the truck. He groaned and his eyelids fluttered, but he remained limp. Hatch knew he was close to coming to and used the cord to tie him up. She bound his hands behind his back. She used the extra rope to bind his feet, leaving him hog-tied but upright in a seated position, making it nearly impossible for him to reach the pedals. Unlike the knots they'd used, the ones Hatch tied would tighten if he moved.

The driver's head remained slumped forward. A whistling sound from his nose followed each of his labored breaths' exhales. Hatch then went back to retrieve the dead man.

Hatch squatted low and hooked her arms under his, locking them across his sternum. Pulling his upper body against her chest and leaning back, she was able to distribute his bodyweight. Hatch dragged the man around the back of the pickup truck to the passenger side. It took several attempts to get his lifeless body back into the passenger seat. Hatch shut the door and then returned to the driver, who was still head down and unconscious.

She slapped the man on the back of the head. He didn't fully rouse, so Hatch applied a little bit of pressure to the bridge of his nose. He squirmed and his eyes opened wide. Hatch released him and wiped the blood on his shirt. His eyes watered. He spat a mixture of blood and frothy saliva. Hatch stepped back and gave him a second to comprehend his situation. He lunged for her and then screamed out in pain. The effort caused the pain to his damaged right arm as the binding tightened.

"You bitch! I'm going to kill you! You're dead. Do you hear me? Dead!"

Hatch leveled a steely eyed gaze at the man and calmly said, "I've been hearing that a lot lately. But here I am. And there you sit." Hatch held up the large knife, the same one he'd tried to plunge into her midsection. "How'd that work out for you the last time?"

His eyes widened at the sight of it. "What're you gonna do to me with that?"

"I don't know. What were you going to do to me with it?" Hatch asked with heavy-handed sarcasm.

He licked the blood from his lips. "I was just following orders, ya know? I was doing what I was told."

"I know a thing or two about following orders, but it looks to me like you failed to carry them out." Hatch looked past him at the dead man in the passenger seat. "Your friend already paid the price. Will you, too?"

"You're crazy, lady! What the hell are you talking about?"

"You know exactly what I mean." Hatch cocked her head to the side and overtly eyed the parking brake release set just off to the left underneath the steering column. "What was it you were planning to do to me?" She scrunched her face in a feigned pensive nature. "Oh yeah, I remember. You were going to take my unconscious body and put it in the driver's seat and then roll me down into the ravine, so I could be crushed to death. You were told to make it look like an accident. Am I missing anything?"

The tough biker's eyes began to water. This time Hatch didn't think it was because of the searing pain of his broken nose.

"Please don't do this." He was frantic. "Listen, you could just go. I won't say nothin'. I swear!"

"I know you won't." Hatch had no intention of murdering the man. Cold-blooded killing wasn't her thing. But she needed him to believe she was capable. All interrogations depended on leverage. In this case, and under the pressing time constraints, hers was the imminent threat of death.

"But before I go, I need to better understand what's going on in this town. What hold do you have over the town of Luna Vista? Why do you guys get a free pass?"

The man squirmed and then immediately winced. Every movement tightened his bindings further and pulled at his damaged arm.

"Moving only makes it worse. There's no point in you trying to get out of the knots I tied, unlike the half-assed job you guys did." The threat of death made real, her second layer of psychological pressure was his perception of no plausible escape. She could see both were now completely understood by her detainee.

"Who the hell are you, lady?"

"I was just somebody passing through, somebody looking for something of a personal nature. And then you had to go and kill that young girl at the motel."

He shook his head. "That wasn't me. I didn't do that!"

"Somebody just following orders, right?" she mimicked.

The man put his head down.

"That's how it always goes. People love to pass the buck. But following orders doesn't excuse the fact that your club was responsible. To me that means every Savage Renegade is directly responsible. To top it off, you made the mistake of trying to clean up your mess by getting rid of me. And you failed. You're now staring at the consequences."

"Then why don't you just kill me and get it over with," the man whimpered.

"Consider yourself already dead and this is your opportunity for penance."

"Penance? God doesn't forgive guys like me for the things I've done."

"Then let's treat this like a karmic opportunity. A point where you get to do some good in the miniscule amount of time you have left on Earth." She cocked an eyebrow. "Tell me what hold the gang has over the town."

"What? You think it's some kind of blackmail thing?"

"I don't know what it is. Why don't you enlighten me?"

"It's simple. No big conspiracy. We, our club, needed a place where things could be stored and moved. Like a central hub for our distribution network to clean up our cash flow. Luna Vista was close enough to the border and small enough to control."

"By clean up, you mean laundering the money?"

"It's all about the money. You can't do what we do and make the money we make without having a place to clean it."

"What are you saying? The businesses in Luna Vista wash your money for you, for your club? Why would they do that?"

"So we don't burn them to the ground." The bound man smiled. His teeth were coated with blood.

Hatch was quiet for a moment as she thought about the well-dressed man she'd seen in the clubhouse.

"How do the Outlaws factor in? What's their role in all this?"

"Every club needs guys like them to handle the smaller distribution efforts. They're just low-level shitheads."

"And what about the man in the clubhouse? The guy in the suit?"

"It's all about money, lady. Hell, I'm sure if you want, I can broker a deal for you. Ya know, tell them to cut you a break. Make a cash trade for my life and call it even. You've proven yourself to be tough as shit. Cain will respect that."

"You think they're gonna pay me to let you go?"

"Sure, why not? I've been in the club for a while. Earned my stripes."

"But you failed," Hatch said. "You failed to do your job. That makes you a substandard employee where I come from. Why would they waste any money on someone like you?"

The man shrugged. Even that subtle movement caused him to wince.

She'd gotten everything she could out of him and knew his banter now was done partly out of self-preservation, but more so out of biding time until his friends showed up. "How long until they were supposed to pick you up on the main road?"

The man was silent. Even his nasally whistle stopped.

"Don't make this pleasant conversation we're having transition to a much more painful style of interrogation." Hatch played with the knife in her hand as if examining the blade's sharpness.

"One hour. Figured it would give us enough time to handle business and verify you were dead. And then we'd walk our way back to the meet location."

Hatch read the man's face and body, searching for any sign of deception. Finding none, she made a judgment call he was telling the truth. She looked at her watch. Making an educated guess at the time since their arrival, the fight, and her short interrogation, Hatch had, at best, thirty minutes left before the next wave of bikers would be arriving.

"Well, it's been fun. But I guess it's time I get going."

"What are you going to do to me?"

"I'm going to give you a better chance at life than you were going to give me."

"What's that supposed to mean?" He swiveled his head and looked down at the rope securing him. Anger replaced the defeated look of moments ago. "When I get out of here, I swear to God, I'm gonna kill you. I'll kill everyone you've ever known! You think we're just here? The Savage Renegades are everywhere. Word'll be out. There's a hit list. And you've just made number one on it!"

"Sounds like I've got a lot of work ahead of me." Unphased by the threat, Hatch turned and walked away. "Good luck getting out of those knots."

The man bucked wildly. He screamed in pain and then followed with a long list of profanity, stringing together words in a fashion that would make most sailors blush.

She was about ten feet away when she heard a loud mechanical thunk. Hatch recognized it and spun on her heels just in time to see the man's eyes wide with unbridled terror.

The vehicle rolled away, quickly picking up speed. Hatch

watched as Manuel's truck, containing the two bikers—one dead and one soon to be, disappear over the edge.

His chance of survival was slightly better than hers would've been. Their plan had been to send her to her death bound and unconscious. At least he would see it coming.

TWENTY-THREE

HATCH, battered and bruised from her altercation at the hands of the Savage Renegades MC Club, made steady progress on her mile and a half walk back to the main road. She continually checked her watch and figured, at best, she had no more than ten minutes before the recovery team arrived. The two dead men didn't have guns on them, but she was sure the others would. Hatch was now unarmed. Both of her weapons, the Sig and the Smith & Wesson, had been taken from her.

At least she could see for miles down the road in both directions. The downside to that was so could they. Hatch visually scanned her horizon in the direction from which the bikers would most likely arrive. Following the truck's tracks in the dirt, she'd deemed they'd taken a right off the main road, which meant the extraction team would be coming from the south.

Hatch listened for the sound of engines, motorcycle or otherwise. It was hard to hear anything over the howl of the wind. It was unlikely she would be able to hear them before they were close enough to see her, but she strained her senses and remained vigilant.

The only weapon at her disposal was the long-bladed knife. She had removed the torn pocket from her sweatshirt and created a sheath with it, wrapping the blade. Hatch tucked it into her pants on the right side of her hip. Her left hand was swollen, especially around the broken index finger. She would have to put to use ambidexterity, should the need to use the weapon arise.

Staying close to the shrubs lining the main road, she continued her long walk back to Luna Vista. She heard a loud rumble from behind her. *Had I miscalculated the direction?* She wondered. It was unlikely. She'd completed numerous land navigation courses during her military career, the most challenging of which being the Special Forces Q Course land nav evaluation. It was a grueling test of mental and physical ability. Hatch passed not once, but twice. She had an excellent sense of direction but being unconscious for the better part of her captivity in the back of the truck's cab could've disoriented her.

Hatch turned quickly and dipped behind a cluster of spiny cacti. Crouching low, she looked toward the north. The sound grew louder. She was relatively exposed. The cacti weren't thick enough to adequately conceal her from view, should they look her way. In the distance, she saw a solitary tree. It would provide some stopping power should bullets start to fly, but there was no way she could make it there before being spotted.

She gripped the handle sticking out from her waist. *I've committed the cardinal sin of literally bringing a knife to a gun fight.* Hatch laughed at herself. Play the hand you're dealt and if you can't laugh when death comes for you, then you haven't accepted the most important rule of war. She squared herself to the approaching threat, if for no other reason than to take it head on. She mentally committed herself to the battle. If she was going to die, here and now in this vast wasteland, then she was going to do it on her feet and on her terms.

She stared intently at the rise of the road to the north. Over the horizon, the sun began to set. Beams of light bounced off the source of the noise. In an instant, she saw the cause of it.

The noise came from a large multi-passenger bus. Hatch let out a sigh of relief and released the grip on the knife's handle. She stood from behind the cacti and stepped closer to the road.

Hatch stuck her thumb out as it approached. In the desolate expanse, the driver would have to be blind to miss her.

The loud burping sound of the bus's air brakes drowned out the noise of the engine. It began to slow twenty feet away from her but didn't come to a complete stop until it passed her. A loud squeak and hiss signified it was fully stopped.

Hatch took up a brisk pace, ignoring her body's pain, as she walked to the door. It opened and she was met with loud cheers. The bus driver leaned in her direction, balancing himself with the crank handle he'd used to open up the folding door.

She looked at the banner sign on the side of the bus. In big gold lettering it read, Lounge Lizard Tour Bus, in smaller print underneath was, Wine and Beer Tours of New Mexico.

The bus driver yelled over the boisterous conversations of the passengers and said, "We're heading into Las Cruces if you need a lift." His face then must've registered her damaged condition because he mouthed, "Are you okay?"

Hatch caught a glimpse of herself in the glass of the bus doors just before they opened and what she saw was not good. Lacerations along her forehead and cheeks were coated in dried blood. Her clothes were tattered with an equal combination of blood and dirt. And her left index finger was the size of a plantain.

She gave a nonchalant shrug and dismissive laugh to calm the man's startled reaction. "Thank God you came along. I was doing a long bike ride. I went off course and hit a ditch. Wrecked my bike and, as you can plainly see, banged myself up pretty good in the process."

The bus driver evaluated her, visually scanning her from head to toe. By the slight squint of his eye, he probably took into account the fact she was not remotely dressed like a cyclist, but for whatever the reason, he didn't press any further. He offered a shake of his head and shrugged. "Well, not going to say it's going to be a quiet ride, but at least you'll get where you're going a whole lot faster. Hop on in."

Hatch stepped up on the metallic step of the bus and gave a soft smile to the driver. "I appreciate this more than you'll ever know."

"Las Cruces okay for you?" He eyed the passengers through the wide rearview mirror. "The toilet's broke in back. So, I might be needin' to make a pit stop before then."

"Fine by me either way." Hatch stepped the rest of the way into the bus and looked down the aisle. It was filled to capacity, or at least close to. The passengers were predominantly men with only a few women present. And all looked to be very much inebriated. They drank from plastic cups as bottles of wine were being passed around.

Nobody seemed to notice her injured face. Whether it was due to their intoxication, or that they flat out didn't care, Hatch was grateful. An older man sitting alone in the front of the bus looked up at her and took notice. He had neatly combed gray hair covering a bald spot at the top and his cheeks were a bright red. He gave a smile and said, "We're with the plumber's union. The Local 193. Headin' into Las Cruces to do our annual drinking tour."

Hatch smiled. "Looks like everybody's getting a head start on the fun."

The man laughed. "Pull up a seat and let me get you a drink." He scooted over, giving as much room as his girth would allow, and patted the seat cushion.

Hatch obliged and sat next to the cordial man. She decided to take him up on his offer of both the seat and the drink.

DARKNESS BEGAN to fall as they lurched forward down the roadway. Hatch took a sip of her drink. She'd assumed it would be wine after seeing several bottles in the hands of some of the other travelers. Hatch was surprised when she tasted the vodka and cranberry mixture. She tapped her plastic cup to her temporary drinking partner's.

The vodka burned her dry throat, but the juice softened the blow. The liquor immediately went to work on her empty stomach and sent a warm sensation through her mauled body.

Hatch listened to the songs and jeering of loud conversations, each person making great effort to outdo the other. The cacophony of chatter blurred into one indecipherable sound that mixed with the vibration of the bus.

It wasn't long before the bus passed by the Savage Renegades' clubhouse giving confirmation she'd been heading in the right direction. The miles of walking would've taken its toll, especially in her current condition. Doable, but not without great effort.

She noticed there were only a few bikes parked in front. Presumably the missed rendezvous and likely discovery of the two dead bikers had stirred the hornet's nest. Like the man said before careening off into the ravine, Hatch would be number one on their hit list. She had to assume a large-scale search party was now underway. Doubtful they'd be looking for her on a bus full of drunk plumbers. Hatch used this lull to recharge before her next move.

The bus rolled along for several more miles before pulling off the road and into a gas station. Hatch sat in her seat and the man offered to refill her cup. This time she respectfully declined. She knew better than to indulge herself, especially when so much was at risk. One drink was good for taking the edge off, but any more might dull her reaction time. Hatch was well aware of the need to have her wits and strength operating at full speed.

"Just a quick pit stop before we get on Highway 70 and head on into Las Cruces," the bus driver announced.

A ripple of cheers sounded from the crowd. Several passengers stood and began making their way toward the door. Hatch was bumped by the unsteady members of the Local 193 as they wobbled off the bus.

A few of the plumbers went into the convenience store while

others formed a line at the bathroom door located outside on the right of the building. Hatch relaxed, her eyes suddenly heavy, deciding now was as good a time to rest as any. As she began to drift into what would no doubt be an interrupted sleep, she thought of the man who'd lent her his own truck. A truck totaled at the bottom of a ravine. She imagined breaking the news. *"Thanks for the loaner, Manuel. It's in a ditch with two dead bikers. And, oh yeah, thanks for putting me up in your motel. Sorry it's burned to a crisp."* Hatch cursed to herself. *How much more damage could she do to this family?*

Her eyes fluttered and she began to give way to her body's need for recuperation. Just as her head dipped under the weight of exhaustion, she heard a loud rumble. Its sound was distinctly different, and it was one she recognized immediately.

Her eyes shot open wide, and she peered out the tinted windows of the bus. A single headlight illuminated the path of the approaching motorcycle. It pulled up to the gas station's store and parked along the curb.

Hatch recognized the man. He was at the table closest to her when she addressed the clubhouse. Undoubtedly, he'd been one of the men responsible for extensive damage to her face and body. And now he was alone.

In the light of the store, she watched the biker enter the store.

Hatch stood and thanked the rotund gentleman who had provided her with a seat and drink. Before stepping off the bus, she thanked the driver.

The bus driver looked confused and said, "You gettin' back on?"

Hatch turned and gave a pleasant smile. "No. I really appreciate you picking me up." She looked out toward the parked chopper. "But my ride's just arrived."

The man cocked an eyebrow high, wrinkling the smooth brown skin of his forehead. Hatch provided no answer and stepped out into the cold evening air.

Hatch walked outside the cone of light provided by the pump area and, under the cover of darkness, she made her way toward the corner of the detached store. She kept watch on the biker who was inside talking with the clerk. Hatch felt the knife at her side. It rubbed the outside of her right thigh as she moved. Her right hand touched her sweatshirt where the handle was.

The passengers began returning to the bus. The line in front of the bathroom had diminished. As she continued to watch the biker, the last person exited the restroom carrying a keychain connected to a rectangular block of wood roughly six inches long. The man, a fifty-something-year-old with wire-rimmed glasses set against his gaunt features, pressed the homemade keychain out toward Hatch and said, "Need to use it?" His breath was a mix of onion and red wine. Not a winning combination.

Hatch took the wood block. It was damp where the man had been holding it. "Thanks."

The man wiped his wet hands through his jet-black hair, slicking it back. "You're the last one. Just make sure you return the key to the lady at the counter when you're done."

"Sure thing," Hatch said. Her attention was still focused toward the store and the long-haired biker inside.

The man walked away and headed back to the bus humming the tune to a song Hatch didn't recognize. She didn't go to the bathroom. She didn't need to. She waited at the corner of the gas station store. The biker was asking the clerk something. The young Hispanic woman behind the counter responded with a shrug and a shake of her head. The biker did not seem pleased, slamming his fist down before storming out.

The last of the passengers who'd gotten off the bus made their unsteady navigation back and re-boarded. The biker stood outside the store's entrance and eyed the bus of drunk plumbers. As the door closed to the bus, he walked to his Harley Roadster.

Hatch noticed a dent in the right side of the fuel tank and smiled. Hatch whistled above the howl of the wind.

The biker whipped his head in Hatch's direction.

The man's eyes went wide as if he were a caged tiger and had just been prodded. He moved quickly at a half-sprint.

Hatch disappeared around the corner to the side of the building and, using the key, unlocked the bathroom door and slipped inside. She left it ajar and tucked herself alongside the frame on the hinge side.

A moment later, the door swung wide. Hatch remained pressed against the wall and the opened door covered her as the man stepped in.

The biker went straight for the closed stall along the adjacent wall. Hatch stepped from her concealment with the rectangular block in hand, still damp from the last passenger's use. The solid piece of wood poked out from the bottom of her right hand. Hatch brought the oversized keychain crashing down on the side of the man's neck. As the biker fell, she followed with a swift upward swing of her leg. Hatch's shin struck across the man's forehead. The compounded effect of the combination attack rocked the biker, and he landed face down on the floor, slamming his cheekbone onto the filthy tile with a sickening thwack.

She checked the man's pulse. Not dead, but definitely unconscious. Hatch then quickly set about searching him. Something she'd done countless times before as an MP, stateside and abroad. She was confident this man would have brought a weapon with him. It took only seconds to find it. A Glock 22 .40 caliber pistol was tucked into the front of his pants near his belt buckle. Hatch found it ironic. The criminal had chosen the most common weapon used by law enforcement agencies across the country.

Hatch took the keys to his motorcycle. She pulled his cell phone out of his pocket and stomped on it before tossing it into the toilet. She left the restroom and used the block as a wedge, kicking it into the gap under the bottom of the door. The pressure would delay the man's exit. It would only be temporary, but under the circumstances, every second counted.

The bus pulled away as Hatch walked over to the motorcycle.

She couldn't see inside, but she waved to her companions anyway. She then kicked her leg across the Harley-Davidson and put the key into the ignition. The bike was a good fit.

She rumbled away from the gas station and out into the night.

Hatch watched the taillights of the bus heading toward Las Cruces. At the fork in the road, she turned left and headed west, back into Luna Vista.

TWENTY-FOUR

HATCH ROLLED into Luna Vista with the borrowed motorcycle vibrating her inner thighs. It had been a while since she'd ridden, but it didn't take long before she had her bearings. She worked to balance the chopper as she took the bend in the road leading to the Moonbeam. Hatch passed the motel but refused to look in its direction. She didn't need any further reminders of that tragedy to resurface and derail her. The last time it had nearly cost her life. She thundered ahead and continued toward Main Street, and in particular, the police station which sat at its invisible dividing line.

Her plan had been a simple one: confront Chief Porter about what she had seen at the motel crime scene. She would give him the ultimatum of coming clean about his involvement and bring an end to the alliance with the bikers or Hatch would expose it to the media. She wasn't sure how the chief would receive this, but with the additional leverage of knowing about the laundering operation, it could tip things in her favor. The truth of Wendy's death needed to come out. And as corrupt as the chief might've become over the years, she hoped deep down he still held some of the values of a cop. Maybe she could unearth them and help bring about a change of perspective. And with it, justice for Wendy and the town of Luna Vista itself.

As she rode through Main Street, the few people out and about did a double take. It was obvious they recognized the chopper or what it represented but seeing a woman on it seemed to perplex them. Hatch paid them no mind and continued on. She brought the motorcycle to a stop in front of Harry's diner, deciding it might not be the best idea to pull up to the police station on a stolen Harley. She doubted the biker she'd left unconscious on the filthy bathroom floor would file a report, but it would've been suspicious, nonetheless, and diminish her standing when confronting the chief if he happened to notice.

Hatch got off the motorcycle and set it on its kickstand. Her thighs tingled from the aftershock of the continual vibration. She saw Harry through the diner's front window. He was busy wiping down the counter. There were a few patrons inside, most of which looked to be finishing up their meals. The diner would be closing within the hour.

Harry looked up from his work. His eyes widened and his jaw dropped open slightly. He was either shocked by her damaged face, visible from the light cast from the restaurant's interior, or by her new mode of transportation.

She didn't enter. Hatch held out a modicum of hope that the next time she spoke with Harry, it would be to share the fact she'd begun the process of righting his niece's death. The first step in bringing order to the chaos was across the street in the hands of the town's police chief.

Hatch crossed the street. She passed the closed gun shop and made her way to the station. She neared the same steps where earlier in the day Hatch had witnessed Porter spewing lies. Just as she began her ascent, she saw the chief exit.

Perfect. Maybe out here, in the open, he'll feel more exposed. Maybe he'll feel compelled to listen, Hatch thought as she quickened her pace. Chief Porter stood just outside the station and held the door open. Hatch slowed and stood just outside the streetlight's yellow glow. She halted altogether when she saw for whom he held the door. The chief laughed at something the man behind him had said.

Chief Porter gave a hearty backslap as the man stepped alongside him. Hatch recognized him. It was none other than the man she'd seen earlier in the biker's clubhouse. The well-dressed man stood abreast with the chief, wearing the exact same suit he had when she'd last seen him. She remembered the apathetic look on the man's face when Cain sicced his underlings on her. He'd done nothing to prevent it or to stop the savage beating she had taken at the hands of the bikers. He must've witnessed it all, including her being dragged away to be murdered.

And here he stood, once again side-by-side with the chief. Any hopes of leveraging compliance from the chief through threat of exposure were immediately dashed.

Who this well-dressed man was mattered to Hatch a great deal but confronting the chief now with this man alongside him would do nothing more than immediately alert the bikers as to her whereabouts. She would quickly be surrounded and outnumbered within a matter of minutes. No, this was definitely not the right time.

Hatch pushed herself further into the cover of darkness, making sure she stayed out of eyeshot. She ducked down, tucking her tall slender frame under the rise of the concrete steps.

From her position, she couldn't hear the conversation. She could only discern its tone, the lighthearted nature of it. *What did they have to be happy about? Two dead teenagers and a town under siege?* Hatch bit her lower lip.

Seeing the chief with the well-dressed man proved, without a shadow of doubt, the depth of the allegiance with the Savage Renegades. Hatch wondered who, if anybody, she could trust. The whole town laundered money for the gang. There must have been an agreement among the business owners. *Harry's diner? Or the Moonbeam?* she wondered. She didn't want to fathom it. Harry and Manuel seemed like men who would stand their ground. But if there's one thing Hatch learned in her short time in Luna Vista, it was nothing was as it seemed.

Hatch knew she was outgunned. The MC club, although now a few short, were coming for her. She still had to contend with the Outlaws, and Psycho was wounded but not out of the fight. Hatch crunched the numbers. She had somewhere between ten to fifteen adversaries of varying degree of skill closing in on her. The small town of Luna Vista suddenly seemed smaller. More disturbing was when she factored in law enforcement. The odds didn't tip any closer in her direction.

Hatch needed to put her trust in somebody. She weighed her options and took a leap of faith, trusting her gut.

Hatch had survived numerous encounters which would've left most others dead. Her saving grace was she trusted her instincts above all else. She had an uncanny ability to discern threats, to know friend from foe, and to follow her heart. Call it what you will, she had a good eye for people. Hatch had applied it in Hawk's Landing, and she had put her trust in Dalton Savage.

Here she was in a new battle zone and in desperate need of an ally. Hatch thought of Officer Cartwright. She didn't even know his first name, but regardless, knew he could be trusted. Without it, without his support, she was all alone.

Cartwright already helped her once when he pointed out the biker's clubhouse location. In hindsight, he was right about warning her not to go it alone. He'd made a judgment call in bringing her to the motel crime scene. And now it was her turn to put her trust in him.

From her squatting position, she heard as the two men walked away in the opposite direction, their voices trailing off. She flipped open her cell phone and dialed her only ally's number.

"Hey, Cartwright. It's me."

"Hatch? Wholly crap! Thank God you're alive," he said.

"Why so surprised? Did you hear something to the contrary?"

"No. Nothing, but the way you left and where you were headed

—I was worried. And it's been a while since I last saw you. I don't know—I guess I thought the worst."

"Where are you right now?"

"You won't believe it, but I was starting to make the drive out to the clubhouse."

Hatch smiled at the thought of Cartwright kicking in the door to a biker's den. "I thought it was out of your jurisdiction?" she teased.

"It is, but not when I'm off duty." Cartwright chuckled.

As foolhardy as it would've been for him to take on a biker gang, she was grateful for the sentiment. And any percentile of mistrust she held evaporated instantly.

"Well, you won't believe where I am."

"Are you going to make me guess?"

"I'm at your police station. Actually, I'm crouched down along-side it."

"Hatch, please tell me you're not going to pick a fight with the chief again?"

"For somebody who's only known me a matter of days, you're a pretty good judge of character," Hatch said.

"Let's meet up and regroup on this thing. Figure some semblance of a plan."

"What's to figure out? I think I've got a good handle on the way things work here in Luna Vista. Might be a little bit too big for me to handle, but if the right people were put into play, maybe it'll get sorted out."

"Whatever you're thinking of doing, don't go it alone," Cartwright pleaded.

Hatch knew the young officer was right. As tough as she was, to disregard the odds stacked against her and proceed without support would be a death sentence, even for someone as well-trained as Rachel Hatch.

"I'm going to wait across the street at Harry's. You won't be able to miss me." Hatch touched the dry blood caked to her fore-head and traced it back to its source. A gash, approximately one inch long extending down from her hair line. It would need stitches. A new scar to add to the many she'd accumulated over the years.

She heard the roar of Cartwright's engine through the phone. "I'll be there as soon as I can. Couple minutes out."

Hatch stood and walked back to where the Roadster sat. Harry was still inside cleaning up. She decided not to bother him. She leaned against the motorcycle's cantered seat and waited while the wind died down a bit.

Cartwright was right about his timeline. He actually pulled up five minutes after ending the call. He drove a red Toyota Tercel. Coming to a stop in the street alongside Hatch, he lowered his window and, giving his best impression of a creeper, said, "Hey stranger, can I give you a lift?"

He then noticed her face and the motorcycle she rested herself against. Cartwright mouthed the word *shit* as his expression begged for answers. Hatch just laughed and walked over to him. She opened the passenger door, but stopped before getting in. She turned and went back to the bike. Pulling the blade from the makeshift sheath on her hip, Hatch punctured the rear tire. Then did the same to the front one. The frame sunk lower. She then entered the Toyota without saying a word.

"That's a big knife." Cartwright pointed to the blade in her hand.

Hatch straightened her body and to slide it back into place along her right hip. "It was a gift."

"And that's an interesting mode of transportation you got there."

Hatch batted her eyelashes. "People in this town have been extremely generous."

"From the looks of things, and in particular your face, it would appear that you've been quite busy since I last saw you."

"What can I say—these guys are givers." She looked out the window.

Cartwright pulled away as Harry walked out of the diner. He looked over at the motorcycle and then toward the departing Toyota.

"So, where to now? You mentioned wanting to regroup," Hatch said. "Do you have some type of game plan?"

He gave a shake of his head. "No, but I figured two good brains could come up with something."

"I can fill you in on what I've learned during my conversation with some of the more talkative members of the Savage Renegades."

"This, I've gotta hear."

Hatch spent the next short chunk of time explaining what she'd learned without divulging exactly how she had extracted the information, much to Cartwright's chagrin.

From the look on the young officer's face, it was obvious to Hatch he had no idea about the money laundering scheme being used.

"If I describe somebody to you, do you think you'd be able to give me a name?"

Cartwright shrugged. "Small town. I'll give it my best shot."

"I put them around fifty years old. Maybe fifty-five. A little bit soft in the midsection. I'd put his height to be about 5'7". Bald, but he keeps a horseshoe of steely gray hair around the sides. He's got a thin mustache and wears wire-rimmed glasses."

Cartwright's jaw went slack and he pulled the car over to the right side of the roadway. "You just described Mitch Collins, the Mayor of Luna Vista. Why are you interested in him?"

It was Hatch's turn to be surprised. She anticipated the man to be a council member, a bigwig in the town. But realizing the mayor stood by while she was beaten and hauled off to be killed went beyond her comprehension.

"He was there."

"Where?" Cartwright asked.

"Your mayor was at the biker's clubhouse when I went in. He appeared from the back and was at a table with Cain, their leader, and his one-percenter."

Cartwright rubbed the space between his eyebrows and closed his eyes momentarily. He looked to be doing some type of deep meditation. Hatch knew she just dropped a mind-blowing bit of information on him. The head of their town was in collaboration with the gang directly responsible for two murders.

"I always just figured it was some unspoken truce. We look the other way and they don't turn this town into a war zone. Ya know, like some type of conciliatory agreement. I didn't think it could be as collusive a plan. Now you tell me the mayor's in on it? The man who runs this town is tied to the people destroying it."

"Corruption lives and breathes everywhere. Money influences. Crumbs for the cockroaches. Small towns are just as accessible to greed as bigger ones. Actually, the size of a place like Luna Vista makes it easier to control."

"I guess I just never thought it was this bad. Or maybe I somehow knew and refused to believe it. If the mayor's a part of it, that means so is the chief." Cartwright's voice trailed off.

"I know it's a lot to take in right now." Hatch twisted in her seat. The Glock dug into the small of her back. "I really appreciate all you've done to help me along this far. And I don't want you to feel obligated to go any further. But I really do need your help. I don't think I can do the rest of this alone. At least, not without a little bit of support."

"I'm still a cop," he offered weakly.

"You work for a dirty chief, but yes you're still a cop. I don't want to compromise that." Hatch gave a smile but felt it must've looked more like a frown. "It's refreshing to see somebody who still has their integrity. Let's come up with a plan that works for both of us."

Relief washed over him. "Do you have something in mind?"

"There's a house in town. I saw Psycho meet up with two of the bikers there the other day. If I had to guess, it's either a stash house for drugs or weapons. Maybe both. Whatever it is, I'm guessing it's an important piece of their business."

"So, what do you want to do about it?"

"I want to put a dent in their operation," Hatch said.

"A dent? And how do you plan to go about doing that?"

"I don't know yet. I'll do a little recon. We'll take it from there."

Cartwright drummed his fingers on the steering wheel.

"I know this is a lot to ask of you, but I want you to know I had intended to handle this a different way. I was on my way to confront your chief. I planned to tell him the evidentiary truth of Wendy's death. All done with the intent of forcing his hand with the threat of media exposure. I thought it might be enough to motivate him to take some action. If nothing else, bring about some justice." Hatch paused. "But when I saw him with the man from the clubhouse, I realized any direct approach would be a mistake, probably a fatal one."

"Then what now?"

"Now? I'm going to hit them where it hurts the most. If they're like every other gang in the world, that place is in their wallets. I want every business in town that's supported this criminal network to feel the pain when the money stops flowing in."

Without saying a word, Cartwright put the car into drive and pulled forward. "Right is right. I'll back your play as best I can. Tell me where the stash house is."

"Not far from here." Hatch looked ahead at the street, eyeing the roads she had committed to memory. "It's three streets down. Take the right and it's the fourth house in on the right-hand side."

They rounded the corner onto Bushnell Street. Up ahead she saw Macho's rust-colored Cadillac Fleetwood Brougham and the Honda Psycho had chased her in. She noted its new tires. Two motorcycles parked on the driveway closest to the street.

Hatch looked over at Cartwright with a big smile.

"I don't know what you're smiling about. But the fact that you are makes me absolutely terrified," he said.

"That's a good thing. Adrenaline will help you focus," Hatch said. Seriousness returned and her affect flattened. "From this point forward, you will have to be on your absolute A-game."

"Once again, the things you say scare the crap out of me."

"Don't worry, yet. Right now, I'm just gonna do a little recon. How about you loop the block and we'll park on the street that runs parallel behind this one."

He did as she instructed and drove around to the backside. Cartwright pulled up along the curb of an unlit house. There was a for sale sign posted in the overgrown yard. "I'm going to get out and take a little looksee. You stay put and keep your phone on."

She opened the door and stepped out into the cold night air.

"Are you sure about this?" he asked.

"No."

Hatch disappeared into the darkness between the houses.

TWENTY-FIVE

HATCH CREPT UP to the back of the house. The strong odor of marijuana and cigarette smoke, similar to the warehouse where she first encountered the Outlaws, permeated the space around the house. The temperature had dropped rapidly. She used the poorly maintained trees scattered throughout the backyard to conceal her movement. Hatch moved slowly under the assumption there could be a potential motion sensor. Most homes had them these days. She closed to a distance where she could clearly see the exterior walls on the back and left side. No sensors were visible. She continued her methodical approach. There was no timeline on this mission, so caution was used.

Approximately ten feet from the back of the house, she could hear angry voices. The wind reduced her ability to make out the details. Then one voice stood out among the rest. Hatch recognized the raspy crackle of Psycho. She pictured his face and envisioned it as he lit Wendy's room on fire. She no longer felt the cold. Her rage burned bright.

There was no more tree cover between where she stood and the back wall. Hatch committed. She moved quickly in a low crouch, staying beneath the window's sill. No motion sensor activated. The only light she needed to avoid came by way of the two back windows of the house. Hatch pressed herself against the rough stucco coat of the wall's exterior.

"That stupid bitch shot me in my foot! Ain't no way I'm letting you guys take her out! You've already failed once." His rant was cut short by a loud slapping sound.

"You're not in a position to give us orders. Or tell us how things are going to be handled. That's not the way it works!" an unrecognizable voice boomed. "I'm telling you right now this is a Savage Renegade problem. You Outlaws are done until we say otherwise. Go back to doing your job. Sell our drugs, bring us our money, and we'll take care of the rest."

Hatch remained pressed against the wall and continued listening. An orange-yellow glow seeped out from the window through a gap in the curtain. She was beneath the one closest to the left corner. She slowly stood. Edging her way to the gap, Hatch got her first glimpse inside. They were standing in the living room. It was sparsely furnished, making the abandoned warehouse look like a five-star luxury apartment. A couple of lawn chairs were set near a flat screen television that hung on an otherwise bare wall. Wires hung down to the floor and connected to a gaming console. Aside from that, the room was empty.

The two bikers stood with their backs to her and were facing the Outlaws. Each person's body language spoke of the tension in the air. Hatch was pleased, knowing she was at the root of it. On the shag carpet between them was a large, open duffle bag. Peeking out from within, Hatch could see stacks of cash.

Hatch decided to get a closer look at the layout so she could better prepare her next move. She stayed low and moved to the next window. She stepped up onto the slight rise of the concrete slab patio. This window was smaller, and instead of curtains, it had cheap blinds. Looking through the slats, she saw the tight confines of a small kitchen area, there were small boxes set aside on the floor with a couple chairs placed around a cardboard table. It looked like a poor version of a man cave card game, minus the cards.

A money counter machine was in the center of the cardboard table. It was of high quality, the type one might find in the back room of a banking facility capable of accurately counting large sums of cash in a matter of seconds. Around it was binding materials and clear plastic bags. A vacuum sealer was on the floor. Stacks of shrink-wrapped cash were set in varying heights.

On the same table as the cash machine were two white powdered bricks, most likely cocaine. One was opened, and around it was cutting agents and a scale. There were smaller bags scattered nearby. Hatch knew, without a doubt, this was a stash house. She was looking at a major arterial component in the heart of the Savage Renegades' operation. Her pulse quickened at the thought of destroying its contents.

One of the bikers entered the kitchen. Hatch remained absolutely still. The human eye is more likely to pick up movement. He didn't notice her. He was preoccupied grabbing up two bags containing broken-up white bits of powder. The contents of the Ziploc bags looked like drywall, but Hatch knew better. It was cocaine, cut and cooked into crack. It was a cheap and easy way to stretch the powder and increase profit. The biker then quickly returned to the other room.

Hatch returned to her original position at the first window. She looked through the gap and watched as the biker handed over one bag to Psycho and the other to Blaze. The biker shooed them away. "Don't know why you two are still standing around. Get to work."

Hatch was happy to see Xavier was not among them. But neither was Macho. It appeared the leader of the local gang was smart enough to distance himself from this part of the business and let his underlings handle the supply.

The two Outlaws departed without protest.

The biker with his back to her turned to face the one she'd seen in the kitchen. She recognized him immediately by the half-moon scar across the left side of his face.

Mongoose, the one-percenter, stood with the smug look of indignation etched across his face.

Hatch thought of Wendy, the girl whose burned silhouette still lay on the Moonbeam's floor, her anguish seared into the carpet fibers of room number two and forever into Hatch's mind. Now, only the stucco wall separated her from the man responsible. She fought against the urge to act, battling against the sense of urgency to take the fight to her enemy here and now. The opportunity might not present itself again, or with the odds she faced now. Two on one was a manageable feat. She'd faced worse and come out on top. She decided to seize it.

Hatch crept along the back wall, keeping beneath the kitchen window. She walked along the concrete slab porch to the rear door which accessed the home through the kitchen. She checked the knob. Always check the door before breaching. She'd learned that lesson well. As foolish as it would be to leave a door unlocked to a house filled with drugs, money, and weapons, criminals are human and sometimes they forgot. No luck. Locked.

She withdrew the large knife from her homemade cloth sheath. Hatch carefully worked the thick, sturdy blade into the gap between the door and its frame. She pried it apart and looked at the deadbolt. It was not locked, which meant her task of gaining access would now be markedly easier.

Hatch slid the knife down until the sharpened edge made contact with the top of the doorknob's latch. She moved the blade downward and inward in an arc. The blade scraped against the metal latch. The blade caught it and she felt the resistance of the spring-loaded lock. Hatch pressed harder. With the extra added pressure, she forced the separation. The door popped open a quarter of an inch.

She kept the knife in place with her left hand, which throbbed painfully at its use, and with her right, she slowly opened the door. Hatch listened carefully. With the door open a few inches, she could hear more clearly inside the structure. She waited to ensure no sign of her enemy appeared.

Hearing the conversation between the two bikers still taking place in the living room area, Hatch slipped inside. She closed the door quietly behind her. With the wind as unpredictable as it was, she didn't want it slamming closed and alerting them to her presence.

Inside, she felt exposed. She set the knife down gently on the counter near the door and withdrew the Glock from the small of her back.

Pressing the gun forward but keeping it tight, Hatch moved across the linoleum floor, taking care to walk heel-to-toe and rolling each step on the outside of her foot. She moved with the controlled silence of a ninja. Her elbows were tight to her body and she maintained a level firing position, keeping a slight bend in her knees while she moved slowly forward.

She pressed up against the wall separating the kitchen from a narrow hallway. The left led to the living room where the two bikers stood. Hatch was close.

"You heard what Cain said. Once the Outlaws make that last run, we're closing up shop here in town and moving on." The man spoke with authority. Hatch assumed it was the one-percenter.

"I don't get it. We've had problems before. We're always able to squash 'em. Luna Vista's been a real win for us," the other man said.

"I don't call the shots. I follow orders. If Cain says we're moving on, then we're moving on. No need to question it," Mongoose said.

"I'm not questioning it. I'm just saying," the other biker grumbled.

"I know what you're saying. But I guess it's a little different this time." Hatch heard the flick of a lighter and then the one-percenter continued, "That crazy bitch killed two of our guys, beat the crap out of Chisel and stole his chopper. There's no telling what she'll do next. She's making this complicated."

"What about the Outlaws? When we up and leave, their protection goes with us. What if they start talking to save their asses?"

"That's why we're going to leave them a little surprise." The one-percenter laughed. "Another tragic accident in the increasingly dangerous town of Luna Vista."

Heavy footsteps approached and Hatch moved back from the room's entrance a step. Mongoose, the one-percenter, walked past the opening a split second later. He proceeded down the hallway. From her angle, she couldn't see where he went. But a moment later she heard a door open followed by a draft of cool air. She guessed he must have gone to the attached garage. During her surveillance of the house the other day, she had noticed the one-car garage. *What did he need to get from it?* she wondered.

She thought about stepping out on the solitary man in the living room. They were temporarily divided. But it would leave her in the middle and make her ability to confront both men, both threats, impossible. Hatch tempered her need to act and continued to play the waiting game.

A moment later, she heard the door at the end of the hallway slam closed and the one-percenter walked back. His gait was labored. As each plodding step grew louder and closer, Hatch heard an accompanying bang and a sloshing sound. Sight unseen, she couldn't quite decipher it by sound alone. But as he passed the kitchen opening, she smelled the distinct odor of gasoline.

"Oh, man! You're gonna burn those sons of bitches?" the other man asked in a pitchy, excited tone.

"It's a crack house, right? Dumb things happen to crackheads. A fire here won't draw nearly as much attention as the fire at the motel."

Hatch heard the man set both drums down in the living room.

"How're you going to do it?" the other biker asked.

"Oh, I'm not doing it. You are. Cain's going to call a meeting with the Outlaws. Tell 'em to meet here. Once they're all inside—poof," the one-percenter said matter-of-factly. "There's no way I'm going to be anywhere near here when this one goes up in flames. That bitch saw me at the last fire. Who knows, maybe the cop did, too. Both are liabilities now. And will have to be dealt with to ensure we have a clean break from this town."

"I've got this, brother. You can count on me." the other biker offered.

"I'll take this cash out to my bike. Go get the rest of the stash bagged up."

Hatch looked behind her to the table with the two kilos of cocaine and the stacked cash.

TWENTY-SIX

HATCH PREPARED for what was coming. She could hear the biker's footsteps approaching. The knife was still on the counter. Although she had a gun, the shot would be loud, and she preferred the idea of leveling the playing field and giving her a one-on-one shot with the one-percenter.

It would be a more silent weapon of choice under the circumstances, but if she were to go for the knife now, it would be too big a move, too risky. Hatch held the Glock in her right hand, keeping it at the ready while using her damaged left hand to balance it. The swelling in her left index finger had subsided a bit. It was a deep purple at the break near the joint. Painful, but not unbearable. The current threat facing her enabled her to push away the thought of its discomfort as she focused intently on the task at hand. She now relied solely on the steadiness of her right hand connected to her burned and damaged arm, the one the Army had told her was no longer at full capacity. Although, during her recovery, she had trained to use it again, the gun in it now felt foreign to her.

The man was close now, maybe a foot away, within a second or two he'd be visible. Maybe she'd get lucky and both men would enter.

Hatch pressed out the weapon, centering it at her solar plexus. Everything at this close range would be pointblank shooting. No sights needed. She remained pressed flat against the wall and breathed slowly, controlling the pump of adrenaline,

The biker entered. It was not the one-percenter and he walked in alone. His hair was pulled back in a messy ponytail with a couple tendrils of greasy, curly black hair hanging down over his face. The man's face was lined with scars telling of a violent nature. It was dented with pock marks ravaged by years of adolescent cystic acne.

Seeing the man was alone, Hatch changed her game plan. She needed to control him silently without alerting the others. The front door slammed and she heard the slosh of gasoline in the other room. The one-percenter must be dousing the walls and carpet.

The pock-marked biker passed by and went to the refrigerator. He didn't notice her standing there with a gun. His attention was on the open fridge. Hatch was out of his peripheral vision and stepped off from the wall.

The man turned suddenly and stood facing down the barrel of her gun with a cold beer in his hand. They were separated by a mere four feet distance. But Hatch had him dead to rights.

His eyes were wide with fear and he dropped the bottle. It shattered on the linoleum, sending a shower of beer onto her pants. With her damaged left hand, Hatch brought her broken finger up to her lips and gave the universal symbol for *shut your damn mouth*. Her eyes intensely punctuated the importance of his compliance.

The man said nothing. He was frozen in place as the beer bubbled on the ground between them. His eyes darted between the table full of cash and drugs and the open doorway to the hallway. She watched as the man weighed his options.

Hatch then took her finger from her lip and pointed down to the ground while keeping the weapon centered on the man's head. He remained frozen and didn't follow her non-verbal command.

She was left with only one choice: eliminate this threat so she could deal with the other. But she knew in doing so, she would give the other man an advantage. Plus, Hatch didn't like the idea of thinking of herself as an executioner, even though these men had it coming. They sealed their death warrant when they murdered Wendy. The girl's memory momentarily unlocked her anger but not in an unbalanced sort of way as it had done during her misguided attempt at the clubhouse. It now gave her the strength to make the difficult decision on what needed to be done.

In the split second it took to commit to the act, the pock-marked biker did something she hadn't expected. Especially in his frozen state. He raised his hands in surrender. Hatch exhaled as the man moved them slightly above his midline. He then began slowly making his way to the floor. He went down on his right knee, keeping his eyes on her the whole time.

Good. He's come to his senses, she thought. At least she could control him, reposition the man to create a human shield if need be, and then in turn address the secondary threat in the other room more effectively. As the man's left knee touched down, Hatch got a better look at him. She realized he was slightly older than she'd anticipated. The long hair wasn't as black as she first thought. There were bits of gray strands scattered amongst it and she guessed him to be somewhere in his mid-forties. His hard life had taken a toll on his body and his knees cracked loudly as he shifted his weight back on his ankles. She could see the strain in his eyes. With the man on his knees and hands halfway up between his waistline his shoulders, she pointed to the ground again, signaling for him to prone himself face flat on the floor.

There was a moment of hesitation before the man began to do as instructed. He bent forward and placed his left hand on the ground like a three-legged dog. Loose strands of squiggly hair partially blocked his face from view. His right hand moved but not to the floor. Instead, it slapped back his leather cut and moved to his hip.

He moved faster than she'd anticipated. He retrieved a gun as he fell to his right side, landing in broken glass and spilled beer. He fired without aiming. Hatch dodged to the right as the round impacted the wall behind her. "She's in here!" he yelled as he scooted back against the open refrigerator.

Hatch circled to the right as the man fired a second, equally sloppy shot. She dipped low, changing elevation. Her movements made it hard for the man to track her as she squeezed the trigger. A deafening bang preceded the silence that followed.

The pock-marked man's head rocked back. Blood spatter coated the interior of the fridge, painting a leftover Chinese food container in a bright red. The effectiveness of her single shot was evident.

She prepared herself for her next attacker, taking up position against the back door. Her Glock was pressed out in the direction of the hallway entrance. The trigger reset and was ready to deploy another round.

An eerie silence followed. No one-percenter.

Seconds passed like minutes. She cast a quick glance to the dead man. No more waiting. She stepped forward toward the open doorway, walking over the pock-marked man's body. Her feet crunched the broken glass. The linoleum was slick with a combination of beer and blood.

As she got closer, Hatch began to slice the pie of the door, moving wide toward the right side of the kitchen so she could get a vantage point into the hallway. Step by careful step, she slowly began to clear the hall leading to the living room.

If the man they called Mongoose wasn't going to come to her, then she would bring the fight to him. Not an optimal plan of action, but sometimes in battle you have to engage your enemy head on.

She'd cleared as much of the hallway as she could from within the kitchen and still no sign of the man. She prepared to step through the fatal funnel when she heard the front door slam.

Damnit! He's on the run! she thought.

Hatch stepped into the hallway. As soon as she did, she was met by an intense heat. She'd been hyper-focused on preparing for the fight. She'd forgotten about the gasoline. She quickly understood why the one-percenter hadn't come in after her. After the gunshot, he must've decided to finish what he had started at the motel. He'd lit it on fire. But she didn't hear the rumble of his motorcycle. *Where was he?*

She turned and rushed to the back door, the one she'd pried open with the knife. As she turned the knob, Hatch heard a loud bang. A bullet ripped through the door, just missing her head. She retreated, taking cover behind the open door of the refrigerator. With the heat of the fire at her back and the unseen gunman in the rear, she was effectively pinned down. Hatch sought to find a remedy to the situation.

Hatch couldn't see out the kitchen window. She darted to the switch on the wall near the doorway and cut the lights. The room went dark. It would take a moment for her vision to adjust so she'd be better able to see outside. Either way, the one-percenter had a much better point of aim. He could fire in from multiple vantage points where she only had the one.

Smoke began to pour in from under the gap in the backdoor. He had doused the backside of the house. She was now trapped on two sides and from two threats.

Hatch began a low crawl across the poorly maintained linoleum. Her elbow slipped slightly on the blood-covered floor. She slogged through, squirming forward on her knees and elbows. Hatch stayed below the rapidly descending black smoke and hoped her sprawl kept her out of his gunsights. The back wall was now engulfed in flame, further shielding her from view.

There was only one avenue of escape left: down the hallway to the garage.

The flames were making quick work of the house, burning their way along the carpet and walls. The fire was already at the kitchen's threshold, consuming the oxygen and seeking more. Hatch crossed into the hallway and took up a hunched crouch, trading speed for oxygen.

The paint along the hallway walls blistered and bubbled. The drywall underneath went up like a tinderbox. The heat was unbearable and worse was the thick layer of smoke. The top three feet from the ceiling was now an impenetrable cloud of smoke.

As Hatch made her way down the hall, the tingle in her damaged right arm returned as if the fire's taunt awakened the physical memory. It brought her back to the months of agonizing recovery, and it didn't paralyze her with fear. In the moment, it was the first time she'd faced fire as an enemy since that day. And if she were to be honest with herself, the thought of it terrified her.

Hatch took two quick inhales followed by a long slow exhale. Combat breathing. *Get the oxygen to the brain get so you can make good decisions. Take yourself out of the fight or flight mode. Survive.* She willed herself to listen.

Hatch immediately withdrew back into the kitchen and grabbed a dirty rag from the sink. She ran it under water, saturating the rag and then pressing it over her nose and mouth with her damaged hand. Her right still held the Glock. The stink of the rag was almost unbearable, but she endured. The odor was trivial in comparison to its alternative. *Survive.*

With the rag pressed to her face, she crept low and moved quickly toward the opening. Hatch ran into the hallway as the flames gave chase. She came upon a bedroom on the right. She looked to the window as it shattered. A flaming gas can landed on the bed and the room erupted in flames. Another potential avenue of escape was effectively cut off. She was being driven forward toward the garage. He was forcing her there.

Whatever his plan, it ended in that garage. *Where the hell was Cartwright? He must've heard the gunshots or seen the fire. Didn't matter now.*

Hatch paused and felt the door. No heat. She turned the knob and pushed the door open.

The garage was dark. No windows. Worse, it was filled with junk stacked on other junk. A proverbial hoarder's paradise. There was no room for a car. There was barely enough room for Hatch to navigate her way. She did her best to keep the weapon pointed out as she cleared the space in front like a blind person without a cane. The fire had made it hard for her eyes to adjust to the darkness. She bumped her way to the left toward where the overhead door would be.

The closer she got, the more Hatch's vision began to clear. On the far side was a door leading out the front to the driveway area. She made her way, climbing over the piles. Sharp objects of an unknown and unseen variety stabbed at her as she desperately crawled to her only possible salvation. In a matter of seconds, the fire from the interior of the house would make its way into the garage, following the same path she'd taken.

She wedged herself in alongside the door. Hatch gripped the knob. She knew the one-percenter would be waiting for her on the other side. With her broken finger, she began a slow turn. Feeling the latch give way, she pushed. Nothing. The door held fast.

Something was blocking it. Squaring herself to the door, Hatch leveled her shoulder, striking hard against the wood. As poorly constructed as this house seemed to be, the door was made of a heavy wood. She turned her back to it, and donkey kicked with her right leg. Her heel struck hard alongside the knob. The shock of the impact reverberated up her leg and into in her torso, yet it didn't budge an inch.

Hatch spun when she heard a sound from the other side of the door. A loud rumble of a motorcycle.

"Burn in hell, bitch!" she heard over the engine.

The sound of the chopper faded away until it was gone. Hatch was left in silence.

As if on cue, the flames tore their way into the garage. This room, this hoarder's heaven, was a sea of flammable items. Desperate, she slammed herself into the door again. Still nothing. She wished she hadn't set the knife on the counter. She might've been able to pop the hinge bolt and dismantle the door.

Whatever he'd placed in front of it was heavy enough that no matter how much she battered the door, it wouldn't give.

The fire lit the room up and Hatch could make out her surroundings. She then looked to the garage door and seeing the lower lip metal handle at the base, worked her way over to it. She tucked the pistol away and, squatting low, pulled up with all her might. It was an awkward angle and it didn't lift. Frustrated, she saw why the door didn't move. The rollers were off their track. The overhead door was completely jammed.

Not one for giving up, Hatch was quickly running out of ideas as she scanned the room of junk, looking for anything she could use to bash her way out. And then she heard a sound outside.

The firelight dimmed as smoke began to fill the room. In the flickering darkness, she suddenly felt dizzy. Her oxygen was quickly being eaten by the fiery monster approaching. The back of the garage was already fully engulfed. It would only be a matter of minutes, maybe less, before the whole place would be consumed. Her legs buckled and her eyes burned. And then she heard the sound again coming from outside. It was louder than the fire's crackle, louder than the junk being swallowed up by the flames. From outside came a scratching sound of metal on wood. Hatch wondered if she was starting to hallucinate.

It was from outside the door. She climbed back over to it.

A loud crashing sound. Hatch reached for her gun but was slow on the draw as the door opened.

Hatch could barely make out his features through the blur of her eyes. Standing in front of her, his face illuminated by the approaching flames, was Cartwright.

The insertion of fresh air fed the fire and it burned wildly out of control, making a last-ditch effort to grab hold of Hatch. She clumsily lunged forward and fell into the officer's arms. Her body suddenly gave way to the exertion and lack of oxygen.

Cartwright caught her underneath her armpits and did a modified dummy drag, pulling her away from the house. Her leg banged against metal and she looked at the cause. The thing securing the door and preventing her escape was the other biker's motorcycle. The dead man's motorcycle had been pushed up against the door, sealing her in the fiery tomb.

She coughed and spit up. Her saliva was dark like charcoal.

Cartwright crouched down beside her. She was hunched over with her hands on her knees, gasping. She fought to get air into her lungs and clear the crud that was coating her throat. Hatch wiped her eyes on her sleeve. Through it all, she could still smell the nastiness of the damp rag she used to cover her face.

It took a few minutes of filling her lungs with fresh air before Hatch felt functional. The cool helped. Hatch felt a surge of energy, more likely fueled by anger, and she rose up. Cartwright stood with her.

"I looped the block after I dropped you off. I figured I could reposition myself better. I didn't want to draw attention. I wanted to get a better angle on the house, but when I came around the corner, I had seen the two cars leave, so I followed them for a minute, trying to get an idea of where they were going. When I returned, the whole front of the house was on fire. One of the bikers was riding off, but when I didn't see you, I didn't chase him. I figured you were in trouble. I saw the chopper leaning against the door and I heard the banging." He was quiet for a moment and looked down at his feet. "I'm sorry."

"I'm just glad you came back," Hatch said. And then broke into an uncontrollable coughing spree. "I owe you my life. Would've been dead if you didn't."

"I'm just sorry I didn't come back sooner."

She looked around. "I'm going after him." And then eyeing Cartwright, Hatch said, "I don't think you should come on this one."

He looked hurt.

"You'll need to keep your distance from me on this. Call in the fire." She coughed again. "And there's a dead man inside."

He gave a puzzled look and then eyed the motorcycle on the ground. She could see he put two and two together.

"What are you going to do?" Cartwright asked.

"If you have to ask, then you definitely should stay behind."

Hatch walked over to the motorcycle and righted it. The keys were in the ignition, dangling from a metallic skull keychain. *How fitting for a dead man's bike,* she thought.

"How will I know you're okay?" Cartwright fidgeted with nerves.

"I'll meet you at Harry's in an hour. If I'm not there—"

Hatch fired up the bike. She headed down the driveway and onto the road, leaving Cartwright and the burning house behind her.

TWENTY-SEVEN

HATCH PUSHED the limits of the motorcycle. Not completely comfortable with her mode of transportation, she found herself fighting for balance as she accelerated into the night. She passed by the road leading to Moonbeam. As she left the town behind, she saw in the distance, maybe just shy of a mile, the red of a single taillight. The one-percenter.

There was no traffic, and Hatch knew her headlights would give her away. After a toggle of the switch, she was cast in darkness. The only light, minimal as it was, came from the cloud-covered moon above. Focusing on the red light ahead, she began closing the distance.

His chopper's roar was louder than the bike she rode. It masked the sound of her approach.

Hatch was smart enough to know that, at some point, whether accidental or intentional, he would likely pick her up in his side mirrors. She just wanted to ensure she was as close as possible before he did.

They were nearing what she now knew was the halfway point between Luna Vista and the Savage Renegades' clubhouse. Undoubtedly, reinforcements would be there, if not small in number, enough to unbalance any advantage she might have over this killer. She decided there was no way she could allow him to get there.

Stopping him wouldn't be easy. Hatch was trained to use the pursuit intervention technique, or as it was more commonly known as, the PIT maneuver. She had deployed it on numerous occasions and with varying degrees of success. But she'd used a car, and one time a Humvee. Deploying such a tactic with a motorcycle would undoubtedly send both into a dangerous and potentially deadly spin out.

With ten feet of distance between, he hadn't seen her in the side mirror. His lack of awareness was most likely attributed to overconfidence, believing Hatch was still entombed in her fiery coffin.

Hatch seized the element of surprise and opened up the throttle. The bike bucked and propelled her forward. She closed the last few feet between them, pulling up alongside his left. Her front wheel passed the metal studded black leather saddlebags hung near the back end of the custom chopper. At this point, her proximity to him was unmissable. He turned his head. Hatch gave a wink. His face displayed as much surprise as it did anger.

Before he separated himself from her, Hatch did something crazy, even for her. She kicked out with her right foot, striking hard against the leather saddlebag. The explosive movement pushed her to the left and the bike wiggled wildly out of control. She used all of her strength to maintain purchase with the roadway and to keep her from laying the bike down.

She slowed and watched the aftermath of her kick.

The one-percenter fishtailed. In an effort to adjust, he overcorrected, and in the process went off the main road and into the uneven paving on the side. The loose dirt and gravel exacerbated the situation and threw the chopper into a vicious spin. Hatch watched the MC club's most dangerous member lose control and hit a deep divot in the ground. The angle at which the front wheel struck the pothole brought the front end to an immediate halt. The momentum flipped the bike up to the right. The man and his motorcycle were one mass hurtling upward. He was airborne for a moment. Then both collided with the hard ground with a bang. The engines roared as the bike continued to slide sideways with the one-percenter trapped underneath. The screech of metal against pavement was deafening, an indescribable amplification of a nail being dragged across a chalkboard.

The rear wheel continued to rotate, kicking up a wild swirl of dust. Her target and the wrecked chopper momentarily disappeared into the surrounding cloud.

Hatch rolled to a stop on the side of the road approximately twenty feet from the biker. The spinning wheel stopped its rotations and the dust settled enough for her to clearly see the man. She now understood what had brought the sliding bike to a stop. He'd slid into a large boulder. The biker was wedged between a rock and the dirt ground. *He's literally between a rock and a hard place,* Hatch thought, laughing to herself.

The one-percenter was on his back. From the distance and in the darkness of the unlit road, it was impossible for Hatch to tell if the man was alive or dead.

She rested the bike on its kickstand and left the engine running. Hatch then pulled the pistol from the small of her back. She aimed the gun at the man. The air was ripe with burned rubber and dust. As she got closer to the downed chopper, Hatch smelled something else. Gasoline.

At first, Hatch wasn't sure if the odor was coming from her, having just escaped the gasoline-doused shack of a house. But as her eyes settled into the darkness, she saw a pool of fluid covering both the biker and the ground around the crash site. Fuel emptied from the cracked tank, leaking onto its rider and the area surrounding him. The man, the Savage Renegades' one-percenter, Mongoose, the person directly responsible for Wendy's death, remained unmoving, pinned between the heavy weight of the custom-made motorcycle. Hatch kept the gun trained on the man's center mass.

She slowed her approach. Outside of the fuel-soaked ground, she stopped. Hatch watched him. The answer to her question was given in the gentle rise and fall of his chest.

The man's eyes suddenly shot open wide. He gasped and then coughed violently. Even in the dark, Hatch could see he was severely wounded. In her early days as an MP, she'd worked more than her fair share of fatal and nonfatal crashes. Looking at the man now, she was uncertain which category this might fall.

"You bitch!" he yelled. After getting the two words out, he made a gurgling, choking sound. He spat to clear it. His saliva was thick with blood. "I'm gonna kill you!"

"I think I've heard that before. Too many times to count since I got to this little town." Hatch snarked. "Come to think of it, a lot of dead men have said that to me."

Hatch kept the Glock pressed forward. The Trijicon sight glowed green and the center dot at the end of the barrel hovered over the wounded biker's bloodstained nametag. He was unable to move, or at least hadn't moved yet. His left hand was free from the wreckage, but his right was pinned underneath, trapped below the bike in a similar fashion to the rest of his lower extremities.

She knew the man had a weapon. He'd fired at her in the house. She didn't know if he was right-handed or left, but assumed he was most likely a righty. By percentile, the majority of the world's population was right-handed. "Show me your right hand. Do it now!" Hatch commanded.

The man spit again. "I can't move it."

THE SAVAGE RENEGADES enforcer struggled against the weight of the chassis. His right leg was barely visible under the twisted chrome. His left was flipped out to the side in an unnatural position. He was effectively pinned to the ground and it was unlikely that he'd be able to get the leverage needed to lift the bike off him. In his disabled status, Hatch faced another dilemma.

The pad of her finger rubbed gently against the half-moon polymer trigger. She thought for a moment about sending a bullet into the center of the man's chest, bringing an end to this now. But killing someone in cold blood, as deservedly as it might be, didn't sit with Hatch.

The man groaned loudly in pain as he moved his left hand and pushed at the bike ineffectively.

"Stop moving!" Hatch commanded.

"It hurts," he muttered. The man ignored her command and thrust his left arm across his body.

The law of averages proved wrong, as the injured biker was left-handed. He pushed back his leather vest and accessed a shoulder holster tucked under his right arm. His movement was surprisingly quick considering his circumstance. The one-percenter pulled the gun free.

Hatch fired and then dove to the right as the biker sent a hail of bullets her way. She landed on the dirt and rolled into a water runoff area. The recessed ground gave her cover.

She counted five or six rounds. He'd been quick with the gun, and so Hatch didn't see the make or model. She could tell it was a semi-automatic. No telling how many rounds the weapon had left.

Hatch was confident her shot had hit the mark. She'd fired quickly, but accurately. Lying on the cool dirt, she heard the man scream out. *Still alive.*

Another rapid burst of gunfire. One round struck nearby, but there was no focus to the shots. She crawled along the dirt gulley, working her way back closer to the man.

"Give it up," Hatch said.

Her voice did as intended, drawing fire from the man. She stayed low. Three gunshots boomed out, sending rounds her way. The volley of fire was followed by a sound she was hoping to hear. A mechanical click.

Hatch stood. The man looked horrified at the sight of her standing only a few feet away, unharmed.

"Get it over with then," the man wheezed. The white of his tank top was saturated in his blood. Her one shot had found its mark. Center mass.

"You're already dead. You just don't know it yet," Hatch said.

"So, what, you're just going to leave me here?"

Hatch shrugged. "Yup. Maybe you should spend your last few minutes of life thinking about the young girl you killed. Her name was Wendy."

One eye fluttered out of sync with the other. Blood loss had taken hold. His motor functions were starting to fail.

As she turned to leave, the connecting wire to the motorcycle's battery sparked. Hatch dove back into the ditch. The chopper erupted into a ball of fire. The heat and light flashed overhead as Hatch ducked for cover. The one-percenter screamed. His voice was high pitched, almost lyrical sounding.

The fire quickly dissipated, and Hatch stood back up and dusted herself off.

The man on the ground was now a burned char not unlike Wendy in her final moments. Karmic justice prevailed.

She evaluated the man. This time, she noticed no rise and fall to his chest. Hatch slipped the weapon back into her waistline and began walking toward her borrowed motorcycle. Just as she was about to mount it, a thought occurred as she looked at the black leather saddlebags hung from the back end of the dead man's chopper.

Hatch walked over to the bags and unhooked them. They were still warm to the touch but not as badly damaged as one might've thought. She popped the latch open and peered inside. Each bag contained several shrink-wrapped stacks of cash. The top and bottom of each stack was a one-hundred-dollar bill. By her glancing calculation, the money within was substantial.

Returning to her motorcycle, Hatch strapped the saddlebags to the bike. She drove away, heading south, back toward Luna Vista as the wind began to kick up in wild blasts around her.

TWENTY-EIGHT

SHE PULLED the motorcycle around the back of Harry's restaurant. Hatch figured now was not the time to draw any unnecessary attention. It was dark and late as she parked between a dumpster and the building's wall.

Hatch walked around the alley up to the front entrance and was happy to see that the light was still on inside. Harry hadn't left for the evening. As she eyed him through the door's glass, she wasn't sure whether he'd be happy to see her. But he deserved to know the man behind his niece's death had been brought to justice. The Outlaws were still out there somewhere, but Hatch needed a moment to reset before she went back on the hunt. Harry's coffee would help.

The smell of the one-percenter's fiery death still clung to her clothes. She felt somewhat self-conscious of it as she entered the diner with the biker's duel saddlebags hoisted over her left shoulder.

The door provided its usual chimed alert, but the sound of it didn't have the familiar cheerful note as it had during her other visits to the diner. The weight of the events of the last couple days was starting to wear Luna Vista's charm thin.

Harry barely looked up from the counter. But when he saw it was

Hatch, he made his best effort to right himself. He gave the satchel on her shoulder a double take as she approached. Without waiting for her to indicate otherwise, he took a mug, set it in front of her and filled it with piping hot coffee.

"You look like hell warmed over, Hatch. Are you okay?"

Hatch thought about that question and really didn't know the answer but offered one anyway. "I've been a lot worse."

Harry gave a slight non-judgmental shake of his head. "Hungry?"

"Not tonight. Coffee's fine." Hatch sat in her usual spot and set the saddlebags on the seat typically occupied by the chief of police. *Fitting*, she thought.

"I'll get you some ice. That finger of yours looks pretty bad."

Hatch had almost forgotten about it. The initial pain of it had subsided and now its dull throb melded with the sea of other injuries she'd amassed in the last twenty-four hours. She was running on fumes. "Thanks.'

Before Harry could walk away to retrieve the ice, she stopped him. "Hold on a sec. Harry, I came here for a reason tonight. I wanted to look you in the eyes and let you know the guy responsible for Wendy's death paid in full for that crime."

Harry's eyes watered. And this time he didn't have the strength to hold back the emotional tidal wave. Tears streamed down the big man's face as he reached across the counter and grabbed her non-damaged hand with a gentle firmness. "I don't know what it is you did. And I'm not sure I want to know. But thank you."

Hatch silently received the man's gratitude.

"So, what now? They're not going to just let this go," he said with a sniffle.

Hatch shrugged. "I don't know. I still haven't got what I came to this town for yet. But once I do, I'll be moving on." Hatch left out the part about finding the three members of the Outlaws but figured there was no point in burdening the man with that worry. "After I go, I think the town's gotta come together and decide what kind of place Luna Vista's going to be. I know for a fact the people that have been running it don't have the community's best interest in mind. And the only way that's ever going to change is if the people in this town push back. And if what I heard tonight was true, it looks like your biker problem is going to be moving on as well. The heat I've brought down on them was too much." Hatch thought about explaining the double meaning in her last comment, having just left the burned biker, but it was a joke only she would find funny.

"I think you're absolutely right. We've stood by too long and allowed council members to make decisions on our behalf that aren't for our benefit. Thanks for lifting the veil of lies and exposing it to us. Just wish it hadn't taken such tragedy to bring it to light. Sadder still is the call to arms came from you, an outsider with no personal connection to this town or its people." Harry gave a slight squeeze of her hand before letting go. "You're a unique person, Rachel Hatch."

She had no response, awkward in the face of such a compliment. The jingle sounded at the door and she spun. Hatch's right hand was already moving toward the gun at the small of her back. She stopped when she caught sight of the newcomer. She was relieved to see Officer Cartwright standing in the entranceway.

Cartwright walked up to the counter and took a seat on the stool to the left of Hatch. "Glad to see you're okay." Cartwright's eyes then scanned the numerous visible injuries. "Okay might be an overstatement, but at least you're alive."

Harry looked at the two of them. "You both smell like you've been sittin' around an outdoor fire pit all night."

Hatch and Cartwright looked at each other. There was no smile in their faces, just the knowing glance of two people who'd faced death and come out the other side unscathed.

Harry filled a cup and slid it across the counter to Cartwright before disappearing into the kitchen area. "I'll grab you that ice and let you two talk."

"I don't even want to know, do I?" Cartwright asked quietly.

"It wouldn't matter anyway. It's not your jurisdiction," Hatch said with a wink, accompanied by a very weak smile. Her attempt at humor fell flat.

"What now?" he asked.

"Funny, Harry just asked me the same thing." Hatch took a sip from her mug. "I think it's time for me to get out of here. I've got somebody to see in the morning. It's what I came here for. After that, who knows. Not sure where it's going to lead me."

"Feels a bit strange to say this, but it's going to be weird without having you around. You've done something to this town. It's changed. I can see the differences already because I see them in me."

"I just realized I don't even know your first name," Hatch said.

"It's Dale."

"Well, Dale, you're smart enough to fix what's wrong with your agency. Run it. Lead it. If not by rank, by action. You'd be surprised. I think a lot of people around this town are looking for somebody to step up. I really think you could be that person." Hatch paused for a moment. She found it strange to give someone else life advice when hers was in a constant state of unbalance. "That's got to come from you. If you don't like something, change it. If it's not right, make it right."

The man slurped his coffee and then looked at her. "You're right. And I will."

Hatch stirred a little sugar into her coffee. She needed the boost. Her adrenaline ran wild tonight and she needed it to help balance her system. Hatch set the spoon down and took a long pull from the mug, tipping it back to get the last drops when she caught something out of the corner of her eye. Somebody standing in the front window of Harry's diner. As she turned, Cartwright did the same. His eyes wide.

Cartwright dove to his right, knocking her mug out of her hand as he tackled Hatch to the ground. An explosion of gunfire erupted, shattering the diner's windowpane.

Hatch pushed the young officer off her and scrambled back. She withdrew the Glock and aimed it out toward the threat, but the shooter was gone. She looked over at the man who had knocked her down, Hatch saw the blood emptying out onto the black and white porcelain checkered floor around him.

Hatch launched herself up and ran toward the main door. She called back to Harry, who had ducked behind the grill in the kitchen. "Check on Cartwright. He's hit. Looks bad. Put pressure on the wound and call for help!"

She rushed out into the night. The shooter was out there some-where. It was Psycho. She'd caught a glimpse of the man. His hair back in the tight cornrows he'd had during their first encounter. *I should've killed him when I had the chance*, Hatch seethed. She wouldn't make that mistake again.

Cartwright lay wounded, possibly dead, on the floor of the diner after putting himself in the line of fire to save her. Thanks to his quick thinking and heroic valor, she was alive. Psycho had made a critical error. He hadn't finished the job. And now Hatch planned to settle the score. No shots to non-vital areas like his foot. When the dust settled, only one of them would be standing. Hatch committed her mind and focused her energy.

Standing on the sidewalk in front of the broken window of the diner, Hatch looked for a trace of the man. He was nowhere to be seen. She was about to double-back through the diner and out the back to her stolen motorcycle when she heard the squeal of tires. A drumming sound of near equal volume accompanied it. Hatch heard the familiar booming bass as Macho's rust-colored Cadillac whipped around the corner.

The windows were down and Blaze was half out of the driver's side rear passenger window with a shotgun in hand. He'd snaked his thick frame through and cradled the weapon under his forearm. He used the roof of the Caddy to act as a support while he took aim. At the helm was Macho, sitting in the driver's side seat. The sight of the front passenger made Hatch see red. In the seat next to the local gang leader was Psycho. He had an unabashed smugness to him. It took all of a split second for her mind to take in the approaching threat.

They must've been parked around the side of the building and looped the block after the first attack. But Hatch was glad they came back. Her nerves were steady. She was the calm in the coming storm.

Macho drove the Cadillac in a direct path, aiming for Hatch. They were coming fast. She thought about diving out of the way at the last second and making a break for the corner of the building. *No! It ends here. And now!* Her inner voice boomed, drowning out the sound of the approaching car. Drowning out everything but the deep, controlled exhalation of her breath.

Hatch committed herself and widened her stance, bringing the Glock up on target. The reign of terror would end here, at the invisible dividing line that separated the town of Luna Vista.

The car was less than twenty feet away and approaching fast. Hatch aimed carefully and picked her mark as the vehicle hurtled toward her. Psycho was now also sticking a gun out the window. Hatch's heart sank when she saw the person behind him in the back-passenger seat. As the car continued its relentless beeline for her, she made out the young face of Xavier Fuentes.

End it! her mind called to her. Hatch fired two quick shots as the vehicle closed to ten feet. Her rounds impacted the driver's side of the windshield. Two small holes, nearly touching, spidered the glass as they penetrated the interior compartment. The vehicle then jerked wildly, spinning and deviating course away from Hatch. The two gunmen in the car never fired a shot as the vehicle veered hard ninety degrees to the right and crashed into the front of the building only feet from Hatch.

Macho was slumped over the steering wheel and bleeding profusely. Hatch couldn't determine if his condition was fatal or if his current state was caused by the gunshot or the crash. Whatever the causative factor, the result incapacitated him. The vehicle was completely totaled, removing any chance of escape. The remaining occupants were dazed for the moment. Blaze's back was arced half out of the window, the shotgun surprisingly still gripped in his left hand, but his eyes were closed, and he had a nasty laceration along the orbital bone under his right eye. A steady trickle of blood dripped onto the sidewalk below. Psycho's head wobbled from side to side and he appeared to be searching the area around his feet. *He must've lost his gun in the crash*, Hatch thought.

Hatch aimed at the front passenger's bobbing head and pulled the trigger. Nothing. In the focused intensity of the last moment, Hatch didn't feel the Glock's slide lock back. The weapon was empty. She cursed. Angry at herself for not remembering the weapon's bullet count.

Hatch quickly retreated back inside the diner, forgoing the door and jumping over the low retaining wall and through the shattered window. She landed on the padded seat of a booth and scampered across it. She knew there were potentially seconds remaining before the gunmen would be on the move again. Hatch sprinted through the diner.

Harry had dragged Cartwright around behind the counter and was down on his knees next to him. The diner owner pressed a table-cloth onto the shoulder of the injured man. Harry looked up at her as she came over.

"He's alive. I'm no doctor, but I think he'll live. I'm just trying to keep pressure on it," he said.

"Keep doing that, Harry," Hatch said as she knelt beside the unconscious Cartwright. She ran her hand along his hip line and breathed an audible sigh of relief when she found his off-duty holster. Hatch pulled out the Glock 23 subcompact pistol inside. She ejected the magazine. It was at full capacity. Reseating it, she did a press check, pulling slightly back on the rear of the slide and looking in the chamber. Seeing the round's casing, she released the slide. The weapon was good to go.

"Harry, they're going to be coming. Do you have something in here to protect yourself if they do?" Hatch asked.

Harry released one blood-covered hand from Cartwright's shoul-der. He then reached under the lip of the counter and withdrew a long-barreled shotgun. He laid it down beside the injured man and immediately went back to tending his wound, keeping the pressure and slowing the blood flow.

Hatch set out through the kitchen to the back door. Outside in the cold air a few seconds later, Hatch ran around the end of the building, hoping to flank the Outlaws' position. As she came around the side of the diner near the intersection with the Main Street sidewalk, she halted. Peeking around the corner, she could see Macho still slumped in the same position she'd left him in. Hatch focused on her primary threat, the other two gunmen. Except as she scanned the area around the car, she was disheartened to see the third member of their group standing beside Blaze. Xavier stood nearby with a gun in his hand. Hatch hoped he would not make the mistake of forcing her hand.

She brought Cartwright's weapon up. Psycho's door was pinned shut by the crash. He pushed back Macho's body and climbed over him and out the driver side window. The three men were in a tight cluster, obviously trying to figure out their next move.

Hatch brought the weapon up and took aim. She had Psycho in her sights, deeming him the most dangerous of the three. Her finger pulled the trigger back, finding the sweet spot before the break point. Just as she prepared to unleash the round, a gust of wind came down. It was like a hurricane force gale. The wind had to be seventy or eighty miles per hour. Hatch had never experienced something like this before. Overseas, dust devils whipped up with some regularity, but this was different. The wind didn't swirl. It was a direct pressure blast of dust filled wind. The effect was devastating. Not only did it blind her, rendering her aim useless. It hit her with enough force that Hatch was knocked to the ground.

She was forced to cover her eyes and mouth, pulling the collar of her sweatshirt up. Hatch could barely breathe in the direct blast of the wind and dirt. The only thing she took solace in is that meant neither could they. Her enemy was under attack from the same weather phenomena.

Hatch pushed forward, fighting her way through it and hoping under the cover of this wild elemental event she would be able to close the distance. Using the sandstorm like a shield of invisibility, she staggered forward. Hatch couldn't see a foot in front of her face. She felt as though she were Dorothy being transported to Oz. She was thrown from side to side while simultaneously being pressed downward.

Just when she'd felt she was making a modicum of progress, the force of the wind increased, knocking her off balance again. Hatch was pressed to the ground on all fours. She maintained her grip on the pistol, holding it firmly as she worked to fight her way back to her feet. And then, just as quickly as it had started, it was over.

Hatch stood exposed on the street, facing the last three members of the Outlaws. They too were getting their bearings again. But they had the benefit of being able to retreat to the protection of the Cadillac, so they weren't as unsteady in their recovery.

Hatch rubbed her eyes and worked to clear the dirt. Through her cloudy vision, she saw Psycho crawl out from the back-passenger side of the vehicle and duck low, taking cover behind the boxy rear fender. Blaze stepped out from the driver's side passenger door. He brought the shotgun up and over the open door.

Hatch did her best to concentrate her focus through the burning sensation in her eyes. Her vision still blurred, the thick stocky man made an ample target. She fired three rounds in rapid succession. Then sidestepped to the right as she worked to continue to clear away chunks of dirt from her eyes. Getting her vision back to workable levels, she saw Blaze was no longer standing behind the door. Her eyes found his dark mass on the ground where he, only moments before, had stood ready to kill her.

She quickly darted forward and crouched low at the front end of the Cadillac. The engine block of the heavy metal rectangular vehicle would stop or slow most rounds. It would serve as a barrier of protection for her while she engaged the other gunmen.

Hatch looked under the car in the hopes of being able to give Psycho a matching pair of holes in his feet. But the crazy gang banger must've learned from his first shootout and kept himself behind the tire. She could fire blindly, but the likelihood of a bullet working its way through the tire to find his foot or leg was slim at best. Hatch didn't have the ammo to expend on sightless targets.

Hatch stayed low and began moving alongside the Cadillac, keeping her profile below the windows. She pushed out with her damaged left hand, still swollen from the beating she'd taken at the bikers' clubhouse and pressed it along the driver's door in the event Macho wasn't dead. He remained still. Hatch focused her attention on the active threat as she continued forward to the midsection of the vehicle. Hatch slowly pushed the open back passenger door. It squeaked loudly and Hatch cringed at the sound of it.

Keeping her weapon at the ready and eyes in the direction of her known threat, Hatch felt her way with her left. She worked her hand along Blaze's body until she found his neck. No pulse.

Hatch kept herself tucked tight and low as she neared the rear window of the Cadillac. She was at the point where the car would no longer provide ample cover. She was too close. More battles were won and lost in the critical split second before confrontation. Indecisiveness killed more people than action. So, Hatch decided to act.

The wind had died down almost completely. In the silence that followed, Hatch heard Psycho's voice in a raspy whisper, but his words were not clear. She assumed he must be talking to Xavier, coaching the boy on his plan. Whatever it was, nervous chatter or a quick huddle, he had given away his position. And she now had a reference point for her aim.

Hatch popped up quickly and saw the wild-eyed Psycho. He was caught off-guard at the back corner of the Cadillac. His face even more deranged and twisted than she'd remembered, cast in the red of the taillights, he looked maniacal.

Hatch fired twice. She kept the gun trained in the direction of the man as he disappeared from her sight, down behind the car.

Hatch then worked herself around the back. Xavier cowered near the trunk latch. His hands were up. The gun she'd seen him holding was on the ground. She breathed a sigh of relief. She was grateful Xavier didn't force her hand. If she had to make that choice, it would've undoubtedly haunted her forever.

She brought her Glock to the low ready after seeing her rounds had found their mark. Psycho lay dead with two bullet holes in him. One in the chest and one in the head. Both men who'd doused Wendy's room and the man who'd overseen the order were now all dead.

Xavier slowly stood. He was trembling uncontrollably. "I didn't want to do it! I didn't want to go with them. Hatch, you gotta believe me! They forced me, but I was never going to hurt you. I swear on my mother," he stammered.

"I know," Hatch said. "I hoped you wouldn't force my hand. I'm glad you made the right choice." Hatch slipped the borrowed Glock in the small of her back and put a comforting hand on the boy's shoulder. His body continued to tremble and he broke eye contact, looking down at his feet. Hatch watched him. "At least you're free from them now," Hatch offered.

Xavier looked up. "How do I explain this to my parents?" he whispered.

As Hatch was about to offer some conciliatory advice, she watched the boy's eyes widen in fear.

Hatch spun. As she did, she saw the bloodied face of Macho standing only a few feet from her. His gun was up and pointed at the center of her forehead. Hatch's gun was still tucked at her back. The rounds she'd fired into the car obviously hadn't killed the local gang leader. One had grazed his neck, but not in a way that had ended his life. The blood from the wound had covered his face in a dark spatter. The dust from the storm clung to it, giving him glittery highlights. The other round struck him in the chest. If left on his own, he would've eventually succumbed to the slow bleed out. She had missed the mark as sometimes happens when firing into the convex bend of a windshield. The rounds must've changed the trajectory and moved off mark.

Hatch was not in a winning position. And although it seemed like a long time since she had turned to face this unforeseen threat, only seconds had passed. But in those seconds, Hatch frantically weighed her options. She ran possible outcomes in a matter of milliseconds, calling upon every ounce of her training to find a solution to this unsolvable equation. She had none.

One thing was certain, Rachel Hatch was not going to die without a fight.

"I told you when we first met. Take my kindness and walk away. But you had to go mess it up." His voice was strangely calm.

Hatch watched the man's finger. It was already on the trigger when she had first turned to face him. And it was still there now. *Die on your feet!* Hatch commanded to herself. She moved her hand toward the small of her back as the gang leader pulled the trigger.

Hatch was momentarily frozen. The gun pointed in her face went *click.*

Drawing her gun and bringing it to bear on the man who had just tried to kill her, she heard a deafening bang as Macho was flung to the left.

Hatch looked to the right, in the direction of the blast that leveled the gunman and conclusively ended the standoff. From inside the broken front window of the diner, Harry stood with the butt of his shotgun resting on his thigh. Smoke trailed out of the front end of its long barrel.

Hatch returned Cartwright's Glock to the small of her back. She knelt beside the now dead Macho and looked down at the gun in his hand. She immediately recognized it. A Smith & Wesson M&P. The same type of weapon she'd found in the abandoned warehouse. Hatch only had time to disable two of them by removing the firing pin. *Talk about karmic justice*, she thought.

"I thought you were a goner."

Hatch stood and turned to see the scared teen standing behind her.

"Me too." She looked back to where Harry had been standing.

He was gone. Most likely back behind the counter, continuing his efforts to save Dale Cartwright.

Hatch went inside the diner with Xavier in tow, leaving the three dead men in the dust-covered street in front of the diner. She heard sirens in the distance, signaling the responding units would undoubtedly be arriving shortly.

"It's a busy night for the Luna Vista emergency services," Hatch said as she came around the counter.

Hatch's only concern was for the man who had taken a bullet to save her life.

She squatted down next to Harry, who was still applying pressure. His grease-soaked apron was now covered in Cartwright's blood.

Hatch gave him a break and took over applying the pressure. She ran her right index finger up and checked his pulse. Faint but steady. The sirens drew closer and she looked at Harry. "Call and tell them to focus their attention here first. They've got an officer down. They're going to need to expedite. He's got a through and through in his upper shoulder, but he's lost a lot of blood."

Harry grabbed the phone from the wall and relayed the information to the dispatcher as Hatch continued to put pressure on the wound.

Hatch put the Glock next to Cartwright. Harry returned and saw the weapon. "What do I tell 'em?" he asked.

"The truth. There's been enough lies in this town to choke a horse," Hatch said.

The sirens filled the air as blue and red flashed against the walls of the diner.

TWENTY-NINE

IT HAD BEEN a day since the shootout at the diner. Harry had done much in the way of clearing any potential fallout for Hatch. He described the attack as being unprovoked. He went on record saying she and Cartwright were having a cup of coffee when the gang members targeted them. Had it not been for the heroic efforts of Officer Cartwright, Hatch would've been killed. Harry described how she found his gun and used it to defend them.

The state police had come in to assist due to the overwhelming nature of the violent crimes occurring in the town over the last few days. The chief was insulted and requested to oversee the investigation himself. He was overridden by members of the town council. A little birdy had whispered in the ear of the lead investigator. Chief Porter had already been placed on administrative leave pending further inquiry. Hatch knew his termination was soon to follow.

Hatch knew that as the state began digging their way through the town's many coverups, the exposure would likely result in both state and federal indictments. But Hatch wasn't in the law enforcement game anymore, and proceedings to follow in the coming months, and potentially years afterward, were not of her concern. Her concern rested in the well-being of Xavier Fuentes and his family, Harry, and of course, Officer Cartwright.

Hatch sat in the diner. It was a bit darker than usual with the main window covered in plywood. She waited as her order was whipped up by the man who'd shot another to save her life. Being served by somebody who had just saved your life was a humbling moment.

The norm of routine was already working its way back into the town. Hatch smelled the home fries cooking on the griddle. The man cooking them had shown hope that the town was capable of fighting their way back to whatever humble beginnings it once had. And this time without the control of an outlaw motorcycle gang and their lesser counterparts. Without those influences, Luna Vista had a real chance at survival.

Hatch watched as Harry worked the spatula. A few minutes later, he appeared from the galley and placed the Luna Vista Special down in front of her. It would be her last meal before leaving the small town. And one that would keep her satiated long after she left.

"So, this is it, huh?" Harry asked.

Hatch looked down at the plate. Steam arose from the home fried potatoes and scrambled eggs covered in cheese. Her stomach rumbled as she inhaled the delicious aroma. "Yup. Looks that way." Hatch took a forkful of egg with her right hand. Her left finger was now splinted and the gash on her forehead was stitched. Before taking a bite, she said, "I've got a question about last night."

"Go ahead and fire away," Harry said. Then catching himself, he raised his hands in surrender. "Sorry, wrong phrase to use around you."

She cocked an eyebrow. "Same goes for you, too." They both chuckled softly.

"So, what's your question?"

"That freak windstorm last night. I've never experienced

anything like it. Was it a tornado?" Hatch asked and then filled her mouth with the hot food.

"No. You're right about one thing, it's a freak occurrence. I personally haven't seen one in years." Harry poured himself a cup of coffee. "It's called a downburst."

Hatch added a little ketchup to the potatoes. "Never heard of it."

"Well, like I said, they're rare. It's a strong localized blast of wind. Some people call them microbursts." He took a sip of his coffee and cleared his throat. "They come down fast and hard. Then they're gone. They can be pretty devastating." The man's cheeks softened, and he smiled.

"What are you smiling about?" Hatch said with a mouthful of food.

"I pretty much just described you."

Hatch almost spit out her food as they both broke into a hearty laugh. As sore as her ribs were, she hadn't felt this good in days.

Harry went about serving some of the other customers as Hatch finished her meal. He returned to clear her plate and top off her coffee mug.

"I have faith in you, Harry. I think people like you can bring this town back to life and knock down the dividing line that has separated this community for too long."

Harry nodded. His face was solemn. "I really can't thank you enough for what you did for me."

She silently absorbed the compliment. Hatch felt a pang of guilt at hearing his words. She picked a fight with a gang and that ultimately cost the life of Harry's niece. She would shoulder that burden for a long time to come.

"I know you don't see it right now, but you saved a lot of people by what you did."

"I just wished I could've saved—." Hatch didn't finish the sentence. She didn't need to. Harry knew. To say her name aloud would do neither of them any good. So, she left it unsaid.

"Are you going to go see him before you leave?" Harry asked.

"I already did. I stopped by the hospital before coming here. He's gonna make a full recovery. It'll take a little bit of time, but he'll be back out protecting these citizens soon enough." Hatch gave a knowing smile. "Ya know, he's got the makings of a great chief someday."

"I agree. Maybe sooner rather than later." Harry chuckled. "There's already talk of Porter stepping down."

Hatch drained the rest of her coffee and stood as Harry set her empty plate in the sink. Before leaving, she walked around behind the counter and gave Harry a hug. She then released him and walked out the front door.

Hatch had ditched the stolen motorcycle outside of town and had gotten a replacement rental car. She drove the teal Honda Accord away from Harry's diner, knowing she would never see her friend again.

Hatch headed back to where it all began, the Moonbeam motel. The darkened char still scarred the area where room number two once stood. Manuel was out front and was beginning the process of gutting the space. Hatch was happy to see his son, Xavier, by his father's side as the two worked together to remove a plank of damaged wood.

Hatch pulled up and stopped in front of her old room. Both men looked at her and smiled. Gone from the younger Fuentes boy's face was the false bravado. As Hatch approached, she saw nothing but a teenager.

They set the burnt piece of wood down and walked over to her.

Hatch popped the trunk of the car. She lifted its contents onto her shoulder and closed it. She saw the confusion in their eyes.

Hatch dropped the saddlebags in front of Manuel.

He looked down at it, further lining the deep brown of his forehead. "What's this?" he asked.

"It's something you deserve to have," she said.

Hatch bent and unlatched one of the satchels so that the man could see its contents. He staggered back and his eyes went wide in shock.

"There's enough in there to fix this motel three times over. You'll have what you need to get it the way you want. And there should be enough to float things for your family during the lean times."

Manuel Fuentes was a man who'd earned everything in his life by working his hands to the bone. She could readily see from the look on his face he was not accustomed to receiving gifts, especially ones of this nature and in this amount. She guessed the contents of the two satchels to be in the ballpark of three hundred thousand dollars. A significant boost in their current financial situation. And an equally significant dent in that of the Savage Renegades, who were now fugitives on the run from the New Mexico State Police.

"I can't accept this."

"Well, I'm leaving it here regardless." Hatch kicked the bag closer to him. "You're going to take it. You're a good hard-working man taking care of a family and trying to run a business. The people this money belonged to tried to take that from you. And in the course of that killed a young girl. Put this money to good use."

Manuel must've seen the conviction in her eyes. He nodded.

"You have a chance now, too." Hatch turned her attention to Xavier. "They have no hold on you. They're gone. What you choose to do with your life is solely up to you. Second chances don't come often in life. Seize this one."

"I will," the teen said.

"I can see you're already off to a good start in helping your father. You can learn a lot from him. You're lucky to have a dad like him," Hatch said, thinking of her own father as she spoke.

Hatch opened her car door and was about to get in when Xavier ran around the car to her. "Hatch," he said. "Thank you for everything. And I'm sorry for the things I said and did."

"No need to apologize. But the way you can truly thank me is give your second shot at life the effort it deserves."

The teen nodded and then he did something unexpected. He reached out and pulled her into a hug.

The boy only held the hug for a moment before retreating back to his father.

Hatch left the Moonbeam motel in her rearview mirror as she drove to the last stop on her list. She stared at the address on the back of the card the gun shop owner had given her, not knowing what answers, if any, lay in wait.

THIRTY

HATCH CREPT the Honda Accord up the long driveway of the house. It was set back in the Mayberry section of town almost at the edge, a polar opposite from where the Moonbeam sat. This house was on the outskirts where civilization broke free into the wide expanse that separated Luna Vista from the Organ Mountains. As she made her way here, Hatch realized how close this location was to the place where she had been pulled over by Officer Cartwright. A few blocks separated her from the man who potentially held the first answer to a long list of questions regarding her father's life and mysterious death.

Hatch parked. She sat in the car for a moment as the wind whipped, jostling the Honda ever so slightly. Nothing in comparison to the wind from the other night. She had never seen anything like that before and wondered if she ever would again. *Downburst*, she thought.

For all the decisions she had made in her life up to this point, most were done with minimal hesitation. But here she sat, with her hands teetering on the door handle. Hatch was afraid to get out of the car and face whatever potential answers might lie within. Her fear came in two parts. One, he might not hold any answers, and this would be a quick end to her journey. Or two, the answers might be something she didn't want to hear. Does learning something bad about somebody you love change your memory of them? Would it alter everything she knew about herself?

Regardless of her hesitancy, Hatch committed to action. She turned the car off and stepped out. Before she reached the first step of the three leading to a wraparound front porch, the door opened.

An older man stood holding it open. He had thick cheeks and a midsection to match. A white handlebar mustache wrapped around his mouth, a throwback to a seventy's western movie actor. The only thing he was missing was his ten-gallon hat. He had a look on his face that was neither off-putting nor overly welcoming.

Hatch stopped in her tracks. "I assume you were told I might be coming to see you. From what I've seen in this town, there is not much in the way of secrets. At least not when it comes to an outsider," Hatch said.

"I was. Wilbur Smith called me up. Told me about a young woman looking for answers." He paused to evaluate Hatch, eyeing her from head to toe. "You look like him."

Hatch cocked an eyebrow, caught off guard by the man's comment. "Him?" she asked.

"Your father. He was a little bit taller, but everything else is the spitting image. You even got that same look in your eye. Like violence is just beneath the surface."

Hatch's heart skipped a beat for the first time since she'd contemplated searching out her father's life and tracking down anyone who may have been responsible for his death. She'd found her first real connection to his past. It had been nearly twenty-one years since her father had been killed. Retracing the steps leading up to it was a daunting task, but she'd just taken the first step of hopefully many.

When she first set out with an address written on an envelope from two decades ago, it seemed improbable it would lead anywhere. But here she was. The man recognized her. Better yet, he recognized her father in her.

"Do you think you can help me out?"

"Depends what you mean by help," the man said.

Hatch understood the man's reservation in welcoming her with open arms. If he was linked in any way to the people who had killed her father, then this man would be cautious. He'd obviously outlived her dad. She had to assume he did that by being very particular with what information he released and to whom. And yet he hadn't left the town, which piqued Hatch's interest.

"Anything you can tell me that might point me in the right direction."

The man raised a hand, stopping her short. They were on an isolated street at the end of a long driveway and he looked around as if there could be a neighbor within earshot. Two decades and this man feared a simple conversation on his front porch in the middle of nowhere.

Hatch nodded and stepped up the wooden steps to the porch. He stepped aside and she entered the house.

He guided her over to a living room area where a grand piano was set in the corner. Plush couches and a loveseat were at the center of the sitting room. He gestured to the loveseat. "Can I get you something to eat or drink?" he asked.

Hatch shook her head no. "No, thank you. I just came from Harry's."

The man's cheeks reddened and he gave a bit of a chuckle. He patted his midline and said, "How do you think I got this? I was about forty pounds lighter before he opened up shop."

He sat in a high-backed rocking chair as Hatch sank into the loveseat. Whatever fabric it was made of, it was probably the most comfortable thing she'd ever sat on. Whatever the man did for a living, or had done, he had amassed a small fortune, as was evident in his decor.

"Nice place," she said.

"Thanks. It's quiet now. The kids are grown and gone, blazing their own trails. And my wife's gone. Her trail is one I hope to meet her on someday. This house, this stuff, it means so little now. It's funny. I used to think it did."

"How'd you come to know my father?"

"Listen, Rachel. Whatever I'm going to tell you now can't come back on me. And the only reason I'm doing it at all is because of who your father was to me." He rubbed the palms of his hands against his thighs. "I'm putting myself at great risk in doing this. Even now, and after so many years."

"Then why do it?"

"Because I'm old. The people that mattered to me are gone. But more importantly, it's the right thing to do." The man unbuttoned the top two buttons of his shirt near the collar. He pulled it aside to reveal a thick jagged scar running from his clavicle, around the side of his neck, and disappearing down toward the center of his back. "And then there's this reason."

Hatch looked at the scar. She'd seen many like it during her time in service and guessed the cause was a massive piece of shrapnel or maybe even a knife.

"I'd be dead if it wasn't for your father. I want to repay my debt to him before I'm packed into a box and buried deep. If I can honor his life and give you some peace in doing so, then maybe I can feel, in some small way, I've repaid him."

Hatch nodded, understanding better than most the significance without asking for the particulars about the how or why her father had saved him. Those details mattered more to him than her. Combat left few things to cherish. And in those rare moments when life touched death on the battlefield, the memories of such events were kept tightly locked away. Hatch had several of her own.

Not long ago, she'd opened herself to Dalton Savage. Even then, she held back. Hatch had told him of the woman who detonated the bomb that had ravaged her arm and cost the life of a teammate. She spoke of how her hesitancy to take the shot had resulted in the death of a friend. But what she had never told him, the thing she had held back in that disclosure, was the little girl in tow. The real reason behind her delay in pulling the trigger. The girl's face still haunted her. And probably always would.

The older man continued, "All the men in our unit were ex-Army. We all had special ops experience. Some of us had even served together overseas, during Vietnam. There was a time after the war where corporations saw the need for privatized military groups. Mercenaries was the term they liked to throw around back then. But we were contractors. Not so different from the ones nowadays. Anyway, these organizations were springing up left and right, and men like myself and your father filled their ranks."

Hatch edged closer, listening to the man's voice. He had the soft but gruff manner of speaking similar to that of Wilford Brimley narrating a Quaker oatmeal commercial. As secretive as the man was, he was warm and engaging. But it wasn't his way of talking that drew Hatch in. It was the things he said. For the first time in her life, she was hearing somebody who really knew her father before their life in Hawk's Landing.

"Is that what the warehouse was used for? A training ground for contractors?" Hatch asked.

"Yes. The company bought the space. There wasn't much out here at the time. It was set up to look like a paper distribution factory. When we had the occasional walk-in, we told them our company only handled international orders. Small town. It didn't take long before the locals stopped asking and we were left alone."

"I saw the indoor gun range in the back."

"We used it for a variety of mission preps and workups. Eventually, the company saw value in being more mobile. After a few years, the unit moved out of Luna Vista."

"But you didn't?" Hatch asked.

"I had fallen in love with a girl. Of course, she knew nothing about me aside from the fact that I had served in the Army and worked at a paper factory. Secrets upon secrets. Hard way to begin a life. I decided to stay behind. I bought the place for a song. And for a time used it as an actual gun range. Ran it as a local business. Did pretty well for myself and then sold it before the economy around here collapsed."

Hatch didn't really care to dig any deeper into how he made his fortune. All she cared about was finding out more about her father and where he went from here. "You stayed behind. And then what?"

"You know how it is when you get out of it. You become an island unto yourself." The man re-buttoned his shirt.

"I just need to know where to go from here." Hatch leaned in. "I need to know who killed my father. And why."

"I don't know who killed your father. That much I can tell you."

"Maybe not, but you did know that it happened."

"Yes." He nodded. "But there was nothing I could do about it."

"There's always something you can do," Hatch said in a hushed tone.

"I guess that's what I'm doing now. A little late, but it's better than never," the man conceded.

"Where did they go from here? How do I find the next piece, the next person involved? What's the name of the group? How about we start there." Hatch shot off the questions in rapid-fire succession.

"I'm sure the name has changed from when we were in. Back then it was called the Gibson Consortium, named after the founding member, Caldwell Gibson. He wasn't ex-military. He was a businessman. To him, it was all about the money. Died about ten years back. Like I said, the company's probably changed hands multiple times since."

"What I've got so far is my dad was a contractor. And for some unknown reason he was killed. Was it the company?"

"That's what I'm telling you. I don't know who killed him. We did a lot of off-the-books ops. We upset a lot of people. The work we did, if it were ever to be exposed, would bring a shitstorm down on every one of us."

Hatch thought about the media frenzy, broadcasting her father's image. He'd made national headlines when he rescued a stranded family trapped in the mountains. The spotlight of one good deed exposed him, and shortly after, he was dead. That's all it took. A blip on the radar of exposure and they had come for him.

"I don't even know if they're still active," the man uttered.

"You do. Or at least you assume enough to hold out giving me any more information."

"I told you, your father and I were close. We kept in touch until his death. I had one more friend like him. Somebody I trusted, and we remained in contact after I went legit."

Hatch leaned forward and almost at the edge of the soft cushion. "You're still in contact with him. I can see it in your eyes."

The man breathed slowly and then nodded. "Not often. But yes. I still have somebody who may be in the know."

Hatch fought the excitement rising up.

"I don't call him. There is no number by which I can reach him. Every once in a while, I receive a letter from him, and in turn, I send him one back." He began to sweat and dabbed his forehead with the end of his sleeve. "Not like you're probably used to, but yes, we maintained contact the old-fashioned way."

"And he's still alive?" Hatch asked.

"Yes."

"Is he still with the contracting group?" Hatch asked.

"No. At least he told me he wasn't. He's as old as me. Not sure anybody wants us dinosaurs running around fighting the bad guys. If he lied to me and he's still involved, then I'm sure it would be administratively at this point. But several years back he sent me a letter saying he was trying to atone for what we'd done."

"And how does one do that?" Hatch asked, wondering herself.

"He became a priest."

"A priest?"

"He turned to the cloth. He told me he felt a calling. His theory was that if he did enough good before he died, maybe some of the awful things could be washed away."

Hatch thought on this for a moment and then asked, "Did he find what he was looking for?"

The man's shoulders hunched up into a shrug. She noticed the side with the scar didn't raise as high. "I honestly don't know. Do any of us ever really find peace? Are warriors able to let go of the violence they've done on behalf of God and country? I know one thing, I never have," he said.

"Me neither," Hatch offered.

Silence hung in the air. Hatch interrupted it. "So, where can I find your priest friend?"

"Africa," the man said flatly.

Hatch's eyes widened. "He's in Africa?"

"Yes. He joined the church and his mission work took him to Kenya. He's been there for a while."

Hatch sat back, sinking deep into the cushion. She felt somewhat defeated. She hadn't imagined traipsing the world. She figured this might take her to another state or maybe even Washington DC. But Africa wasn't even on her radar.

"I'm sorry, but he's the only person in the world who may know anything more than what I told you. He stayed with the group a lot longer than me. All I have is an address in Mombasa. But he spends most of his time in a small village outside of the city. At least that's where he was six months ago when I got his last letter."

Hatch felt the embers of hope being rekindled. A lead is a lead no matter where it took her. She'd been everywhere and nowhere. Africa was just another link in the chain. "May I have his address?"

"I'm not sure how he'll receive you. Over the years, he's gone to great lengths to distance himself both physically and emotionally from the things we did. Be mindful of that."

"Consider me warned. I guess I don't have to worry about you calling in advance and warning him of my pending arrival."

"Not sure I would risk that—for your sake as well as mine."

"You think your long-time friend would send somebody for you?"

The man didn't react to the question. He sat motionless.

His silence answered her question. And the answer was a resounding yes. If the priest in Kenya was still somehow involved with the contractor unit and felt exposed, he wouldn't hesitate to eliminate the threat, regardless of friendship or passage of time. *What had my father been involved with?* Hatch wondered.

The mustached man got up from his rocker and moved along the tiled floor, disappearing from view for a moment into an adjacent room. She heard the open and close of a cabinet door. He returned again with a slip of paper. On it was a name, Dermot McCarthy, and below it was the international address for a P.O. Box in Mombasa, Kenya.

Hatch pocketed the information and stood. The man extended his hand and said, "I don't know what it is you're hoping to find, but whatever it is, I hope you do, and you finally get some closure. You and your family deserve that."

Hatch shook his hand. "Me too," she said softly. She turned toward the door. "I'll let myself out."

Hatch opened the door as he said, "You take care of yourself Rachel Hatch. Because nobody else will."

She closed it behind her. Hatch got into the Honda. Her return to Hawk's Landing would be postponed. Her next destination was set.

Hatch had no idea what to expect or where this journey would eventually lead. But she had no choice. It had to be made. Without it, she would never be capable of truly returning home.

The few days spent in the small town of Luna Vista had nearly cost her life. She thought of the people she connected with there and the lives forever changed by tragedy. A town now in a rebirth. Not unlike the tragic death of her sister and the new relationships born from it. Hatch let her mind drift to her niece and nephew as the desolate landscape passed by around her. She thought of the things left unsaid between her and Dalton Savage.

She hoped this next trip would bring an end to her quest for vengeance and allow her a clear conscience to return home so she could begin her life anew.

Hatch would be heading to Africa soon. But not before stopping by Fort Bragg, North Carolina. She knew it was a longshot, but if anybody from her prior inner circle could shed some light on this latest bit of information, it would be her former team leader, Chris Bennett.

Read on for a sneak peak at *Fever Burn (Rachel Hatch book 3)*, or get your copy now:
https://www.amazon.com/Fever-Burn-Rachel-Hatch-Book-ebook/dp/B085VNJ9SY/

Join the LT Ryan reader family & receive a free copy of the Rachel Hatch story, *Fractured*. Click the link below to get started:
https://ltryan.com/rachel-hatch-newsletter-signup-1

Join the L.T. Ryan private reader's group on Facebook here:
https://www.facebook.com/groups/1727449564174357

LOVE HATCH? **Noble? Maddie? Cassie?** Get your very own
Rachel Hatch merchandise today! Click the link below to find coffee
mugs, t-shirts, and even signed copies of your favorite L.T. Ryan
thrillers! https://ltryan.ink/EvG_

THE RACHEL HATCH SERIES

Drift

Downburst

Fever Burn

Smoke Signal

Firewalk

Whitewater

Aftershock

Whirlwind

Tsunami

Fastrope

Sidewinder (Coming Soon)

RACHEL HATCH SHORT STORIES

Fractured

Proving Ground

The Gauntlet

Join the LT Ryan reader family & receive a free copy of the Rachel Hatch story, Fractured. Click the link below to get started:

https://ltryan.com/rachel-hatch-newsletter-signup-1

Love Hatch? Noble? Maddie? Cassie? Get your very own Rachel Hatch merchandise today! Click the link below to find coffee mugs, t-shirts, and even signed copies of your favorite L.T. Ryan thrillers! https://ltryan. ink/EvG_

FEVER BURN

RACHEL HATCH BOOK THREE

by L.T. Ryan & Brian Shea

FEVER BURN PROLOGUE

Mombasa, Kenya

The boy was hunched over, digging hard at the ground before him. He wasn't playing. Although, as his mother watched from nearby, she wished more than anything that he would. Masika hung a sheet from a clothesline stretched between two trees. But as was the way of things here, childhood was a fleeting fancy, one stolen by circumstances. It had been over a year since her eldest son had been taken. Zaire, at age twelve, had taken it upon himself to fill the void. His mother looked on sadly as the morning's mist surrounded him and the sun began to rise up beyond the dense tree line. He'd been at it since before dawn. A long line of upturned earth was the result of the last hour of toil.

Masika finished hanging the several sheets, spreading them evenly along the line and knotting the ends to the line to secure them in place. The brightly colored cotton fabric flapped in the gentle breeze.

She walked over to the well and filled a bucket. A group of engineers had come to the village some years back and dug out the well. It was life changing for them. No longer did they have to make the trek through the pass down to the river to get a drink. Plus, the water tapped from an underground source was much cleaner and therefore better for drinking. Although they still used the river to bathe and launder their clothes.

The tar-sealed wooden bucket banged into her knee as she walked, sloshing the water and wetting her embroidered kitenge dress. The coolness of the liquid felt good as morning temps began to climb. She knelt on the soft ground beside her son and, using a hand-made ladle, scooped out some of the water.

"Drink, my son. It will be hot soon. You need to keep your strength up."

The boy shifted and looked at his mother, his dark hands caked with soft mud.

She brought the ladle close and Zaire slurped it up noisily. The excess spilled out from his mouth and dribbled down his chin. She scooped more from the pail.

Zaire held up his hand. "No more for now. I've got to get back to work. The ground is softer now with the rain, and I want to get the seeds in before sundown."

Light had just broken and her son was already preparing for a day of work that would take him all day long. Masika remembered when his days were filled with exploration and wonder. And prayed daily that someday they would be again. With the extraction of most of the able-bodied young men who'd been taken and forced into servitude, the village was left to rely on each member, young and old, to pull their weight. A harmonized synchronicity existed.

Inside their hut, she prepared the morning's meal. The villagers usually consumed two meals a day. Breakfast was done in the privacy of each individual hut, but the village shared a communal dinner after the day's work was done. That meal had been, until recent events, a time of great celebration. When the workday ended, singing, dancing and storytelling took place around the fire. It was a joyous time. Then Dakarai rose to power and life in the village changed. Wives lost their husbands, children lost their fathers, and mothers lost their children. The village was stripped of its men who were sent to serve a warlord whose purpose was malevolent at best.

Most mornings Masika served mkate, a simple flatbread. The children liked it when she added sesame seeds. She'd plate it with some fresh fruit. It was simple enough to make and hearty enough to provide energy for the day's work. When feeding her seven children, simple was essential. All breakfasts came with the sweetened Chai tea. Today would be different. One day a week, when she'd gone to the market and had the materials, Masika would treat her family to mandazi. It was a deep-fried pastry similar in taste and texture to an unsweetened doughnut.

Masika set about boiling the oil. She knew once the scent of the pastry floated out to her son it would bring him in. Zaire couldn't resist the treat, no matter how dedicated he was to his chores. As she went to the cabinet and pulled out the flour, she heard the rumble of trucks.

There were two entrance and exit points, one that could be made by vehicle and the other, which was a footpath, led down to the river. Her heart began to beat faster. She hoped the arriving vehicle would belong to Father McCarthy, the priest who served their villages and several others in the area. Maybe he was bringing others with him, which he did on occasion. Humanitarian workers had come to the village several times over the years, delivering food and medicine. One group had put in the well years back. The priest came quite frequently, and they'd come to enjoy his visits, but he wasn't scheduled to be back for another day or so.

Her optimism was dashed as she realized that the more likely reason for the trucks arrival was the return of the warlord and his men for some reason. And this thought made her panic.

The abduction of her eldest son one year ago left an unfillable hole in her heart.

There were other boys reaching the age of maturity. Her 12-year-old son was very close to being on the warlord's list if he chose their village to replenish his resources.

Masika knew what happened when their men disappeared. They'd heard stories of the conditioning--the psychological and physical tortures they endured. And the drugs Darakai used to keep them in line and addicted. They were changed. As if their souls had been ripped from their bodies, the men became empty vessels.

She had caught a glimpse of her son six months ago on a convoy when she was in Mombasa town center. He was riding with a group of men in the back of a Jeep. Her eyes brightened at the sight of him and she waved, hoping he would jump out and run to her. Masika knew her son had seen her. His eyes momentarily locked with hers. But to her dismay, he had no reaction, not even a wink, a secret half smile, anything to tell her that the boy she knew was still inside. He was just a shell of the son she'd raised, his mind corrupted by the warlord who controlled him now.

Masika was determined not to let that happen to her next oldest boy, Zaire, who was out toiling in the field.

She rushed to the door as the roar of the truck engines grew louder. It was custom that the villagers would greet any and all arriving guests. It was something they'd always done. But now, at Dakarai's decree, all were ordered to come to the center point of the village. The fire pit where jovial gatherings had once taken place was now a place where atrocities were carried out. This past year had soured the affinity of the gathering point.

By Dakarai's edict, everybody was to be out of their huts and in visible sight when they came. It was done to control the masses, and make sure that there was no subversion. A few villages had fought back in the early days of his rise to power. The end result carried with it devastating consequences. Her village had heard the tales and offered little in the way of resistance. When time came for a selection of some of their men or the stealing of their food and supplies, the resistance came in the form of a scream or a whimper of protest or simply a tear rolling down a cheek. But no formal attempts to stop the warlord's soldiers were ever made. Bravery was a foolhardy thing at best. Life trumped death, making the decision to comply easy.

Masika stepped out onto the dirt path and started making her way with the others toward the center of the village. With her other children clinging closely to her, she looked around for Zaire. Their scared faces were hidden behind her brightly colored dress. They were young, but they knew the threat.

Her heart sank, as her fear was confirmed. This visit would not be the priest or any humanitarian efforts. Any hope was dashed, as the two-vehicle caravan of the warlord's men moved forward. Guns poked out from several points in their Jeeps with a few men riding high on the top. The second Jeep had a large machine gun fixed to the roof and a man standing behind it at the ready, his eyes bloodshot and wild. She did not like these men. She did not trust them and worried for her village, and more importantly, her family every time they came. There was no sign of her eldest boy among the soldiers.

Where was Zaire? she thought, frantically scanning, looking for him among her people. She cast a glance back to the garden area where he had been troweling with his hands just a short while ago. His diligent work, churning the soft earth and creating a little repository for the seeds to be sowed was evident. She thought of the tender exchange they'd shared as she served him water from the ladle.

But his small body was not crouched where it once was. He wasn't in the crowd. He knew better than to wander off. Whenever the trucks came, he was supposed to find her, to tuck himself deep behind her, making himself small so he wouldn't be worthy of selection, hiding in plain sight. But he was nowhere to be seen, and this worried her.

Without Zaire present, she was suddenly filled with a wholly different prospect. A sense of relief rushed over her. Maybe he had run, taking the back path down toward the river and hiding somewhere down there away from Dakarai's soldiers.

The soldiers rarely went down to the river. On occasion they took some of the female villagers down there for things that she dared not

278 FEVER BURN PROLOGUE

think about. Even if that were the case today, they would undoubtedly be too preoccupied, and her son would be safe.

She tried to calm herself and take solace in the fact that he wasn't here. He couldn't be selected if he wasn't here. *Would they notice Zaire's absence?* If they did, she would be punished. They'd need to make an example for the others.

The soldiers exited their vehicles as the jeeps came to a stop. All except for the man standing behind the mounted machine gun.

The yelling began, ordering the villagers to tightly huddle up. They surrounded them like a pack of rabid dogs. Most chewing khat, the drug Dakarai used to influence his soldiers. And one that added to their deranged state of mind.

The rifles were used to prod them. The clink of metal and bone and flesh as the elderly and infirmed moved slower, displeased them. One of the younger soldiers used the butt of his weapon to strike a man using a cane, sending him to the ground.

A young woman ran over to help, and the soldier shoved her from behind, sending her down on top of him.

Laughter amongst some of the men broke out as they jeered the two with taunts. Dakarai wasn't present, but his lieutenant belted out in Swahili for them to stop.

The barrel chested lieutenant with a penchant for young girls turned his attention to the crowd. "We need three volunteers."

His terse voice and succinct command drew silence from the villagers. Volunteers. They all knew what it meant. And nothing about it was voluntary.

Now Masika was grateful. She couldn't send forward Zaire because he wasn't there. Her other children were far too young to join the ranks. As painful as it would be to watch another family endure such hardship, she was glad this time it wouldn't be hers.

It didn't take long before the soldiers picked their recruits. A tall boy nearby was grabbed by one of the armed men and dragged away from his mother. Masika listened to the anguished screams of the mothers as they made a last-ditch plea, begging for them to stop, trying to remind the soldiers that they were once boys, that they weren't always under the warlord's command.

But it happened regardless of protests as it had in the past and would undoubtedly happen again in the future, these cries for humanity fell on deaf ears.

One of the soldiers went door to door checking each hut, making sure that nobody was hiding. Masika could hear the crash of pots. The clang and bang of overturned tables as the man rummaged his way around, sending another message. Don't hide. But no one was hiding. Nobody except her son. *Please be at the river*, she prayed. She tried to calm herself, to remain steady in the face of such danger.

The soldier exited the last hut and shook his head, looking at the leader, saying something to the effect of "nobody's here."

The lieutenant looked at the group, turned to his men and said, "Let's go."

The three boys who had been selected, none of them much older than her son, were shoved toward the awaiting jeep. In fact, the youngest of the three was only six months older than Zaire, although he was taller and a bit lankier, giving the impression of being maybe a year or two older.

Masika felt blessed her son was born small and that he had remained so as he grew. Maybe he could avoid their interest for another year or two if luck favored? Maybe something would happen to change the course of this current situation and they'd be free from oppression.

As she stood shoulder to shoulder with her people Masika made a silent prayer that these men would leave and never return. Then movement caught her attention out of the corner of her eye. It was her son. Zaire peeked out from behind the side of one of the huts nearest the jeep where the young men were being loaded.. Whatever she had felt in panic and worry was now giving way to something worse, an impalpable fear. She could taste the bile in her stomach. *What was he doing? Go back to wherever you were. They're leaving.* She willed him to listen, but he wasn't looking at her and she did not want to stare too long in his direction for fear one of the soldiers would notice.

It was too late, he was running now. She held back the scream that she wanted loose into the air. Zaire was running at a dead sprint, a large tree limb in his hand. The branch was held at the ready like a baseball player preparing to take the plate. He rushed forward to the soldier putting the last child, his best friend, into the back of the jeep.

The soldier on the turret, seeing the boy running, yelled something to the soldiers on the ground, who turned and saw the boy. The last to turn was the one forcing the new recruits into the back, and he was the young boy's target. And as the man began to turn slowly to see what the commotion was about, her son swung the stick, like John Henry swinging that mighty hammer. It came crashing down on the soldier's shoulder, who, if she had to guess, his age was not more than 17, the heavy branch striking somewhere between his shoulder and the man's neck.

Her son was strong. The toil of hard work had made him so. The force with which he struck the soldier dropped the gunman to his knee.

Masika watched in horror as her son jumped on the stunned man's back and ripped free the machine gun that he had been holding. Zaire was swinging it wildly about, pointing it in every direction and yelling. "Go! Leave! Leave my friends! Or I'll kill you all!" he shouted. His voice cracked under the strain.

Tears streamed down her son's face. The look of anger in his eyes was one she'd never witnessed in his twelve years of life. He looked like a rabid dog, loose and unchained.

Several of the soldiers took aim. The lieutenant let out a deep laugh.

Zaire was trembling. These men saw it. They were battle hardened and numbed by the khat. Life and death no longer held the same meaning as was evident in their soulless eyes. They knew the look of a killer and the conviction it took to pull the trigger. As angry and desperate as Zaire was, Masika had no doubts these men could see that he didn't have it. She knew her son. He was no murderer.

All the effort he had just made was for naught. He couldn't follow through and they were starting to see that. She wanted to cry out.

Several of the gunmen were now taking their aim on the villagers.

The lieutenant said, "Drop the gun or we kill everyone here. Your family will die today. Is that what you want?"

Zaire looked to the crowd bearing witness to his act of courage. He looked at his mother. Tears fell more rapidly. His lip trembling in both fear and sadness, his failure immediate as the soldier he'd toppled and taken the weapon from, stood up behind him and struck him in the back of his skull. The hard impact could be heard in the silence and it jolted him forward.

Her son's wide eyes, wet with tears, disappeared into the dirt in front of him. His resistance was thwarted as the gun was ripped from his hands.

And then several of the other men surrounded him and began kicking and punching the boy. She wanted to help. She squealed in anguish as a muzzle of a nearby soldier was pointed at her head.

Masika suffered in silence as she watched her son being beaten into unconsciousness by the warlord's men.

The one who had his gun taken from him, shoved the other's back and pointed the rifle at the back of Zaire's head. Just as he was about to pull the trigger, the lieutenant called out, "Stop!"

He walked over and whispered something into the gunman's ear that no one else could hear, a private one-sided conversation. The weapon lowered and the gunman retreated to the truck.

Zaire remained unmoving, face down in the dirt.

A split second later, the soldier who had been embarrassed by the 12-year-old returned with a thick rope. The lieutenant smiled his approval and then several other soldiers grabbed up Zaire. His head hung low.

The lieutenant walked forward toward the villagers, eyeing each one of them slowly and then coming to rest his gaze on Masika. He must've seen her distraught look, the pain in her eyes that only a mother could have at a time like this. And then he said, "This will be the last time something like this ever happens. You will learn not to resist--not to fight. And this boy," he thumbed to Zaire who was being supported by his henchmen, "will serve as a reminder."

FEVER BURN CHAPTER 1
FAYETTEVILLE, NORTH CAROLINA

She stood outside the bar. It had been a long time since she'd frequented this establishment. Years, in fact. The last time was just before her exit from the Army. Standing here now in early spring, where the heat of the day was already starting to climb, seemed surreal. A Deja vu of sorts, yet now she was a wholly different person.

Somebody from the Northeast might feel that it was already summer here, but Hatch knew better. Summer was still months off as far as temperatures went, and by midsummer, the temperature would climb to nearly one hundred degrees with a hundred plus percent humidity. She'd trained in those conditions, and somehow during that time, had acclimated to them. But after leaving New Mexico, the dry, cool climate, and making the drive out here to Fayetteville, North Carolina, she was not accustomed to the change and her early morning run left her pores open as the sweat continued to pour even after the cool shower she'd taken to rinse herself off.

Hatch wasn't exactly sure what she was hoping to find here but figured this was as good a place as any to meet with her former team leader. She wished she could have stayed with the Task Force

Banshee and been allowed to be a member of her team a little bit longer, to find that closure and to complete her military service with the men that she had grown accustomed to serving with. But the incident and the fire that crippled her right side of her arm had left her unfit in the eyes of her former team leader. But she needed him now. She needed to sit down with the man and ask him what he knew before she made the international trip out to Kenya. She needed to know what she was up against, and he was the closest thing to insider trader information she was going to find.

When she had called him, he had been reluctant, to say the least, in agreeing to meet with her. But after some cajoling on Hatch's part, Bennett agreed to meet her. He picked the location, one of neutrality, and somewhere where there would be others around. She could tell in their brief conversation that he was guarded and wasn't sure how Hatch felt about him. That seemed fair. Hatch wasn't sure how she felt about him herself.

Anger had been the first reaction whenever his name popped into her head. Their last interaction had been less than amicable and she felt the ties to him had been severed over a year and a half ago when she walked away to start her life as a civilian. She was still feeling out that title. It didn't quite fit her.

He'd said to be there at 11 o'clock. Hatch knew the bar opened at 10, and she decided to arrive at 10:30. She always liked to be ahead of whatever was coming, and in this particular case, a little bit of advance recon of the bar and its inhabitants, would give her a leg up if Bennett felt her request for a meeting with him was not on the up and up. Obviously, he was nervous about it, and the fact that he had chosen this establishment proved that. If he was nervous, her suspicion was raised also.

Hatch pushed open the door, and although it was bright and warm outside, the bar was warm inside, but dark. A dankness hung in the air, the smell of old beer and spicy chicken wing sauce struck her nostrils as she entered. The owner and proprietor, Trey Daniels, had proudly bragged that he'd created a magical hot wings' sauce. He guarded his recipes as if they were the crown jewels. The wings had made him a legend in the area, winning numerous cook-offs. The walls, besides the military memorabilia, were adorned with photos of him in various hot wing cook-off competitions. His broad smile with his apron smeared with hot sauce and a wing in hand appeared in most of the pictures. He'd always told her, when Hatch used to come to the bar, that he planned to market it, sell his secret ingredient sauce to one of the big corporations, maybe Heinz, and make his millions. But as she walked into the bar and took a closer inspection, it seemed nothing had changed since she left. Everything remained unchanged, and his dreams and aspirations of becoming a hot wing sauce household name appeared to have been tucked neatly away, probably in a mental drawer full of other unrealized endeavors.

The bar owner and saucier, for lack of a better term, looked up as Hatch walked in. He gave her a casual nod and a wink. The two had shared many stories over the years and had forged a bond, although it had been some time since she'd seen him. In her world once out of sight, a person was out of mind as well. But seeing him brought back that comfort and familiarity, that sense of connection to a place, to a time, when things made sense. And in that split second as he poured a glass of beer for a patron, Hatch momentarily forgot that she was a civilian now. She blissfully remembered her time in the service and wanted to stay in that moment as long as she possibly could. She knew as soon as she opened her mouth and spoke to Daniels, the reality of the circumstances that she was just a civilian now, would intrude. She felt that she was a nobody in the world of the military, her service completed and was forgotten.

Hatch pushed aside her hesitation as she entered.

Bellying up to the bar, she said, "Hey, Trey been a while."

Trey Daniels pushed his ample girth over the top of the bar. For a former special operator himself, he had allowed the deliciousness of his wings and probably far too many beers over the course of the years to build a layer of bulk, mostly fat, around what used to be rigid, thick muscles.

Pictures on the wall showed him from back in his Vietnam days. A time when he was a lean, thick, strong man, often cutting the sleeves off of his shirts just to expose his rounded shoulders and bulging biceps. But he was no longer that man, although deep inside, Hatch knew better than most, rubbing absent-mindedly the scar tissue on her right arm, that outward appearances were not always as they seemed, and people like Daniels and Hatch were always tougher than appearances made them out to be. She knew in a throwdown situation that Daniels would be able to hold his own, and she'd seen him on occasion demonstrate that when tossing out some rowdy soldiers who'd had too much to drink and nowhere to spend that amped up testosterone.

She recalled one time when a young infantry sergeant had finished off a bottle of Jack before coming in and apparently felt the need to test the bar owner by ordering a drink. Daniels, recognizing the condition of the sergeant, refused to serve him and poured him a coffee instead. In a fit of anger, the drunken soldier broke the bottle on the counter and proceeded to try to hop over and stab Daniels. As big as Daniel's was, pretty much the same size he was now, he had little trouble dodging the attack and knocking the bottle free from the man's hand.

The young sergeant had, for all intents and purposes, tried to stab the bar owner, but Daniels maintained a poise that could only be acquired by somebody who has faced enemy gunfire. He knew, even though the circumstances were intense, that this young soldier was not in his right mind. And instead of treating him like the enemy, he treated him to a quick punch to the stomach.

As the man doubled over, instead of continuing the beating, he caught him before he hit the ground and carried him like a sack of potatoes over his shoulder. He took him outside to the fresh air. Hatch remembered seeing Daniels go back in, get one of the soldier's friends who had been at the bar with him, and kindly ask him to take their friend home. Daniels never called the police. He went right back to pouring drinks for the other patrons as if it never happened.

That was just one of many times. Hatch saw the bar owner handle an unruly incident with total control. Daniels was not the same size and shape of his youth, but he carried with him a deftness and a depth of character that she found in few others. And seeing him here now reminded her of all that, all those memories, and she smiled back. It felt good seeing him again.

"My God," he said, "Rachel Hatch in my restaurant? And to what do I owe this honor?" He added a pantomimed tip of the hat.

"It looks more like a bar than a restaurant," Hatch said.

Daniels laughed. This was their running joke. He always tried to make his food what people came for, but at Snake Eaters, the drink always outweighed the meal. "What brings you here?" he asked.

"I'm supposed to meet up with Bennett. Hasn't been by, has he?" Hatch asked. Hatch also was gauging whether Bennett had come and done his own precursory recon before the agreed upon meeting.

"I haven't seen Chris in here for a while. Figured he was out saving the world," Daniel said. "Well, look at you, though. You don't look like a day out of uniform."

Hatch again rubbed the scar tissue through her shirt. Although it was warm, she still wore a lightweight Lycra long sleeve shirt. She wasn't sure when her self-conscious mind would let her expose what was underneath that sleeve, but she'd exposed it to very few and had always been guarded when out in public. As confident as she was, the damage to her right arm carried with it not only the strange looks, but always brought up the question of how she got it. That *how* was a very difficult and private thing to share, the damage of which cost some of her teammates their lives. And the image of the mother and girl that had detonated the bomb that burned her flesh still haunted her to this day. She did her best to tuck that memory down deep.

"Well," Hatch said, "I'm definitely not the same person I was. I guess I'm still kind of finding my way in this civilian world. But hell, you know better than me about that journey."

Daniels smiled. "You're right about that. I've been out for thirty plus years and I'm still trying to figure it out. So, if you do before me, please let me know how we're supposed to adjust to normal life after the things we've seen."

Hatch appreciated the man for his experience, his kindness, and more importantly, the fact that even since her separation, in his eyes, she was on equal ground with the other soldiers in the bar. Hatch eyed the private section of the bar and said, "I'm going to take my drink over there," she said.

Daniels nodded. "What'll you be having?" he asked.

"Well, it's 10:30, so maybe just a Coke. You know what?" she added, "Why don't you put a little splash of rum in there?"

Daniels smiled and reached back for a bottle of Captain Morgan's and gave a healthy pour, not eyeing or measuring the shot that he put in the drink. If Hatch was to wager a guess it was probably closer to a shot and a half, maybe two. But her nerves had gotten the best of her and she figured maybe she'd try to calm them a little bit. Although she didn't typically rely on liquid courage, the meeting with Chris Bennett was putting her in an awkward position.

Filling the rest of the glass with Coke, he slid it over to her.

Hatch reached in her back wallet to pull out her money.

"Not here. Not today, Rachel. It's been too long. This first one's on me." Another wink. "It's good to see you."

Hatch thanked him and took her drink over to a reserved seating area on the right side of the restaurant. In it, there was always one glass set in front of an empty chair at the far end table. Every day, Daniels made sure that he poured two fingers of his drink of choice for the day, into that tumbler. It was set for the soldier who would never be able to take that drink. Daniels began the tradition when he first opened the joint.

Hatch sat near the table and, with her back against the wall, faced the door where any moment Chris Bennett would be coming through.

FEVER BURN CHAPTER 2

Hatch sat and took a slow sip from the rum and coke that Daniels had made. It was strong, as she expected, having seen the pour he made into the glass before filling the rest of it with Coke. The soda softened the blow a little bit, but she knew to pace herself. As the liquid hit her stomach, she felt the warmth rush over her. It'd been a while since she'd had a day drink, and although it felt right at the time when she'd had ordered it, it also felt out of place and out of character for her.

She was angry at herself, not for deciding to have the drink, but more because she felt the need to take the edge off. After all the things she'd experienced in her life, a meeting with Bennett was unnerving her. Alcohol was seldom the refuge she sought. Hatch had accustomed herself to physical punishment in the way of a hard workout or a long run. Those were the ways she took the edge off or eased her anxiety, or in some cases, tried to forget some of the past. But today was not one of those days, and the workout that she had put herself through earlier in the morning, hadn't depleted her to the point where the anxiety didn't touch her. So the drink had now found its way of working a little bit of magic and alleviating some of that stress about her pending encounter.

As she sat there in the bar that she had frequented during her years of service, she noticed that one of the soldiers eating a burger in the corner with a few of his friends began eyeing her. At first, she felt maybe he wasn't looking at her directly, but seeing as there was no one else around in the secluded reserved area, it only took a moment for her to realize that he was in fact, giving her the eye. He whispered something to his friends and then stood. Hatch thought to herself, "Well, this isn't going to be good."

The young man with his ginger hair tightly shaped in a high and tight approached in somewhat of a huff. He walked directly to the table she was sitting at, and placed both hands firmly in front of her, jostling the drink, and causing the ice cubes inside to rattle against the glass.

Hatch slowly looked up and then took a sip, silently dismissing whatever this was about.

The ginger looked back at his friends who nodded, and then turned to her and said, "This is reserved seating, operators only. I think you might be a little bit lost."

Hatch looked away, back down towards the glass that was still three quarters full, picked it up and took another small sip. This silent defiance seemed to only enrage the young soldier further, as a little vein began to bulge in his neck and his pale face started to redden.

"Hey lady, I'm trying to be real nice here, but this is a special section of the bar that is reserved for a special type of person."

Hatch set the glass down, droplets of condensation already beginning to pool on the outside in the muggy heat of the room. She pushed back ever so slightly in the chair and readied herself to confront the man. She wasn't quite sure how she intended to address this issue. She was a civilian now, and to try to give her backstory might've come off wrong, and most likely, this man wouldn't believe her if she told him. Her experience was unique, unique not only for the army, but for a female in the army. Few had done what Hatch had. Actually, there was only one other female to successfully complete the selection course, and there had been no other, to her knowledge, that had ever done it twice, male or female.

Hatch folded her arms and said, "I think I'm okay. Thank you." This only seemed to further infuriate the ginger soldier.

He looked back at his friends and threw his hands up, as if to question how this girl could be standing up to him. When he turned his attention back to her with his fists balled. Hatch thought for a second that this soldier was angry enough to possibly take a swing. Maybe he'd been drinking a little bit too long, and his judgment was skewed. It wouldn't be the first brawl that took place between soldiers.

Hatch had plenty of memories from her time as an MP and the fights she'd broken up. Many times the reason was petty. Although she did understand the ginger's desire to protect the sanctity of the reserved area, which was set aside for special operators, those that had served not only in a military capacity, but in some of the most dangerous roles imaginable. And Daniels, being a former Green Beret himself, found that it was important to designate a space just for them. He always gave them a little bit of extra in their drink, and comped them some food, typically one of his extra spicy wing platters, as a way of thanking them.

But what pissed Hatch off was the way this soldier addressed her from the get-go.

Hatch took a deep breath, exhaling slowly as she stood up. Being 5′10″, Hatch was nearly eye to eye with the ginger haired man standing before her. And she could see that when he realized this, that her physical stature was comparable to his, he took a step back. His movement was part fear, but he was also distancing himself, and preparing for what might come.

Hatch didn't make a fist, although she readied herself in case this young soldier made the mistake of getting aggressive with her beyond his words. She stepped back with her right foot, just slightly, just enough to give her balance and put her in a better position to counter anything he might throw her way.

All of a sudden, a voice boomed. It was Daniels. "Hey! Why don't you back off and leave her be?"

"But Trey, this woman, she's sitting in the reserved section! She's got no business, you know better!" The soldier pleaded, half embarrassed. His face turned a blotchy red.

Daniels leveled a stern gaze at the man and said, "She's done more than you've ever done, or ever will do."

Receiving the admonishment, the red in the young soldier's face deepened. A crease of confusion etched his brow as he looked at Daniels. "I don't understand. What are you talking about?"

Daniels smiled as he pointed toward the bar to a framed article from The Army Times hanging on the wall, surrounded by patches and other memorabilia. The article's caption in bold black letters, "First female to ever complete Army Special Forces Selection Course Twice."

Daniels let the man process what he was reading, and although there was no picture, the message was clearly sent.

The man looked at the article, and then at the woman who stood before him. His eyes ping-ponged back and forth, until they settled back on Hatch. His face was red, but the vein along his neck no longer bulged. The remnants of red peppering his cheeks were out of sheer embarrassment. "I...I just thought that I just... I've never seen...," he stammered.

Hatch gave him a break and decided in that split second that he was, although aggressive and intoxicated, nothing more than a young soldier over eager to enforce tradition.

"Listen, I get it. Maybe next time don't come off as such a hothead, but I understand you were looking out for the sanctity of this space, and I never would've sat here had I not earned the right," Hatch said softly.

The ginger soldier said nothing further and turned as if he'd been reprimanded by a principal or parent. If he had a tail, it would've been tightly tucked between his legs. He walked back to his friends, who were looking at him with dismay and shock that he had been reprimanded, and the woman had been defended by the bar owner.

Hatch turned her attention to Daniels, who was making his way back to the bar area. "Thanks. I could've handled myself, ya know," Hatch said.

Daniels shot a glance over his shoulder. "Oh, I know. I just didn't want to clean up blood this early on a Tuesday. His blood."

They both laughed as Hatch resumed her seat. She checked her watch and saw that it was nearing 11 o'clock. The little dump of adrenaline from the potential skirmish with the young soldier had mixed nicely with the little bit of Captain Morgan in her system, and she felt a slight weight lift from her shoulders.

Hatch always felt that combat, the potential or otherwise, always gave her a sense of calm. It was in those moments of chaos she felt most at peace. She was the proverbial calm in the storm, and she realized that about herself. Ever since leaving the army, she'd sought that connection. It had been severed when the army no longer wanted her, and in particular, her old unit.

A few minutes later, just past 11, the door opened, and the familiar face of Chris Bennett entered. He eyed Hatch, then he surveyed the bar, his operator training, even in a safe environment, always on point, as was hers. No amount of time could undo the training they'd been through. Entering any confined space, people of their experience always did a quick check of the surroundings, both people and location.

Satisfied, Bennett moved in. He held up two fingers and nodded at Daniels, who immediately set about lining up two shot glasses, and he filled each of them with a Glenlivet whiskey, Bennett's drink of choice.

Bennett didn't hold eye contact with Hatch for very long. He walked directly to the bar and grabbed his two shots, and then brought them over to where she was sitting. Before he took his seat, he turned back to Daniels, "I'll grab a Miller Lite too. Thanks, Trey."

Hatch eyed the man's two shots in his hands. Ordering a third beverage to wash them down in reverse order meant he was doing whiskey with a beer chaser. Usually it was the other way around.

"I see you're getting a good start to the day. I assume you're not going back to do any range work," Hatch said, eyeing the two shots. Apparently Bennett was just as nervous about this meeting as she was, as he also was not known for heavy drinking, although on occasion he partook, and this was apparently one of those occasions.

"So what are we doing here, Hatch?" he asked, downing the first shot and slamming the glass onto the table.

"Well, I have some questions. I told you when we talked that I needed to see you in person, and it's important," Hatch said.

"Okay then, if it's important, get on with it."

Hatch eyed him carefully. The last time they had spoken to each other, she nearly knocked him unconscious. It had been the last time they had faced each other, and it was a heated and physical altercation. But did he assume that she called him out of the blue to set up round two, or was he just awkward around her since that encounter?

"Listen, Chris, I've got a lead on what happened to my father, and I wanted to see if you knew anything that might be able to help me out--point me in the right direction--give me a heads up before I head off to my next destination," Hatch said bluntly.

"Your father? I don't really understand what you're getting at," he said. "I remember you saying something about a hunting accident when you were a kid. How would I be able to help with that?"

Hatch sighed. "I've come into some new information. My sister died, well, she was murdered recently, and it set in motion some things when I went home. One of which was I found out a little more about the circumstances around my father's death, and I've been tracking those leads since then," she said.

"Sorry to be so cold, but what does this have to do with me?" Bennett asked. His face was contorted in a look of confusion.

"Nothing, not directly, but I know that you're still in the special operations community, and you have access to things that I don't anymore," she said.

"Wait a minute, Rachel. No way am I going to go pulling black ops folders or digging deep. I'm not losing my job and my career over some wild goose chase you may be on," he said.

"I didn't ask you to do that," Hatch snapped. "I didn't ask you to dig anything up. I wanted to ask you what you know about the Gibson Consortium," she said.

"The Gibson Consortium? I don't know. Well, I know of them. There was a unit of private contractors called that, but that was a long time ago. They changed names and I think ownership. They're known as Talon Executive Services now, TES. I've only had a few dealings with them overseas, after you left the unit," he said.

"It's funny that you choose those words," Hatch said. "*Left the unit. If I recall, I didn't leave anything. My decision was made for me.*"

"So you're here to bring that up? We're getting into that now? I thought this was about your father, or are you here to beg to come back? You're a civilian now, Hatch. You're not one of us anymore. I'm sorry that was such a hard pill for you to swallow, but that ended over a year ago," he said.

Hatch took another sip from her drink, this one just a little bit longer than the last. "I'm not looking to get back into the unit, Chris. I know it's over. Trust me. I've already gone down that path. I did what I could to prove my worth to you and it didn't matter. I'm not here to push that issue. Let's drop it for now. I'm sorry I even brought it up," she said.

Bennett threw down the second shot of whiskey as Daniels set the Miller Lite down beside it, collected the two empty shot glasses, and disappeared back behind the bar. He immediately took a pull, the reverse order, whiskey to beer chaser had been complete. "Okay, so what is it you want to know?" Bennett said.

Hatch evaluated him. She remembered the good times they'd had when the team was whole, when they were out there doing it, getting the job done. They were an unstoppable force, and she carried her weight and then some. Then, that day happened, and as if the blast wasn't bad enough, the emotional destruction that moment had for both the team and her, was something that would never be erased. Seeing him sitting here before her now made it hard for her to adjust to the fact that their friendship and comradery had burned up in that blast, leaving invisible scars that both of them carried from that day forward.

"So what do you know about Talon Executive? What's their deal?" she asked.

"They're like any government contractors. They fill some voids and do some private security work. It's like the former Blackwater. They handle details that aren't tasked to military personnel, but they are all ex-military. I haven't heard anything crazy about them, but I will say this, of all the private contractors that I have worked with, they are the most secretive. They rarely are at any of the combined functions on bases. They keep to themselves and operate exclusively with members of their own unit. They never task out, and never ask for support from us," he said.

"You've never had any negative dealings, you've never heard of anything going wrong outside the wire?" she asked.

"Look, Hatch, I know we've got history so I'm just going to say this. Most of the guys in that unit, in that contractor service are ex-Delta, these are next-level guys. I knew a few of them, but when they went in, we lost contact. So really, what I know is limited?" he said with a shrug.

"You don't have any point of contact there? Somebody I could reach out to and speak with?" she asked.

Bennett took a sip of his beer and shook his head, and then he leaned forward just a bit and he cast a quick glance, barely noticeable toward where Daniels was at the bar. He was drying a rinsed mug and tending the bar back duties in between orders. "Listen," he said in a whisper. "I do know this, and what I'm going to tell you is just grumblings. You don't have the clearance anymore for the real stuff, but I'll tell you this, they're not a group to mess with. I've heard stories, guys go missing, ops go bad, nothing happens. There's no press, no paper, nothing. Even in our circles, limited details. So whatever you think you're digging up, you might be crossing swords with the wrong people."

Hatch leaned forward slightly because of his need for secrecy and said, "Why are you whispering? What are you worried about?" she asked.

"Listen, they've got eyes and ears everywhere. They're connected to the military. There's big money in this stuff, you know that. Man, they do some of the stuff that nobody, even the bigger contractors can handle. So yeah, I don't like talking about it, especially to you, who's obviously come here on some half-cocked idea that it's linked to your father's death. I don't even want to know why you think that. The less I know about what you're doing, the better off I am," he said, and then pushed back in his seat and folded his arms.

Hatch eyed him. "So that's it? There's nothing else you can tell me? Okay, well I'm not going to tell you where I'm going next, but I've got a long journey ahead of me, and hopefully that next step won't get me killed. Seeing as how I know almost as little as I did when I walked in this door, you're definitely not setting me up for success," she said.

Bennett sighed and rubbed his temples, took another long pull from his beer, and kept it in his hand and didn't set it back on the table. He looked over at Hatch. "Listen, Daniels might know something more," he said.

Hatch shot a glance over to the thick bartender and the restaurant owner, maker of sauces. "You talking about Trey? Daniels? Him over there?" she asked confused.

Bennett nodded slowly but said nothing.

Hatch said, "Why would he know anything about it?"

"Because he was one of the founding members. Eyes and ears everywhere," he said with a wink.

Hatch sat back absorbing this. The man she'd known for years. She'd come to his establishment, drinking, and eating, and socializing.

To think Daniels had known or may have known something about her father or his death, and had held back, sickened her.

Hatch finished the rest of her rum and Coke. The ice had already melted, the remnants in the cup were more water than anything else. She was grateful for it, because too many drinks, and she didn't know if she would be able to contain the anger rising up. It was misguided anger and she knew it. She didn't know who she was angry at or if Daniels knew anything at all. But here Bennett sat, laying it all out for her, at least hinting at what potentially could've been right in front of her all along.

"Hey, look, maybe he doesn't know anything. Maybe he was in it early, got out early. I don't know. And I don't know what this has to do with your father's death, but what I can tell you is this--some things are better left buried. Sometimes it's just better that way," he said.

Hatch looked at him, then turned and looked at Daniels behind the bar, who nodded and held up a bottle of Crown, and gestured at her glass. She shook her head no, and he went back to his work.

"Yeah, listen, Hatch, I gotta go. I got stuff to do. It was good seeing you," he said.

"Was it?" Hatch asked.

Bennett stood and looked down at her before leaving. "For what it's worth, you were a hell of an operator, and I'm sorry for the way things played out. And whatever it is you're looking for, I hope you find it."

With that, Bennett walked out of the bar, leaving Hatch alone in the private section of Snake Eaters. The lunch wave of people began to trickle in, and tables were starting to fill.

Hatch stood and took her glass over to the bar. She debated on discussing the new information with Daniels right here, right now, but as the man became busy with orders, she didn't want to tip her hand. Hatch decided she would return later, around closing time, and have a little one-on-one with her friend and bartender about the group responsible for her father's death.

Order your copy of Fever Burn now:
https://www.amazon.com/Fever-Burn-Rachel-Hatch-Book-ebook/dp/Bo85VNJ9SY/

Join the LT Ryan reader family & receive a free copy of the Rachel Hatch story, *Fractured*. Click the link below to get started:

https://ltryan.com/rachel-hatch-newsletter-signup-1

ALSO BY LT RYAN

Find All of L.T. Ryan's Books on Amazon Today!

The Jack Noble Series

The Recruit (free)

The First Deception (Prequel 1)

Noble Beginnings

A Deadly Distance

Ripple Effect (Bear Logan)

Thin Line

Noble Intentions

When Dead in Greece

Noble Retribution

Noble Betrayal

Never Go Home

Beyond Betrayal (Clarissa Abbot)

Noble Judgment

Never Cry Mercy

Deadline

End Game

Noble Ultimatum

Noble Legend

Noble Revenge

Never Look Back (Coming Soon)

Bear Logan Series

Ripple Effect

Blowback

Take Down

Deep State

Bear & Mandy Logan Series

Close to Home

Under the Surface

The Last Stop

Over the Edge

Between the Lies (Coming Soon)

Rachel Hatch Series

Drift

Downburst

Fever Burn

Smoke Signal

Firewalk

Whitewater

Aftershock

Whirlwind

Tsunami

Fastrope

Sidewinder (Coming Soon)

Mitch Tanner Series

The Depth of Darkness

Into The Darkness

Deliver Us From Darkness

Cassie Quinn Series

Path of Bones

Whisper of Bones

Symphony of Bones

Etched in Shadow

Concealed in Shadow

Betrayed in Shadow

Born from Ashes

Blake Brier Series

Unmasked

Unleashed

Uncharted

Drawpoint

Contrail

Detachment

Clear

Quarry (Coming Soon)

Dalton Savage Series

Savage Grounds

Scorched Earth

Cold Sky

The Frost Killer (Coming Soon)

Maddie Castle Series

The Handler

Tracking Justice

Hunting Grounds (Coming Soon)

Affliction Z Series

Affliction Z: Patient Zero

Affliction Z: Abandoned Hope

Affliction Z: Descended in Blood

Affliction Z : Fractured Part 1

Affliction Z: Fractured Part 2 (Fall 2021)

Love Hatch? Noble? Maddie? Cassie? Get your very own L.T. Ryan merchandise today! Click the link below to find coffee mugs, t-shirts, and even signed copies of your favorite thrillers! https://ltryan.ink/EvG_

Receive a free copy of The Recruit. Visit:

https://ltryan.com/jack-noble-newsletter-signup-1

ABOUT THE AUTHOR

L.T. RYAN is a Wall Street Journal, USA Today, and Amazon best-selling author of several mysteries and thrillers, including the Wall Street Journal bestselling Jack Noble and Rachel Hatch series. With over eight million books sold, when he's not penning his next adventure, L.T. enjoys traveling, hiking, riding his Peloton,, and spending time with his wife, daughter and four dogs at their home in central Virginia.

* Sign up for his newsletter to hear the latest goings on and receive some free content ➜ https://ltryan.com/jack-noble-newsletter-signup-1
* Join LT's private readers' group ➜ https://www.facebook.com/groups/1727449564174357
* Follow on Instagram ➜ @ltryanauthor
* Visit the website ➜ https://ltryan.com
* Send an email ➜ contact@ltryan.com
* Find him on Goodreads ➜ http://www.goodreads.com/author/show/6151659.L_T_Ryan

***

BRIAN SHEA has spent most of his adult life in service to his country and local community. He honorably served as an officer in the U.S. Navy. In his civilian life, he reached the rank of Detective and accrued eleven years of law enforcement experience between

Texas and Connecticut. Somewhere in the mix he spent five years as a fifth-grade schoolteacher. Brian's myriad of life experience is woven into the tapestry of each character's design. He resides in New England and is blessed with an amazing wife and three beautiful daughters.

Join My Reader List and get a FREE Copy of the Nick Lawrence prequel short story: UNKILLABLE. Go to: brianchristophershea.com/contact/

Connect with Brian through his author website or various social media sites.

www.brianchristophershea.com

www.facebook.com/brianchristophershea

twitter.com/BrianCShea

or reach out by email:

info@brianchristophershea.com

Made in the USA
Las Vegas, NV
08 August 2024

93568327R00182